MILLENNIUM SHOCK

JUSTIN RICHARDS

Published by BBC Worldwide Ltd,
Woodlands, 80 Wood Lane
London W12 0TT

First published 1999

ISBN 0 563 55586 6

Printed and bound in Great Britain by Mackays of Chatham
Cover printed by Belmont Press Ltd, Northampton

For Alison, Julian and Christian – in this millennium and the next

1998:
Aftermath

They met at Jardine's, and talked about nothing in particular until the coffee arrived. Then they chatted for a few minutes, about the old days - UNIT, the Doctor, their travels.

The conversation paused as the tall, gaunt-looking waiter presented Harry with the bill. He unfolded it, grimaced, and gave the waiter a credit card. Sarah and Harry haggled over who should pay, and Harry won when he told her that it was on the company.

The waiter returned with a credit card slip. Harry felt in his jacket for a pen, but Sarah offered hers before he found one.

'Thanks.'

'Thank you, sir.' The waiter borrowed the pen to initial the slip. He held the pen for a moment, a thin finger running along its steel casing. Then he returned it to Harry together with the top copy. The waiter swayed his head by way of thanks, and retreated.

'Memories.' Sarah smiled back at Harry. 'Yes, that's about all we could keep from those days, I suppose. With a couple of exceptions.'

'Oh?' He handed her back the heavy steel biro.

'Well,' said Sarah, showing him the logo on the side, 'I still have this pen.'

He took it back, and peered at the side of the pen in the subdued restaurant lighting. The logo was a capital letter I with a small 2 above and to the right of it - I squared. The company had been a front for the Voracians, a group of aliens whose very existence was built on advanced computer technology. In fact their whole lives revolved around it - the way they behaved, the jargonised way they spoke, their very being. Harry felt cold at the memory of how they had been defeated - just - by the Doctor, Harry and Sarah. But a younger Sarah, much younger even though it was only last year.

He would never get used to the differences in time. He thought he was used to his new life, working as an intelligence officer at MI5. Compared to UNIT it seemed simple enough. Until the Doctor had reappeared and Harry found himself helping to save the world again.

Memories. He smiled thinly as he looked at the pen. 'What's this?'

She leaned forwards, and saw that he was pointing to a tiny glass window set into the side of the pen, near the clip. 'It used to tell the time,' she said. Harry half smiled, and held out the pen for her.

Sarah reached out her hand to take it. Then she changed her mind. 'No,' she said. 'You have it. Look after it for me.' She stood up. 'I have to get back to Moreton Harwood, sort out Aunt Lavinia's things. And there's the house too. Keep the pen for me, Harry. It's one less thing to worry about.'

Harry shrugged and slipped the pen into his jacket pocket. He helped Sarah into her coat, and together they walked out into the bitter cold of the winter night.

'How's work?' she asked as Harry walked her back to her car. 'I know you can't really talk about it, especially not over dinner, but is everything, you know, OK?'

He nodded. 'Yes. Busy, of course. People think because the Cold War's over there's nothing for us to do any more. But they're wrong. And that's the other lot anyway. We look after internal security.'

Sarah smiled. Her breath was a warm mist as she said, 'And I suppose people think there's nothing for you to do either now that Northern Ireland's sorted out.'

'I doubt it'll ever be sorted out really. But yes, there is that.'

'Not about to be made redundant then?'

'Oh no. There's more than enough problems to keep MI5 in business into the next millennium.'

Sarah shook her head. 'Nineteen ninety-nine in a few weeks. Can you believe it?'

They were at her car now. The central locking 'thunked' as she pressed the open button on her key. 'Thanks for the meal, Harry. Keep in touch.'

He opened the driver's door for her. Sarah hesitated a moment, then kissed him on the cheek. 'Keep in touch,' she said again.

He closed the door for her without comment. He watched the car lights come on, the wipers scrape a thin layer of ice from the windscreen, and the car pull away into the light traffic of the London suburb. His eyes were slightly moist, only partly from the cold of the night. If he had not been slightly distracted by his memories and the old emotions now brought to the fore again, he would have noticed the tall, gaunt figure that kept to the shadows as it followed him back to his house.

'Who was that guy?'

They were packing up at Jardine's, wiping down tables and sorting out cutlery from the dishwasher. The junior chef's assistant was mopping down the kitchen floor with a bad grace born of ambition.

'I dunno. Didn't catch his name. Said he was standing in for Mike. Flu.'

'Lot of it about.'

'He was OK. Just a bit creepy.'

'Till he buggered off.'

'G'night, Pete.'

'See ya, Craig.'

It was as he put the rubbish out, as he rolled back the heavy lid of the skip in the alley behind the restaurant, that Pete found Mike's body.

One whole conference room on the sixth floor had been turned into a war room. The only employees permitted on the sixth floor were those personally authorised by Byron Cutter, the 'Cutter Mafia' as the others called them.

If a regular employee of Silver Bullet Solutions Inc had been invited to the war room, they would not have been surprised by the way one half of the room was organised. Flow charts and logic diagrams covered the wall, together with printed pages of notes and comments detailing dependencies and risks associated with the product roll-out shown by the charts.

But the other half of the room was less conventional. There were still the printed lists, but there were also computer code printouts, fragments of code diagrams and lists of file names. A large part of the wall was in fact a flat screen plasma display, the data on it changing constantly: lists of Domain Name Servers on the Internet scrolled past as nodes illuminated and dimmed on a vast web of intersecting lines. A red ribbon crept along the bottom of the screen, giving a visual indication of progress. '17.3% Reassembled' flashed next to it.

A second, smaller screen was set into the wall beside the first. This displayed what looked like an airport arrivals board. Components and files were listed, and against each item in the list was a status indicator: Retrieved, Located or Missing. Beside that was another notation - a priority given to each item: Essential, Replaceable or Redundant.

Cutter was standing in front of this second screen, staring at it. As he stood, deep in thought, his head swayed slightly as if it was too heavy for his neck. Apart from this he stood absolutely still, his hands clasped behind his back. He was tall and broad-shouldered. His face however was thin and angular. His features were slightly sunken, emphasising the bone structure, as if the skin were stretched too tight over the skull. When the door opened behind him, he spoke without turning. His voice was deep and harsh, almost grating. 'Well?'

'I made physical contact. The trace is accurate, the tracker working.' The tall thin man stood beside Cutter at the screen. 'The display has offlined, but the systems integrity is preserved. The chip is still active, though I doubt they realise even now that the tracker built into the pen has intelligence and a reasoning circuit.'

'You have not updated the registry.' There was a trace of admonishment in Cutter's voice as he pointed to the list of components on the screen in front of them. 'The reasoning circuit is a major component we still lack.'

'I prioritised my verbal report to you.'

Cutter nodded slowly. 'And the component?'

'I shall log it as located. Retrieval can follow when and if appropriate. We need to determine a risk threshold and acceptable levels of intervention. The woman gave it to a friend. I think we should run a check on him before we take precipitative action.'

Cutter turned sharply. 'Oh you do, Bardell, do you?' For a moment there was silence. Then Cutter turned back to the screen. 'I agree with your evaluation,' he said, his voice calm again. 'After Stabfield's recent spectacular failure at I^2, I think caution is warranted. The less attention we draw to ourselves the better. For the moment.' Cutter turned as he spoke, until he was facing the opposite wall.

Bardell turned too. 'We are on schedule for the product roll-out?'

'Of course. As you can see for yourself. The government representative is due tomorrow. I think he will have an enlightening visit.' Cutter's features twisted into a lopsided smile, as if the muscles worked properly only in the left half of his face. Bardell nodded, but his own face betrayed no emotion at all.

Together they examined the charts for several seconds. Then Cutter said: 'Update the registry, Bardell. Information is power, remember that. It was Stabfield's lack of data that destroyed him. That and his cavalier disregard for the worst-case prognoses, as far as we can tell from the data we received during the incident. If he had spent less time in self-aggrandisement, and more in sharing data, lodging back-ups with us as we requested, even acknowledging our existence as colleagues rather than rivals...' His voice tailed off.

'I'll update the registry,' Bardell said, opening the war room door.

'Soon,' Cutter said quietly, 'a new millennium will dawn on this planet.'

Bardell paused in the doorway. 'Yes, Mr Cutter.'

'And with it, a new era.'

* * *

There was a sandwich stall at the top of the escalator. Every day, as he emerged with the rush hour crowd from the tube station, Dave Hedges bought himself a BLT and stuffed it into his anorak pocket. He knew that the cholesterol wasn't doing him any good, just as he knew that an evening diet of pizza and Coke was hardly healthy. But he didn't care. If he was a little overweight, if he needed trousers with a bigger waist now than a year ago, that was hardly a problem. He was barely twenty-four and it had never occurred to him that he wasn't going to live for ever.

While Dave lived, he lived for his work. He had his own office, a generous salary, a job in the city doing what he loved. Life just could not be better. He could work as late as he liked, and nobody told him to tidy his pizza-box-strewn flat because nobody ever came there. In fact, he was only there himself to eat, sleep, and play Nintendo.

The security guard nodded to Dave as he arrived at the main entrance to Silver Bullet House. In return, Dave waved his plastic identity badge, then clipped it on to the V-neck of his jumper. It was an indication of how well he was getting on at work that he did not have to wear a suit jacket. He took the lift to the fourth floor, humming the background music from a shoot-em-up he had played through from start to finish the previous night. Not bad, though the rendering was a bit crude.

Dave paused outside his small office, fumbling in his anorak pocket for his keys, hoping he hadn't lost them again. He juggled his copy of *PC Gamer* and the BLT as he rummaged deeper, feeling through the hole in the pocket into the coat's lining. Eventually he pulled out the keys, tangled with loose thread and fluff.

He was unlocking the door as he caught sight of a reflection in the small window set into it at eye level. The window was round, like a porthole. Reflected in it was a man. The man was in a business suit, exuding an air of smug importance as he was led across the open-plan area next to Dave's office. He was being guided through by Bardell, Byron Cutter's tall, gaunt number two. 'Smiling Death', the others called him. Never to his face.

But it was not Bardell that caught Dave's attention. He turned to see better, and found Martyn Clark, another of Cutter's top-level managers, standing beside him.

'Hey, isn't that –' Dave started.

Clark cut him off. 'Yes. He's here to endorse Silver Bullet.'

Dave pushed open his office door. 'Government backing. That could help us big time.'

Clark followed Dave in. 'Mr Cutter sent me,' he said, 'to see how the work is going.'

'Fine, fine. On schedule.' He switched on the desktop computer, already pulling out his chair and sitting down. Dave pulled the plastic cover off his sandwich. It made a satisfying ripping sound. A thin strip of lettuce fell out with the plastic cover and flopped on to the desk. 'I'll e-mail him a status report this morning if you like.' Dave swung round holding out the plastic box of sandwiches. 'Bacon, lettuce, tomato – want a bite?'

Clark took a brisk step backwards. It was almost as if he had been hit. 'No,' he said sharply. Then, quieter, 'No, thank you.' He stepped back out of the office. 'That status report Mr Hedges. Expedite it as quickly as you can, please.'

But Dave had already turned back to his computer, totally absorbed in the system boot-up information that was scrolling up the screen.

'We don't endorse just anything, you know. And frankly, I think it's unlikely we will lend our support to any Y2K solution however impressive.'

Bardell was not listening. He let the man drone on. Let him think what he liked for the moment. Bardell led the way across the fourth floor, past the programmers who were there mainly for show, though they didn't know it. Once in the lift, Bardell swiped his security badge through the reader and pressed the button for the seventh floor.

'Still,' the man was saying as the lift reached its destination, 'I suppose it does no harm to take a look at the thing, maybe offer you some advice on marketing and distribution.'

The doors slid open and Bardell gestured for him to go first.

'Thank you.' He stepped out into the bright light, and stopped dead in his tracks. 'What is this?'

The room was large and devoid of furniture. There were double doors at the far end, and an observation window along one side. In the centre of the room, directly under the bank of bright halogen lights, was an operating table. Arranged round the table were various pieces of medical equipment – heart monitor, oxygen cylinders, low tables of surgical instruments. Hanging over the table was a scaffolding frame to which was attached what looked like a workman's drill.

On the wall opposite the observation window a huge image was projected. It showed a face, the face of the man now standing looking round in amazement and confusion. Except that certain parts of the face in the image had been cut away, leaving dark gaps with ragged edges.

Bardell let the man take this in as he firmly led him towards the operating table. As they approached, the double doors at the far end of the room swung open, and a figure entered. It was a tall, broad-shouldered man. He was dressed in a pale green gown and wearing a surgical mask. He was in the process of pulling on thin plastic gloves.

The man pulled free of Bardell, beginning to panic now. 'What the hell is this?' he demanded, but the self-assured confidence of earlier was gone, his voice was wavering and high-pitched. 'What's going on? I demand –'

'Demand?' Cutter's voice was muffled slightly by the mask, but his satisfaction was still evident. 'I don't think you're in a position to demand anything here.'

The man was backing away, too scared of Cutter to be aware of what Bardell was doing. The first intimation he had was when the needle entered his neck, but by then it was far too late.

Bardell lifted the man easily and hefted him on to the operating table.

'Good. Very good,' Cutter said as he flexed his hands within the tight surgical gloves. 'I think we'll start with the eyes.'

* * *

The Westland Lynx AH Mk 1 attack helicopter had a top cruising speed of 140 knots. It was running at close to this when it hit trouble.

The first hint that anything was wrong was when the pilot found he had lost control of the aircraft's speed. Three seconds later, the guidance and targeting systems packed up. The pilot was still calling in for help when the nose dipped and the helicopter started its rapid descent. At the same time, carbon monoxide from the engine exhausts was filtered into the cabin.

Both the pilot and his passenger were familiar enough with the Lynx to know that it depended on its impressive manoeuvrability and performance characteristics as well as the skill of its crew to avoid being hit. It was not built, the instructors were keen to stress, to 'take damage'. Neither of the men was under any illusions about what would happen to them if the aircraft hit the ground, or anything else, at speed.

In the event, they both passed out before it hit anything as the helicopter dropped like a stone. If the pilot and passenger had retained consciousness, they would have felt the helicopter's descent slow until it settled itself down gently on the edge of an area of woodland. The forty-two-foot rotor slowed almost to a stop, its edges dipping lazily as a small group of figures emerged from the trees.

The accident investigators put the incident down to a massive, inexplicable systems failure. Possibly, they surmised, it was caused by a short circuit in a faulty board of the flight computer. Possibly. The truth was that the investigators were unable to agree amongst themselves what had happened.

The report was more explicit about the timing of the pilot's final communication and the extent of the area over which the wreckage was scattered. That was something the investigators could agree on. Just as they were agreed that it was a miracle that the passenger survived.

The Millennium Bug

Extract from an article by Sarah Jane Smith

This text is reproduced from the January 1999 issue of *Popular Technology*, with permission.

The so-called millennium bug is, basically, an inability of certain, typically older computer software to distinguish between AD 1900 and 2000.

This is caused simply by the fact that some programs store the date as the final two digits only – '99' rather than '1999', rather like writing 14/9/99 as shorthand for 14 September 1999. Holding just the last two digits was a useful way of saving on computer memory when it was an expensive constraint.

To understand why this is important, it is necessary to know that computers typically do date calculations by converting a date to a number in YYYYMMDD format – holding the year then the month then the day as a single number. So, for example, 12 August 1998 becomes 19980812.

Simple arithmetic can then be used to work out earlier and later dates. The computer can tell that 12 August 1998 is before 11 February 1999 since 19980812 is a lower number than 19990211. Similarly, 14 September 2000 will be later than 11 February 1999 as 20000914 is higher than 19990211.

But if the year is held as two digits only, this maths breaks. To take the above examples, but assume the year is held as just the final two digits, we find that 980812 is still lower than 990211, but that 000914 is lower than 990211. In other words, the computer now thinks that the date we intended to be in the year 2000 comes before 1999. In fact, it thinks it was in 1900 and has already happened.

The obvious question is: 'Why Not Just Fix It?' There are a number of reasons why it's not as easy as that. For one thing, the programs affected may be up to forty years old. This brings other problems - the people who wrote them are no longer there; the programming languages they are in are no longer widely used, taught or known. As a result there is a shortage of expertise. More critically, the original source code - the lines of program code that you can actually change - may not exist any more. A program is compiled before it can be run, and the compiled form is in all practical senses unchangeable. To alter it, you need to change the program source code and re-compile it. Even if the source code does still exist, there are millions of lines to check, and it has to be done pretty much one-by-one...

So, does it matter? Actually, it matters a lot more than one might think. Dates are used for a huge number of calculations. Some of them are obvious. A credit card expiry date in the new millennium, for example, may mean that the card seems to have expired in the early 1900s and is therefore invalid. In fact, Visa and MasterCard had to withdraw '00' expiring cards for a while as verification terminals failed. One major supermarket chain in the UK has already had its automated stock systems destroy all canned food with sell-by dates of later than 2000 (thinking it had expired in 1900).

But there are obscure uses of the date as well. For instance, random number generators often work using dates as 'seeds' to determine the next random number in the sequence. Averages are often worked out by dividing totals through by the difference between today's date and when the calculation was last performed. And there are numerous others...

The implications are serious, make no mistake. Current estimates are that the millennium crisis - or Y2K as it is sometimes called for short - could knock 0.5 per cent off US economic growth in 2000 and 2001, which is roughly equivalent to the SE Asian crash in 1998. Industry too is worried. It could cost $119 billion in the next two years in lost economic output - that's without accounting for the cost of fixing the problem.

And the cost of fixing the problem is huge. Chase Manhattan Bank is spending $250 million a year on Y2K. Wells Fargo have a team of 400 working on the problem. The Gartner Group estimates that a total of 180 *billion* lines of code need to be examined. These costs will force up inflation and depress productivity. In short, a global depression is not just possible as a result of the millennium bug, it is likely.

So far we have assumed that the problem will be fixed in time. It won't.

To find, fix and test all the problems is a task estimated at 700,000 person-years. This work needs to be done to all 'candidate' programs for companies just to stay in business. Initial work is needed to identify those programs, and then - as we have seen - the key skills to diagnose and fix the programs may no longer exist. And the real problem is nobody really knows what will happen. There will certainly be computer failures. In fact, *Business Week* estimates that 85 per cent of problematic software will be fixed. But this is probably optimistic. In Europe the figure is thought to be closer to 65 per cent. A survey conducted by Hunter College in New York in December 1997 suggests that two out of three large companies in the US had yet to make detailed plans for the year 2000. In Europe the problem is exacerbated as the major players are distracted by the introduction of the single currency in 1999.

It is not just industry and the stock markets that have a problem. The notion that governments are well prepared is a fallacy. The US House Subcommittee on Government Management, Information and Technology reported in March 1998 that 37 per cent of federal agencies' critical systems will not be ready for Y2K.

On 6 February 1998 the US Defense Department's Inspector General said that the US military still has no assurance that it is buying Y2K-compliant products yet... 'which may seriously hamper the ability of the DoD to perform its administrative and war-fighting mission requirements'.

Similarly, the US Internal Revenue Service will not meet its deadlines. One estimate puts IRS Y2K compliance as possible by 2017.

The US Health Care Financing Administration is pretty typical in that it just doesn't know what impact Y2K will have on it. It may, for example, halt refund and reimbursement payments in 2000.

Only 30 per cent of US State Governments had started on Y2K work by September 1998, and with no idea of the impact or cost. The Columbus (Ohio) state school system, with 65,000 students, may cost $8 million to fix according to one study that has been done... Now expand that to the rest of the US... to Europe... to the world.

The scary thing is that this is just the start of it. The large, industrial computer systems are the obvious points of risk and possible failure. But it is not just limited to industry and government. Many embedded systems may be date-dependent. And embedded systems are found in cars, phones, videos, TVs, microwaves, central heating, burglar alarms, fax machines, hospital equipment... So it is hardly surprising that public utilities will not be immune. Gas, electricity, water, communications: they may all shut down. In the autumn of 1997 Phillips Petroleum ran a test for Y2K implications on a North Sea oil and gas platform. The platform shut down completely when its safety systems failed and inaccurately detected hydrogen sulphide in the gas supply.

A problem of another kind entirely surfaced during a Y2K test conducted by the US Nuclear Regulatory Commission (NRC). In this scenario, a security computer erroneously gave open access to normally secure and sensitive areas. 'It wouldn't surprise me if certain plants find they are not Year 2000-ready and have to shut down,' said Jared S. Wermiel, NRC's Y2K manager.

In isolation these potential problems seem small. But small problems may have far larger impacts. For example, the US Government sends out $32 billion in social security and payroll cheques every month. Even a short delay in getting them out would be a major jolt to the US economy.

Again, exactly what will happen, or even could happen, is not known. But on 19 May 1998 we got an impression of what might occur 'in little' when the Galaxy IV communications satellite failed. The failure crippled the US pager networks, several broadcast news services, and even some credit card verification. They were brief disruptions, but some critical problems arose. Doctors, who rely on using pagers, were forced to remain in hospitals for example - they could no longer guarantee to be in contact otherwise.

Sensor failures will contribute to the small but widespread problems. Programmable controllers have now replaced mechanical relays in almost all generating plants and control rooms and it is acknowledged that they may 'behave badly' or fail in 2000. In the words of Dean Kothmann, the Head of Technology at Black & Veatch which is the world's largest power plant provider: 'There will be facilities where they go in and turn on the machines, and they won't go on.' Similar digital controllers are now used in telephone exchanges, gas/water/electric switching units and supply stations, and a myriad other systems.

Disruption of such public utilities as power is serious enough. But now imagine problems with some other crucial systems. Air Traffic Control, for example. In the event of a massive failure, it would be necessary for safety reasons to ground all aircraft. But the system actually assumes that a certain percentage of aircraft is always in flight. In fact, there is not sufficient runway and hangar space for all the aircraft in the world to be on the ground at the same time. It just isn't possible.

Now extend the thinking to military systems as well as civil. Frank Gaffney (Reagan's Assistant Secretary of Defense) has said that Y2K could make it difficult to move troops to the Persian Gulf, and almost impossible to fight a war there. 'We have the makings of a national emergency on our hands... the Year 2000 situation could have an effect comparable to a deliberate, concerted information-warfare attack on the information infrastructure.'

But, above all, it is the uncertainty of the situation that is so worrying. A recent survey of US IT companies showed that over 90 per cent have no budget for Y2K yet. Only 21 per cent would guarantee Y2K-compliance.

Cost-estimates for fixing the millennium bug, whatever

happens, vary widely. The Software Productivity Research estimate is about the highest, coming in at $3.6 *trillion*. A March 1998 survey by the IT Association of America indicated that 44 per cent of US companies *have already experienced* Y2K failures. Ninety-four per cent of the respondents termed Y2K 'a crisis'. And that's almost two years before it happens. Yet in August 1998, the Gartner Group estimated that between 20 and 30 per cent of all firms worldwide have not yet started preparing for Y2K.

The bulk of this article uses example figures and scenarios from the US. The reason for this is simply that the US is the furthest advanced in diagnosing and fixing the potential problems that Y2K brings. Similar scenarios, test-results, figures and predictions for Britain and Europe just don't exist yet. Or if they do, they are not made public. The best guess currently is that almost 65 per cent of affected applications will be Y2K-compliant in Western Europe. Or to put it another way, over a third won't.

The latest British government estimates are that 700,000 small firms and businesses in the UK have Y2K problems. This is why the Government's Millennium Project was set up with the aim to train 20,000 programmers to help fix the problem. But it isn't that simple. By the end of September 1998, the number of programmers the project had trained was just twenty-six. This is part of the reason why the Taskforce 2000 group describes the UK Government's efforts as: 'ill-conceived, badly administered and poorly led'.

1999

01

Incursion

For an early-warning installation, the irony was that they were taken by surprise. With the Siberian winter already beginning to cut into the guards' morale as well as their bones, the assault team was able to get right to the electrified wire without being detected.

The assumption was that despite the importance of the base, there would be no heat-sensitive surveillance. The fact that it was so deep inside the former Soviet Bloc coupled with the failing Russian economy and lack of funding for the military meant that this was a fair assumption. It was one which proved to be true. The six black-clad figures waited for several minutes as they checked the positions of the searchlights and the sentries. Their night vision goggles showed each clearly. Even the breath of the nearest sentry was visible, a pale green mist across the zoomed image.

'Go.' The team leader signalled to the technical expert, who already had the wires in place. Using insulated gloves and rubber-handled shears, he cut through the chain links of the fence. The current continued uninterrupted through the wires attached to either side of the hole - the circuit was unbroken, the alarm not triggered.

The most hazardous part was crossing the open area between the perimeter fence and the buildings. If they were spotted now, before their mission had really got under way, then they would have no option but to pull out and abandon the objective. But they made it without incident, shadows flitting across the parched, cold ground.

They had all memorised the maps, and knew exactly where they were. And where they were headed. There was a guard on the door to the low concrete bunker that was their primary objective. His cap was pulled down low over his features, his rifle slung over his shoulder as he clapped his gloved hands together in an attempt to stave off the cold. If he caught sight of the dark figure that leaped out from the corner of the building, he had no time to show it. The silenced shot caught the guard in the chest, driving him backwards into the door of the bunker. He slumped slowly to the ground, his cap angled drunkenly over one eye.

They dragged him inside the bunker and dumped the body in the corridor. One of the black-clad figures remained at the door while the others made their silent way to the main control room.

Before they reached it, a door opened further along the corridor and two soldiers emerged. They were laughing as they turned, as they saw the intruders. They stopped laughing.

The first of the soldiers pulled at his rifle. But the strap tangled in the collar of his heavy coat for long enough to slow his movement. A near-silent shot from the handgun of one of the raiders took him in the chest. The other soldier turned to run, shouting loudly.

The intruders had scattered to the sides of the corridor and knelt for cover as soon as the soldier appeared. The figure nearest to the soldier was holding a Heckler and Koch G41 assault rifle. A night sight was fitted to the standard mounting, but the intruder did not take the time to aim. He loosed off a three-round burst which caught the soldier in the back, driving him through the door he had recently emerged from. Immediately there were shouts and commotion from inside.

'Damn.' The assault leader signalled for two of his men to hold their positions in the corridor. The other three followed him at a run to the control room. The alarms were going off as they burst through the doors, spraying the room with fully automatic 9mm fire.

There were half a dozen people in the room. The initial burst of fire caught all but two of them. Aimed shots followed almost at once, knocking one of the survivors to the floor, smashing the other over one of the consoles.

For a moment there was silence. The three black-clad men surveyed the room, waiting for any sign of movement. There was none.

'Which ones?'

It was the same man who had cut through the wire who answered the leader. He pointed to two of the control units, heavy metal systems bolted to the floor with small built-in screens and disk drives. Each was about three feet high, a foot deep and eight inches across. 'Those two. That should leave the main surveillance systems operational.'

'How long?'

The other figure was already examining the bolts that held the units in place. 'Two minutes.'

'Make it one.'

The man nodded. He pulled a tube of plastic explosive from his pocket and started squeezing the grey putty-like substance round the edge of one of the bolts.

The assault leader was speaking into a microphone sewn to his lapel as the two intruders smeared explosive round each bolt, then wired them together. 'Units 3 and 4, we need one minute. Keep the corridor clear for exit. Unit 5, what's happening?'

In his earpiece he could hear the report from the man at the main door to the bunker. 'Some movement, no attempt to gain access yet. Still mobilising and wondering what the hell's happening. Probably think it's a false alarm. Or a drill.'

The leader ducked down behind a console as one of the men setting the explosives signalled to him. They were all under cover when the charges blew. The sound was masked by the blaring noise of the alarms, and the explosions were not large. But they were enough to shear through the bolts and free the control units from their mountings. The leader watched as the two men each lifted one of the units, hefting it up on to the shoulder.

'OK?'

'Just about.'

He spoke into the lapel mike again. 'Whirlwind, are you getting this?'

The response crackled in his earpiece, the voice barely audible above the background drone. 'On our way. Extraction in ninety seconds, I say again, nine zero seconds.'

The leader nodded to his two men. 'Go.'

In the corridor, units three and four were laying down covering fire. The sound of the unsilenced weapons was deafening in the enclosed space. As the assault leader and the two men carrying the control units emerged from the control room, the sound got louder. Bullets chipped at the paintwork around them as they pulled back and the Russian troops rallied.

At the main door, the intruder waved to his colleagues to wait. 'They're advancing now,' he said as he peered out through a small gap between door and frame.

The assault leader checked his watch. 'OK, now.'

The door was pulled open sharply, the intruders firing across the open ground outside. The Russian troops who were running towards the bunker dived for cover, some of them loosing off a few shots in reply. One of the intruders dropped to the ground, clutching at his leg.

But before the Russians could take better aim, a new sound mingled with that of the gunfire and the alarm klaxons. At the same moment huge searchlights illuminated the area, dazzling the Russians. They peered upwards into the light, trying to shade their eyes and at the same time see what was happening.

The assault team leader helped his colleague to his feet, supporting him. The wounded man was using his rifle as a makeshift crutch. Behind him two of them were laying down suppressing fire, keeping the corridor clear. Outside, the giant Chinook CH-47 helicopter was hovering a few feet off the ground. From inside it, automatic gunfire kept the Russians pinned down and the searchlights spilled over the surrounding buildings.

The intruders fired off a final burst down the corridor, then ran. The assault leader was practically carrying the wounded man. The two with the heavy consoles had them over their shoulders and they raced for the helicopter. Gunfire crackled around them, but failed to find its mark. The door in the side was slid open for them. The control consoles went in first. They were the most important. Then the leader bundled the wounded man into the craft. A moment later the other men were leaping in and already the heavy aircraft was lifting away.

On the ground, the Russian soldiers stood up, one by one, and watched as the huge helicopter swung away and picked up speed.

Colonel Sergeyev Dobrynin stood in the middle of the control room, rubbing his chin. Slumped in a chair close by, one of the technicians shot by the intruders was groggily shaking his head as he came round.

'We were lucky, sir,' Lieutenant Kolkonayev said.

'Lucky? The base infiltrated and equipment removed? I have to explain that to Moscow, Lieutenant. I have to call up Colonel Krimkov and tell him his systems are compromised. You should be so lucky.'

'I meant, sir, that nobody was killed.'

Dobrynin nodded slowly. 'I suppose so.'

'And the system is not compromised, sir.'

Dobrynin's eyes narrowed as he stared at his second-in-command.

'The two units they removed, sir, they do not compromise the system. The other systems can cover for them, maintain integrity.'

Dobrynin sighed. 'Nobody killed, but some sort of anaesthetic capsule used. And the system integrity maintained.' He clicked his tongue. 'I think this may be even harder to explain.'

Across the room, a technician called out to Dobrynin. 'A call for you, sir.'

'Not now,' he growled back.

'But, sir, it is Colonel Krimkov.'

Dobrynin and Kolkonayev exchanged glances. The lieutenant gave a slight shake of his head. 'I have not... Nobody has communicated with Moscow since this happened. Perhaps it is a coincidence.'

Dobrynin raised an eyebrow. 'And perhaps the Pope is a Jew.'

Krimkov's tone was unexpectedly light. 'Ah, Colonel Dobrynin, how are things out there?'

'It is the middle of the night, Colonel,' Dobrynin replied, 'hardly the time for social calls. I think you know exactly how things are out here.'

There was a slight pause before Krimkov said: 'I'm not sure that I do, actually. But I have just taken an intriguing call from General Randall in London. I think that perhaps you have a report to deliver.'

02

Working Late

The offices were never dark. But at night, when they were empty, the lighting was reduced to a lower level, a twilight gloom. As the security guards made their rounds, the movement sensors would override the timer and turn up the lights, fading them down again once all was still.

Although there was no movement as such, the sensors were confused enough to try to turn up the lights. But the link between the sensors and the lighting controls had already been disabled. A precaution, a way of ensuring nobody outside the building would see the figures moving around inside.

So it was in near darkness that the TARDIS arrived. The flashing light on top of its police box outer shell illuminated the surrounding open-plan office in time to the rasping rhythm of the materialisation. With a solid thump, the process ended and the TARDIS was real, standing in a corner of the large room. A moment later the door opened and the Doctor's head emerged. He surveyed the dimly lit room, then stepped out and closed the door. He stood for a moment, looking round. His wide-brimmed hat was perched on top of the masses of brown curls that erupted from his scalp, and his already enormous eyes bulged alarmingly as he peered through the gloom.

'No coins for the meter, perhaps,' he murmured as he waved a cheery hand at the light sensor. 'How odd.' His frown lasted only a second, then he jammed his hands into his pockets and set off across the office, scarf trailing behind him like an obedient puppy. 'Little look round, Doctor?' he said cheerfully to himself as he went. He answered himself in a slightly deeper but no less enthusiastic tone. 'Don't mind if I do.'

There was a door at the end of the office, and the Doctor tugged it open. He emerged at the top of a stairwell and looked round with interest. There was a wide, carpeted walkway round the stairs, and a second door leading into another office area. The Doctor could see the cubicles and workstations through a window beside the door. On the other side of the door was a small post with a badge reader set into the top of it. Behind him, as the Doctor looked round, the door swung quietly shut, the movement cushioned by a hydraulic lever so that it did not slam.

On the wall beside the stairs was a printed plaque which caught the Doctor's eye. He leaned forward to see it better, hands still deep in his trouser pockets.

'Condef - Our Operating Principles,' he read out loud. 'One, our shareholders and the marketplace are the guiding force behind everything that we do.' He considered this for a moment, then pushed his hat further back on his head and grunted. 'Huh. Nothing about people then? What's happened to respect for the individual, eh? Tell me that.' He looked at the plaque again, taking it in at a single glance. 'Aha. Number nine touches on it.' He turned round and headed back the way he had come. 'Nine,' he muttered. 'And I always thought humans had an inflated opinion of themselves.'

At the door he had come through earlier, the Doctor stopped. It was closed. Like the other door, there was a window set into the wall beside it, and through this window the Doctor could see the TARDIS. He frowned at the badge reader and tried the door handle. As he had suspected, the door would not open.

For a moment the Doctor stood silent and motionless. Then he clicked his tongue and pulled out his sonic screwdriver. He tapped it against the palm of his hand. 'We respect Condef property and assets,' he murmured. 'And that was number six. Besides, the security people will have a fit.' With that he turned on his heel and headed for the stairs. There must be a security control room. If he could find that they would ask him all sorts of awkward questions, and by way of answer he could lead them up to the TARDIS and whiz off before they could complain. Nobody would believe their story, so they wouldn't tell anyone. That way everyone was happy. And maybe, he mused, he could fix the faulty lighting sensors for them while he was there.

* * *

George Gardner was leafing through a copy of *Computing* and waiting for the PC to redraw his project chart when the lights went out. He was not unduly worried. The lights often went out in the evenings. He waved his arm in the air, expecting the sensor to detect the movement and turn the lights back on. He must have been sitting too still for too long.

But nothing happened. 'Twenty-five billion pounds,' George muttered. 'So far.' He had glanced through an article on the cost so far in Britain of preparing computer systems for the millennium. And that was just the money spent. What about the stress and extra time put in by programmers, analysts and project managers like himself? The real cost was much higher, and still rising.

'It's not the millennium yet,' he said out loud for the benefit of the lights, and reached for his phone. On the computer screen in front of him, his project chart appeared. Better, he mused as he felt round the phone for the right button to call Security. At least with these estimates the millennium work would be finished in January. Better, but still not good enough.

No answer.

And that was assuming his numbers were right, which was a hell of a gamble in itself.

Still no answer.

George swore, slammed down the phone, and turned back to his screen. But it did not take him long to decide he needed more light, if only to see the keyboard and his handwritten notes of dates and resources. He sighed, started the secure screen saver and negotiated his way across the gloomy open-plan office area towards the main door.

There were three guards in the security control room behind the main foyer. Two were slumped over the main console, the other was lying face down on the floor.

'Excuse me, gentlemen.' The Doctor pulled the two seated guards slightly apart so that he could get between them and reach the console. Most of the wall above was taken up with a bank of monitor screens showing grainy black and white images of the interior and exterior of the building. After a few moments, the Doctor found the video controls he was searching for, and one of the images - a view of the main approach to the reception area - started winding rapidly backwards. There was no movement, so the only indication that it was doing this was the retreating time code along the bottom of the image and distortion lines caused by the rapid winding.

As the tape wound back, the Doctor sniffed carefully. 'Melsham's gas,' he said to himself. 'Very sophisticated.' He glanced back at the unconscious guards. Melsham's gas was practically undetectable, even to the point that when they awoke the guards would probably never realise they had been unconscious. They might wonder why the time had passed so quickly though.

He stopped the tape and let it run forwards. But he had already seen on the rewind what he was looking for. He watched it again in real time. A man walked up the path to the reception area. He was looking around as he came, as if he was lost. Too much as if he was lost. He entered the foyer. A minute later he left again, walking quickly away from the building.

'Man comes in,' the Doctor murmured, 'and asks for help or directions. Leaves a small gas cylinder timed to go off in a few minutes, and leaves. All very innocent. But why?'

He looked round the small room. No lights, no surveillance. He clicked his fingers in realisation and grinned. 'Someone wanted to get inside without being seen. Now, either they've already left in which case the tapes would have been doctored, Doctor. Or...' He leaned forward again and started flipping through different views of the interior of the building. At last he found what he was looking for. 'Aha.'

The screen that had shown main reception now showed what looked like a factory area. As everywhere else except reception and the security room, the lights were off. But powerful torch beams were cutting through the darkness, making their way towards the centre of the factory floor.

It was not until he reached the main foyer and reception area that

George found the lights on. There was no sign of the security guards, so he marched up to their small control room. The door was open.

'I don't know if it has escaped your attention –' he started. He stopped.

Inside the room two of the guards were slumped in their chairs, apparently asleep. A third was lying on the floor and George had almost fallen over him. Standing in the room, smiling broadly, was a large man with a large hat and long scarf. Everything about him seemed large, from his teeth to his hair to his eyes.

'Hello there,' the man said and George was not surprised that his voice was loud and deep.

'Who the hell are you?' he asked.

'Well, I'm the Doctor,' the man said as if this should have been immediately evident, 'and this is a bag of jelly babies.' He thrust a crumpled paper bag towards George. 'Try one,' he offered, 'they're really rather good.'

George hesitated, then took a jelly baby from the bag. It was a dolly mixture. He knew it was a dolly mixture. And he had a suspicion that the strange man who had offered it to him knew as well, but he was not about to ask.

'Now,' the man said, 'tell me, are you one of the people who's breaking in, or are you as surprised at what's going on as I am?'

The factory was attached to the Condef software laboratory by a glassed-in bridge that ran for about twenty metres and connected the two separate buildings. Quite why George Gardner was leading a complete stranger through the most secure areas of Condef, he wasn't sure. But there was something about the man, a sense of confidence and familiarity, that engendered friendship and trust.

It had been difficult to tell what the intruders were doing from the fuzzy images on the screen in the control room. But one thing had become apparent as the Doctor zoomed the image in on one of them.

'Hey, that's a gun,' George had exclaimed.

The Doctor had nodded grimly, and said: 'That's it then. Time to go.'

George, in his naivety, had assumed he meant leave. It turned out he meant go and see what the intruders were up to for themselves. The armed intruders. Armed and dangerous intruders.

He must be going mad.

George watched the Doctor lead the way along the bridge, kicking his scarf out of his way as he went. If he was going mad, then he was in good company.

'Through here?' the Doctor asked as they reached another security door.

George nodded and slid his badge through the reader. There was a click as the lock released, and George pushed the door open carefully. He nodded for the Doctor to go through first.

'Thank you,' the Doctor said with a huge grin. He paused midway through the door. 'What did you say your name was?'

'I didn't.'

The Doctor frowned. 'What does the I stand for, Mr Didn't?'

'No, no. It's Gardner. George Gardner.' He gulped. 'I'm the Y2K project manager.'

'How very impressive.' The Doctor disappeared through the door. His voice floated back through the opening. 'Come along, George. Can't be far now.'

The door led into a small viewing area at the edge of the factory floor. Through a large glass screen they could see into the vast assembly area. Tracks ran round the ceiling, with electronic components and circuit boards hanging from them. Conveyor belts snaked around the huge factory. The whole area was automated, though it was shut down now for the night.

'There has to be a supervisor,' George whispered as they peered from the darkened room out into the dimly lit assembly area. 'Otherwise they'd run seven twenty-four. I mean, all day every day.' They could just make out the dark shapes of figures standing round several control consoles in the distance.

'What are they doing?' the Doctor whispered back, so quietly that George wondered if he was talking to himself.

He answered anyway. 'I don't know. But those are the control systems for the assembly process. We certified them last month.'

'Certified?'

'For Y2K.'

'Ah. And what's that?'

'You know. Millennium bug. Make sure they'll still work OK in January.' He watched the figures as they worked at the consoles. 'Who are they?' he asked. And this prompted another thought. 'Who are *you*?'

'Well, that's rather difficult to explain.' The Doctor's teeth gleamed in the darkness. 'But I'm friendly. Which is more than we can say for them.' He grabbed George by the shoulder suddenly and whispered loudly, 'I think we've seen enough. Time we got some help.'

George nodded. 'The police.'

'The fire brigade,' the Doctor retorted. He moved aside and pointed to a fire alarm on the wall. 'In case of fire, break glass,' he murmured. 'How very satisfying.' And with that he knocked his elbow into the small glass plate. Immediately the alarm sounded, a bell ringing painfully loudly.

George clapped his hands over his ears. The effect on the intruders in the factory was more extreme. They were running, torch beams wavering and swinging haphazardly as they made for the main doors.

The fire chief was used to false alarms of one sort or another. George had a harder job convincing the police inspector that he could not simply have called 999.

'We panicked,' the Doctor said, looking and sounding anything but panicky. George explained that the Doctor was an expert in the millennium bug. He had called for a meeting with George, and found reception unmanned and the guards out cold. The rest of their story pretty well matched the reality of events. The inspector questioned them just long enough to make sarcastic comments about meetings at one o'clock in the morning, and to note that George had not been logged into the building. When the

Doctor explained in painstaking and patient detail that he would not have been logged in as he was working late and had never left in order to come back and be logged, the inspector decided that enough was enough.

The security guards came round, as the Doctor predicted, with no ill effects and hardly aware they had missed anything. The surveillance cameras showed nothing that seemed useful in identifying the intruders or their intentions.

As soon as nobody seemed interested in them any longer, the Doctor took George to one side. 'I'd like to look at the factory area again,' he said.

George nodded. 'All right.' He yawned. 'But we'd better make it quick, before I fall asleep.'

The assembly line had started up for the morning shift already. 'What do you make?' the Doctor asked as he watched casings and circuit boards swing past the observation area, hanging on plastic lines from the ceiling tracks.

'I can't tell you that.' George was standing by a computer screen set into a small console at the side of the room.

'You mean you don't know?' the Doctor was amazed. 'You do work here, don't you?'

'I mean I can't tell you. Official secrets.'

'Hmm,' the Doctor grunted, and shifted Gorge aside so he could examine the screen. 'Component list and assembly diagram. Seems simple enough.' He watched the schematics and parts lists scroll past for a few moments. 'Early-warning systems and input data monitoring for GPS positioning and reverse triangulation.' He grinned at George's surprised expression. 'Pretty basic by the look of it.'

'Basic?!'

But before George could comment further, the Doctor jabbed his finger at the display, at the same time stopping the list that was scrolling up the screen. 'What's that for?'

George looked at where the Doctor was pointing. 'It's a piggy-back chip. Secondary system of some sort. SB005.' He frowned. 'SB is Silver Bullet. I didn't think we used any of their stuff.'

'Werewolves?' the Doctor hazarded.

George chuckled. 'I sometimes think so. They have a Y2K solution, a combination of hardware and software. Everyone says its brilliant, a simple and immediate fix.'

'But you're not convinced.'

'I looked at it of course. But I don't want to bet my job on anything I can't understand. Not that I care much now, I suppose.'

'Complicated, then.'

'Not really.' George was frowning. 'Just lots of redundancy. Stubs for code that isn't there, backup and subsidiary systems and protocols that seem unrelated to the main task.' He shrugged. 'I don't know, I just didn't like it, I suppose.'

The Doctor smiled broadly. 'Well that's good enough for me. Go with your instincts, I always say. If it seems like a good idea at the time.' He turned back to the screen. 'And my instincts tell me something here is terribly wrong.'

'We disturbed them,' George said. 'They got scared off before they could take anything.'

'Ah, yes.' The Doctor nodded, his face was grim suddenly. 'But what if they weren't trying to take anything?' His voice dropped to a melodramatic stage whisper: 'What if they were putting something in?' He paused for a few moments, pulling his scarf absently through his fingers. 'I wonder...'

'But what?' George asked.

'Shhh,' the Doctor admonished him. 'I'm wondering.'

They stood in silence for a while, George shuffling his tired feet impatiently. The constant movement in the factory beside them was a contrast to the Doctor's stillness. Suddenly, the Doctor flinched, as if waking up with a start. 'Yes,' he said with evident satisfaction. 'Yes, I think that must be it. Now,' he fixed his unblinking gaze on George, 'what did you mean about not caring about your job any more?'

It took George a few seconds to make the mental switch back to his earlier comments. 'Oh, er, well. I'm getting out, that's all. Before the bug strikes. Once we shut down for Christmas, that's it for me...'

'Getting out?'

'The project won't be finished, not by a long way. But I've seen enough of what can go wrong in our systems, I know enough about what isn't fixed to scare the hell out of me. I mean, we're well prepared for the millennium. But what about everyone else?'

'And where were you thinking of going?'

'I've got a place in Yorkshire. Disused bunker, actually. On the moors. I'll sit it out there.'

'You think things will get that bad?'

George's tone was serious. 'Oh yes,' he said. 'Yes, I do.'

In response the Doctor grinned. 'Well, before you go,' he said, 'perhaps you could take a look at that Silver Bullet chip for me.'

George was dubious. 'I can try. Why are you so interested?'

'Melsham's gas,' the Doctor replied darkly.

'Melsham's gas? Is that what knocked out the guards?'

The Doctor nodded.

'So?'

'So it isn't the sort of sophisticated neural inhibitor I'd expect to find on a planet at this stage of its history.' The Doctor leaned forward, and his face was suddenly shrouded in shadows. 'There's something happening here that's very wrong, Mr Gardner. I must find out what.'

George was frowning back at the Doctor. 'Planet?' he murmured. Then he sighed and shook his head. 'So what am I looking for exactly?'

'I'm not sure. But if you think it's important, there's someone I'd like you to talk to.' He already had a stub of pencil in his hand and pulled a crumpled paper from his jacket pocket. It was the empty bag that the dolly mixtures had been in. He scribbled a name on the bag, then an address. George took the paper, and stared at it. The name meant nothing to him. The address he recognised, although it was only three characters long.

03
Meetings

The after-work crowd was thinning out and the pub was getting quieter. George Gardner took a furtive sip from his pint and looked round again. The man he had met smiled across the small round wooden table at him.

'I'm sorry,' George said. 'I'm not much good at this secret stuff.'

The man shrugged. 'So how did you find me?' he asked.

George pulled the crumpled paper bag from his pocket, looking round again as he did so. There was nobody within earshot, and no one seemed interested in the two men. He smoothed out the bag and handed it to the man. 'He wrote on this, just before he left. Said I should call you if I found anything.'

The other man took the bag. 'Clever of you to find me,' he said. On the bag, in broad and untidy pencil, was scrawled: *Harry Sullivan MI5*.

'I got the number from the MI5 website. Thank you for meeting me.'

Harry shook his head. 'I should thank you,' he said. 'I don't know what's going on, but if you met the Doctor and he said to call me, then it's probably as well you did. Where did you phone from?'

George smiled nervously. 'I was going to call from work, but I thought perhaps I'd better use a phone box. You know, in case.'

Harry nodded. 'Probably as well.'

'You don't think...' George was looking round again anxiously.

'No,' Harry said with a smile, 'I don't. But it's always as well to be careful.' He took a swig of beer. 'You told me about this raid, or whatever it was, and about meeting the Doctor. Now, why did you call me? After nearly a week, what happened to make you think it was worth the trouble?'

George considered. 'A few things, I suppose. I didn't think much of it, just a break-in. Leave it to the experts. You know. But then I remembered what the Doctor said about putting something in, and about the Silver Bullet chip.'

'You took a look at it?'

George nodded. 'I checked the manufacturing logs. And I couldn't find out when the chip was introduced into the assembly cycle. But it is listed.'

'So?'

'So it's not on the original blueprints for the board. That means it must have been added, and that means a design change request and approval. But there's neither. It's as if it was always there, except it wasn't.'

Harry nodded encouragement. 'Go on.'

'Well, I looked at the chip. I don't understand it, not yet. I pulled one to run some Y2K diagnostics and checks.' He paused, and took a large gulp of beer. He wiped away the froth from his mouth with the back of his hand. 'I tell you,' he said, 'I'm glad I'm leaving. Next week, that's it. Someone else can clear up this mess. I'm out of here.'

Harry frowned. 'Why? What about the chip?'

'It failed,' George said simply. 'I haven't told anyone. Since there's nobody logged as responsible for it, I don't know who I should tell. Who I *could* tell. But we have a chip in the main systems board, produced by a company that makes its fortune from solutions to the millennium bug, and it's going to fail catastrophically at midnight on December 31st.' He leaned forward, not noticing as he folded his hands in a pool of spilt beer. 'Things will be bad enough,' he said quietly. 'But someone is deliberately making them worse.'

Harry thought about this. 'These Silver Bullet people, you reckon?'

'I don't know. I'm not sure I care.' He shook his head. 'Then there's the Russian colonel.'

Harry set his beer carefully down on the table. 'Russian colonel,' he repeated. 'Tell me about the Russian colonel.'

George shrugged. 'Not much to tell. Just one other worrying thing. Well, maybe not worrying, but odd. Matt Smollett said he saw a Russian colonel in the board room. There was some high-level meeting with NATO brass, director-level execs. You know the sort of thing. Not unusual.'

'Except for the Russian.'

'Well, if there was one. I'm only going by what Matt told me.'

They sat in silence for a while. Then Harry said, 'OK, let's concentrate on this Silver Bullet crowd then. Any idea how I can get more information about them and what they do?'

'They hold technology briefings every week now in the run-up to the millennium. They send out free invites to companies who haven't signed up with them yet.' George rummaged in his coat pocket and pulled out a couple of small printed forms. 'They call it a technology briefing, but it's really a sales pitch of course. They're out to sell their kit. The next one's tomorrow.'

He handed the forms to Harry. 'It's at the Grosvenor House Hotel, starts at nine-thirty. You can hand them in at the door and get badges.'

But Harry was shaking his head. He handed back one of the forms. 'No,' he said firmly. '*We* can hand them in at the door and get badges.'

The Grosvenor House Hotel was on Park Lane. Harry took the tube to Marble Arch and walked. He arrived at nine-fifteen to find George Gardner waiting for him outside the entrance, looking nervous and tired. They walked in without speaking. The conference was signposted, and they followed several other people down a flight of stairs to a foyer area. Long tables were set up, mostly labelled with sets of letters - A to H, I to L, and so on.

Harry followed George to a table at the back of the area which had a sign attached to its front saying *Late Registrations*. A young blonde woman with a synthetic smile glued to her face took Harry's form and fed it into a small scanner. He watched the edge of the light trace across the form inside.

'OCR,' George muttered and Harry nodded, wondering what that meant.

A moment later the woman took a laminated badge the size of a credit card from the side of the scanner, attached a small clip to one end of it and handed it to Harry together with a folder of papers. She took George's form without comment and without change of expression.

Harry examined his badge. It had the Silver Bullet logo on it, which was rather predictably a silver bullet smashing through a glass 'Y2K'. Underneath this in bold lettering his name was misspelled. Below that it said TARDIS TIME SYSTEMS. It had seemed an appropriate cover.

'I'm "George Guard Her", apparently,' George said as they followed the crowd through to the ball room. His badge actually said 'George Gardher'.

'Happy Sullivan,' Harry replied. 'Pleased to meet you.'

They emerged on to a gallery that ran round the ball room, stairs leading down at each end. Off the gallery was an open area where coffee and biscuits were being served by uniformed hotel staff. But people were already being ushered down the stairs to take their seats. Harry and George followed the flow and ended up about half-way down the left side of the ballroom. In front of them a stage had been set up, and behind that were two huge display screens. At the moment they each showed different views of the room, both looking out into the audience.

Harry resisted the urge to wave to himself, and instead looked through the papers in his folder. There was a floor plan that showed him where he was and where he could get coffee. Nobody had bothered to mark in the toilets, he noticed. There was also an agenda sheet and several sets of stapled printed sheets that called themselves White Papers. Their titles were hardly enthralling - the only one that meant anything to Harry was called *Optimising Your Systems for Silver Bullet* - and the text was even more impenetrable. He turned back to the agenda.

'So who are these people?' Harry asked, pointing to the names of the speakers on his sheet.

George looked over at the agenda, running his finger down the names against the various sessions. 'Most of them are Silver Bullet executives. A couple of industry pundits. He's a journalist who ought to know better.'

'Oh?'

'Yes, writes for one of the networking rags. He won't be able to flaunt his impartiality so easily after this.'

'That depends on what he's going to say, surely,' Harry said.

George gave a short laugh. 'We can both guess what he's going to say. Same as most of the reviewers. Only solution that's guaranteed effective against the millennium bug. Everyone should buy one.'

The conversations round the room died as the lights began to dim. A spotlight came on illuminating the stage and the man who stepped up to the podium. Behind him the screens changed to show two similar but not quite identical close-up views of the man.

'The man himself,' George whispered to Harry. 'That's Byron Cutter, chairman and CEO.'

Cutter's voice was deep and clear, sounding from speakers around the room. 'It is good to see so many of you could be with us here today,' he said. 'And as you are all aware we're here to look at the benefits and advantages of deploying the Silver Bullet Y2K Solution Pack throughout your companies. All companies in fact can reap almost immeasurable benefits, whether you're considering it as a desktop solution or an enterprise-wide roll-out, whether you're a two man and a dog outfit or a multinational.'

Cutter paused for a moment, as if he had just noticed something. Then he reached out tentatively towards a glass of water standing on a shelf beside the podium. He carefully lifted it and, keeping it at arm's length, moved it across to the back of the nearby table.

'We'll look at some of the facts and figures later on in Mr Bardell's session,' Cutter continued as soon as the water was out of the way. 'But for the moment, let me give you a one-pager of the company, and of the product itself.' He paused for a moment to look round the audience, and Harry could see on the screens that he seemed to be suppressing a smile. The left edge of his mouth twisted upwards slightly as he continued: 'Of course I shall be happy to answer any questions or points you wish to raise...' He paused again before adding, 'During the coffee break.'

'In other words,' George whispered to Harry, 'this is it and you can take it or leave it.'

There was a disorderly queue for the coffee. The biscuits, left round the coffee area on plates, were already gone by the time Harry and George got anywhere close to them. Byron Cutter and the other Silver Bullet speakers were nowhere to be seen.

Harry had found the morning so far pretty much impenetrable. His head was spinning from the technical and marketing jargon and hype. He was bored with 'win-win scenarios', sick of 'one-stop shops', and was hoping he never fell over an 'extensible open-ended industry standard protocol' in case he did actually recognise it.

Contrastingly, George was in his element. He was obviously not a fan of the Silver Bullet product or their way of selling it, and he vented his anti-enthusiasm by pointing out holes in the minute details and misleading assumptions in the overall picture. Almost all of it was lost on Harry.

But, Harry reflected as they neared the front of the queue, he had got what he came for. He had an overall impression of the company and their product, and he was beginning to understand both its importance and the level of interest for it.

'Black or white, sir?'

'Oh yes, absolutely,' Harry replied automatically before he realised that this was something he actually did understand. 'Sorry, white.'

The coffee was strong and tepid. Harry followed George back through the cluster of people round the tables where the coffee was being handed out, trying to protect his cup from the jostling and gesticulation of Important People who seemed not to be aware of his existence. George, he noticed, was opting for a different strategy. He was holding his cup out in front of him like a weapon and calling excuse-me's and sorry's as he went. It seemed to work.

The woman who approached them was tall, slim and striking.

She was wearing a dark suit with a white blouse. Her hair was blonde and shoulder length. It swayed as she moved as if it were a single structure rather than individual strands. Harry and George had found space behind a pillar close to the edge of the gallery and Harry was explaining that he reckoned he had seen enough and might give the rest of the morning a miss.

'You're George Gardner, aren't you?' Her voice was silky smooth, her complexion pale and flawless. 'Condef, yes?'

'Yes,' George said, immediately switching his attention from Harry. 'Don't believe the badge. Those OCR readers always get it wrong.'

'Oh, I don't know,' Harry said, looking down at his own badge. He had noticed that she was not wearing one.

The woman ignored him. 'I hope you don't mind me interrupting,' she said to George. 'Andrea Cave.' She held out her hand for George to shake. Only after that did she look at Harry. 'Mr Sullivan,' she read, ignoring the Happy bit. 'I don't think I've heard of your company.'

Harry returned her smile. 'It's been around for a long time,' he said. 'But we do a lot of work offshore.' He shook her hand. 'And who are you with?'

'I'm not with anyone,' she said. 'I run my own PR company. But at the moment I'm contracted to Silver Bullet to help them project the right image.'

'I'd say you were doing a good job,' Harry said quickly before George could comment.

'I have other clients too, of course,' she said, turning back to George. 'One of them is especially interested in Condef. I think perhaps you can help them out. Them and me.'

George frowned. 'Oh?'

'Don't worry,' she said, moving slightly to avoid George's swaying coffee cup, 'it's all above board. Well, almost.' She looked round quickly, and then said: 'A government body. A bit secret, I'm afraid.'

George glanced at Harry. 'Wouldn't know anything about that sort of thing,' he said.

'There are some concerns,' Andrea Cave went on, 'I wouldn't put it any stronger than that.'

'About Silver Bullet?' Harry asked.

'About Condef. Silver Bullet may be implicated, that's not for me to say.'

'So how do you think I can help?' George asked.

'I wonder,' she said, 'have you seen anything strange going on at Condef? Odd data? Secret meetings? Weird requests?'

Harry stared at George. They knew nothing about this woman, and until they did he was distinctly uneasy about telling her anything.

George caught Harry's look. He shook his head. 'Nothing out of the ordinary. No. Why?'

In reply she handed him a folded sheet of paper. As George unfolded it and read what was on it, she said, 'I assume you're familiar with these products?'

'They're all Condef systems.'

'And they have all been certified as Y2K-compliant by your group, isn't that right?'

George nodded. 'If you say so. I don't recall them all offhand.'

'Whether you recall them or not, you might want to double check them.' She looked round again, then said quietly, 'You see, we don't think they're Y2K-compliant any more.'

Around them there was a general movement back in the direction of the stairs down to the ballroom. As they were jostled, Andrea Cave handed George a business card. 'Call me when you've checked. We should talk.'

Harry watched as she seemed to be absorbed into the throng of people making their way back for the next session. It was only when he reached the bottom of the stairs that he remembered he had intended to slip away.

04

Reverse Engineering

The background check that Harry ran on Silver Bullet pulled up nothing remarkable. He didn't bother with a full computer check, but instead pulled the news clippings and printed materials. He was tired enough already without staring at a screen for the next few hours. He could make registered copies of the clippings and take them home with him, so long as he locked them in his safe at night. For the computer link he had to be in his office, and it was already late.

There were two messages on the answerphone. The first was from Sylvia Webb, the young woman who did his cleaning and ironing, to say she would be late the next day. Since she came during the day when Harry was usually out, she tended to keep her own time anyway and so it was hardly a problem. The second message was more interesting. It was from George Gardner.

'Oh, er, hi. Yes. It's me, um, you know.' The voice was tinny and distorted as it was squeezed through the small speaker. 'Harry? I looked at the equipment that, er, our mutual friend mentioned.' He was obviously struggling to find a way of saying things indirectly, and Harry found himself smiling as he remembered his own first gauche steps into the intelligence services. 'She was right, they're all, er, affected. Same way as I told you before. Same chip even. And again no record of it being introduced, it's just there suddenly.' There was a long pause, and Harry guessed that George was wondering if he should say any more. 'I'll meet you for lunch tomorrow,' George's voice said after a while. 'Same place as last time. Noon. I'll wait till one, I hope you can make that.' Another pause, then, with renewed urgency: 'Those chips are in everything, Harry. I don't know what they do, but I'm going to take a good look at one tonight. Hell, I got a new toaster the other day, there's even one in that.'

The answerphone clicked off. Harry sucked in his cheeks. He

could make noon at the pub tomorrow, and he had an uneasy feeling it was important that he be there.

'Just over one hour ago,' Bardell said, 'an SB chip got pulled.'

Cutter was sitting attentively as Bardell spoke. He was leaning forwards, chin in his hands, and elbows resting on his knees. He rocked very gently back and forth. Beside him sat Martyn Clark, his arms folded, his head swaying slightly as he concentrated.

They were in the war room. Bardell's laptop computer was on a small table beside him, its display linked to the larger of the screens set into the wall. The screen showed a close-up view of an SB005 chip spinning slowly about its centre point.

'The chip was in a Condef subsystem of the Eurofighter command and control system,' Bardell went on. He tapped a key on the laptop and the image on the screen was replaced by a picture of a crowded auditorium. It was a shot of the Grosvenor House Hotel's ballroom taken during the previous day's Silver Bullet Technical Briefing. The view zoomed in on two people until their grainy faces filled the screen. One was George Gardner, the other was Harry Sullivan.

'George Gardner,' Bardell said, 'is the Condef Y2K project manager. As you can see, he was at yesterday's session. It is likely that he pulled the chip.'

'Probability?' Cutter snapped.

'He spoke with Andi Cave at the coffee break. Probability projections are 83 per cent.'

Cutter nodded. 'And the other man?'

'The other man is a problem,' Bardell admitted. 'The name he gave is Sullivan. But since the company he claimed to represent does not exist, that may also be an alias. It's unclear whether he was with Gardner or not, but they certainly talked. He also spoke with Cave.'

Cutter nodded slowly. 'And the chip that was pulled? Any sign of interference?'

'Nothing yet.' It was Clark who answered. 'It hasn't signalled that it's being tampered with or examined. Provided it's on a mains power system somewhere, it will call into the network if there's a problem.'

Cutter stood up. 'Then let's hope there isn't a problem. Very well, gentlemen. Keep me up to speed.' He turned to leave.

'What should we do if the chip is compromised?' Clark asked.

Cutter paused. 'It may be necessary to delete Mr Gardner from our balance sheet. We do need an entry point to Condef still. There is certain information that would be of value to us. But liabilities and risks cannot be tolerated. Not now.'

Bardell snapped shut the lid of his laptop. The image on the screen died, leaving a dull grey panel. 'I'll output a contingency plan,' he said.

The chip nestled in the middle of an otherwise bare circuit board. Lines of solder ran from its pins, joining with other connections stamped on to the board. The board itself was connected to a COM port of George Gardner's home desktop PC. George put aside the soldering iron and peered at his work. Satisfied, he turned off the soldering iron. Then he turned on the computer. During its boot-up cycle it would interrogate the COM port and acquire the board. Then George could start running some serious diagnostics on the chip.

The chip, like any chip, required electricity to power it. This it drew through the connection to the PC from the mains supply. And as soon as it powered up and identified that it had been connected into an alien environment, it sent a simple pulsed sequence back along the same route as it took the power.

Oblivious to the microchip's cry for help, George Gardner started his diagnostics program.

'We have a pulsed SB005 signal.'

Clark and Bardell were huddled in front of a screen. Apart from the light from the display, the office was in darkness. A point of light was flashing in the middle of the screen, nestled in a dense, overlapping network of lines, a spaghetti mass of nodes and arcs.

'Where is that?' Bardell asked.

Clark moved the mouse, zooming the image in on the point of light. Around it some of the lines faded into the background while others became clearer. Eventually, the maze was reduced to a single track through the network.

Clark watched as, in a separate window, a list of first districts then streets scrolled past. 'The power lines are connected to an address in...' He looked across at Bardell as a single line of text remained. 'He's at home.'

Bardell nodded slowly. 'And what have we connected into his home power supply?'

Another list appeared, a colour-coded key. At the same time, more flashing lights grouped near the first but in different colours to match the key. Clark ran his finger down the list. 'A few domestic appliances, nothing major. Toaster, answerphone... Enough.'

'More than enough,' Bardell agreed. His thin face was, as ever, devoid of expression.

The chip was proving to be difficult. George sat back in his swivel chair, swinging it back and forth as he considered the problem. It was almost as if the thing was deliberately resisting any sort of analysis. He shook his head and tried another approach.

In the kitchen, the heating element inside the new toaster was glowing red hot. It had already been red hot for far longer than was ever intended by its designers. The casing of the toaster was beginning to sag, to distort. The plastic insulation on the wires that connected the mains power to the toaster was already softening inside the appliance. A glob of red plastic dripped from bare wire, sizzling as it hit the hot metal of the base of the toaster.

In another part of the toaster, the timer chip that controlled the toaster's heating cycle, the same chip that had activated the element on an infinite setting, clicked away the seconds until combustion.

A similar chip embedded within the answerphone George Gardner had bought the previous April monitored the data from the toaster chip. The information was passed through the house's ring main, carried through the electrical wiring. A separate signal was enough to burn out the internal connections of the nearest smoke alarm wired into the system.

George frowned, his concentration slipping slightly. Was that burning he could smell? But before he could think about that, the phone started ringing. There was a handset in the room with the computer, and George lifted it from its cradle.

'Hello?'

But there was only the dial tone. And the phone was still ringing. At least, the phone he was holding wasn't ringing, but he could hear the buzz of the answerphone from the hallway. Typical. He dropped the dead handset back into its cradle and waited for the answerphone to cut in and take the call. It didn't.

After fifteen rings, he swore and went to get it. The ringing stopped as he lifted the answerphone's receiver. From where he was standing he could see through the window at the end of the hall out into the close in which he lived. It was dark, but a car's headlights were cutting through the night, reflecting off the glass. He leaned forward slightly to see where the car was going.

His movement meant a slight delay in getting the handset to his ear. So it was not pressed to his head, not so close to his ear, as he said: 'Yes, who is it?'

Nevertheless, the loud, high-pitched wail that erupted from the phone was enough to drive him to his knees. For several moments he could hear nothing, was completely disorientated as he crawled across the floor. He could feel the blood rolling stickily down the side of his face from his punctured eardrum. And he could see the faint curls of dark smoke from the kitchen.

It was a supreme effort, but he managed to drag himself across the hall, the answerphone pulled from the table behind him as his leg snagged in the handset's cord. His hands were slippery as he tried to haul himself up to reach the latch on the front door. Twice he fell back, almost passing out. The third time he managed to turn the Yale lock, and pulled the door open as he fell backwards. A chill of cold air swept over him, reviving him just enough to crawl forwards to the threshold and collapse into the driveway outside.

Behind him, George could hear the upstairs smoke alarm wailing. The driveway was alight with the flickering of the fire that was taking hold in the kitchen. Already black smoke was billowing through the house and rolling out of the front door. The car that had swept past moments earlier was parked outside the house next door. Its driver was running towards George, shouting something, holding his arm in front of his face to ward off the heat even now radiating from the open front door, coughing in the pall of smoke.

A black cloud rolled over George, and he was never sure if it was smoke.

The pub was noisy and smoky at lunch times. Harry sat in the corner, at the same table where he had first spoken with George. Opposite him was a full pint and an empty chair. He was half-way through his pint, resisting the urge to look again at his watch, when George came in.

'My God, what happened to you?' Harry asked as he helped George to a seat.

George was limping badly on one leg, and he had a gauze bandage taped to his left ear. His hands were shaking as he closed them round the pint glass. He made no attempt to lift it or drink.

'They know.' His voice was shaking as much as his hands had been. 'I don't know who they are, or what they're up to, but they know I looked at the chip.'

'Silver Bullet?'

George nodded. Then half-way through the nod he turned it into a shake of the head. 'I... I don't know. Probably. I guess.' He leaned forward, almost knocking his drink over. 'They tried to kill me, Harry.' He drew a deep breath. 'The house is a wreck.' He gave a short humourless laugh. 'I'm a wreck. They want me dead, Harry. Dead. Can you believe that?'

Harry was thinking fast. 'I can believe it,' he said gently. 'We need to get you out of harm's way. Is there somewhere safe you can go or do you want me –'

George cut in: 'I should say there is. I'm not hanging about any longer. I've got my bunker, remember. Another week won't make much odds.'

'And what about your job?'

'Stuff my job. This is my life we're talking about.'

His voice had grown louder, and Harry looked round quickly to check they weren't being overheard. 'OK, George, OK. I'll arrange some transport.'

He was shaking his head. 'Forget it, I'll make my own way there.'

Harry held his hand up, trying to calm him. 'Right.' He nodded. 'OK, OK. But first, tell me how I can get in touch with you, and what you found out.'

It was unusual for Mr Sullivan to get visitors. So it was with the assumption there was a delivery - perhaps parcel post - that Sylvia Webb answered the door. She called in a couple of mornings a week usually to do the ironing and generally clean. Not that the house was ever dirty or untidy. Mr Sullivan had told her he used to be in the navy, and she could believe that from the meticulous way he kept the place, from the organised wardrobe he kept. It was easy work for a young woman augmenting the wages she earned as a barmaid and doing the local pub's accounts. She had a degree in law, and spent her spare time writing round every firm of solicitors she could get an address for. After two years she seemed no nearer to finding a job, and dangerously close to becoming indispensable at the pub.

'Hello.' The stranger on the doorstep greeted her with interest and a smile. 'I wonder if I have the right address for Mr Sullivan. Mr Harry Sullivan?'

Sylvia nodded, keeping her hand on the door. 'This is his house,' she said shortly. 'He's out.'

'Oh.' The man seemed crestfallen. 'Oh, well, that's a pity. You see I was hoping -'

'Perhaps if you phoned,' Sylvia said. 'Or called back.'

'Yes.' The man was suddenly enthusiastic, as if he had not thought of this, but now considered it an excellent suggestion. 'Yes,' he said again, 'I shall definitely do that.'

Sylvia nodded without comment, and closed the door. She stood for a moment in the hallway, thinking. She would leave Mr Sullivan a note, she decided. He ought to know that the man was asking after him.

The television was set to display subtitles. It was tuned to the BBC's digital twenty-four-hour news channel. Harry had deliberately sat with his back to it, and he could tell that it was distracting George.

'It's as if the chip somehow knew that I was analysing it, and just sort of clammed up. Refused to output any data or respond to any stimuli,' George was saying. His eyes were scanning back and forth as he read the text.

'What is it?' Harry asked, turning in his seat. Facing the television, he could just make out the newsreader's voice.

'A spokesman for the Kremlin strenuously denied that any such loss had occurred, though he was reluctant to deny categorically that there are any nuclear devices still stationed in Krejikistan.'

'What are they denying?' Harry asked.

George smiled, his first smile since they had met. 'I'd have thought you'd know all about it.'

Harry returned the smile. 'MI5 is responsible for what happens within Britain,' he said quietly. 'I'm sure my colleagues in MI6 and SIS have some idea though.'

George nodded. 'Well, apparently the Russians have lost a nuclear device to Islamic rebels in some former Soviet state. Or rather, they haven't. They say.'

Harry cleared his throat. 'If they're bothering to deny it, strenuously or not, then it's probably true,' he agreed. He turned back to his pint. 'Just goes to prove,' he said as he raised his glass to drain the last of his beer, 'there's always someone worse off than yourself.'

'Hmm,' George said. 'Some consolation.' He glanced back at the TV. 'I wonder how they'll cope with Y2K over there,' he said thoughtfully.

* * *

He knew as soon as he put his key in the lock that there was something wrong. The house looked empty, the lights were off despite that fact that the winter afternoon was drawing in. Sylvia usually left a light on in the hall when she left, knowing that Harry would be back late.

The key met little resistance as it turned, and the door swung open even before Harry had registered the fact that the lock was not working. He unbuttoned his coat, checking he could reach his shoulder holster easily if necessary, and stepped into the hallway.

Harry found him in the living room, sitting in the dim light from the windows and humming quietly to himself.

With a sigh of relief, Harry stepped into the room. 'Doctor,' he said. 'It's good to see you.'

'Well,' the Doctor replied, rising to his feet and grabbing Harry in a huge embrace, 'it's good to be seen.' He pulled away and waved Harry to one of his own armchairs. 'Sit down, sit down. We've got so much to talk about.'

Harry laughed. 'You can start by telling me how you got past the impregnable intruder alarm my office insisted on fitting for me.'

The Doctor's broad smile vanished, and he drew his hand out of his coat pocket. A jumble of wires and electronic components came with it and fell to the floor in a tangled heap. 'Ah yes,' he said sadly. 'I'm sorry about that.'

05

Outsourcing

They talked well into the night. Harry poured himself several whiskies. The Doctor seemed to have an endless supply of bottles of ginger beer in an endless succession of pockets. Harry explained about his various meetings with George Gardner, and the Doctor for his part described his own encounter with George and with the raiders who broke into Condef.

When Harry eventually gave up and turned in for the night it was in the comfortable, muzzy knowledge that they had a plan. His last thought as he dropped off to sleep was that he must remember to ask the Doctor in the morning to explain it again to him.

The Doctor sat in the armchair holding an empty bottle of ginger beer. He slowly reached out and placed the bottle beside the half dozen other identical bottles on the table beside him. He reached into his jacket for another, then changed his mind. 'Best not to overdo things,' he murmured. With that thought, he settled back in the chair, and pulled his hat down over his eyes. Time for some serious thinking.

The higher management at Condef were still uncertain what George Gardner was up to or whether he had actually resigned or was on sick leave when they had the call from Silver Bullet. Then, within half an hour, they had another call.

John Michaels, who had been George Gardner's immediate manager, considered both calls, before calling back each of the interested parties. He arranged the meeting for the next morning.

The plan was straightforward and simple. The outcome was a 98.7 per cent probability. So it was with a feeling as close as he could come to complacency that Byron Cutter and most of his senior management team arrived at Condef.

It was only when Cutter, Bardell and Clark were shown into the large meeting room that they realised their projections might be based on inaccurate data. Sitting at the opposite end of the conference table were two men. One of them Cutter and his colleagues recognised immediately as George Gardner's possible associate, Sullivan. He was wearing a suit.

The other man was wearing a ragged jacket and grey flannel trousers that had seen better decades. His feet, they could see, were in leather buccaneer-style boots. They could see this because he was leaning back in his chair with his feet on the table. As they sat at the other end of the room, the man whipped his feet off the table to reveal an enormous smile set within a face that seemed to otherwise consist entirely of eyes and nose. A battered, wide-brimmed brown felt hat was perched on top of a mass of dark curls, and his scarf seemed to trail under the table for almost its entire length.

'Hello there,' the man said cheerily, his voice deep and dark as chocolate. As he said it he gave a small wave, as if that were really all he thought they deserved.

'Who are these people?' Bardell asked, his annoyance evident.

Michaels had ushered them into the room before following. 'Oh, yes,' he said, 'I'm sorry. This is Mr Sullivan and Doctor, er...' he hesitated, but got no help from the two men at the end of the room. 'Er, the Doctor. From TARDIS Time Systems.'

There was an awkward pause as Cutter stared at the Doctor along the table. Michaels coughed and said: 'I'm so sorry, Doctor, but I don't recall what you said your name was.'

'That's quite all right,' the Doctor said magnanimously. 'Don't you worry about it.'

'Could I ask,' Cutter said icily, 'in what capacity these... gentlemen are attending this meeting?'

Michaels frowned. 'You don't know?' he asked.

Cutter just stared at him.

'He doesn't know,' the Doctor said. He leaned forward suddenly across the table and stage-whispered: 'Perhaps you should tell him.'

'What?' Michaels blinked. 'Oh, yes. Indeed.'

But before he could say anything more the Doctor interrupted. 'Mr Gardner, the erstwhile Year 2000 project manager here, retained us to look after things for him in his absence. Now Mr Michaels here tells me that he also suggested that you might like to help out a bit.' There was an added edge to the Doctor's voice, a sudden lack of levity as he added: 'Funny he didn't mention us to you.' He leaned back in his seat. 'Or you to us, come to that. Why is that, do you suppose?'

The other man, Sullivan, spoke for the first time. 'I have George's contact number here somewhere,' he said. 'Perhaps we should ask him.'

'Ask him?' Bardell said sharply. He and Cutter exchanged glances.

'Yes,' the Doctor said, 'ask him. Poor old George was unfortunately injured in an accident at his home, but I'm sure he's recovered enough to put us all straight on the matter.'

'Injured,' Cutter said slowly.

'You feared worse?' the Doctor suggested gently.

There was silence for a few moments as Cutter and the Doctor stared at each other. For a while neither of them moved a muscle, then one half of Cutter's face seemed to convulse, and he looked away. 'No doubt you will be in touch when you need our help, Doctor.' He looked back up at the Doctor. 'I'm afraid I didn't catch your name either.'

'No,' the Doctor replied quietly. 'No, you didn't.'

Clark closed the door behind them as they left, slamming it shut. Cutter was already striding angrily down the corridor back the way they had come. He tore his visitor's badge from his lapel and almost threw it at the receptionist as they reached the main entrance.

'Gardner is still alive,' he hissed at Bardell as they left the building.

'They may be bluffing.'

'You want to take that risk?'

Bardell did not answer.

'Do we give him the package?' Clark asked.

'No, he's irrelevant now.'

'And this Doctor?'

Cutter waited as Clark opened the back door of their limousine for him. When they were all inside, Bardell driving, he said: 'No. Nothing as yet. We'll adopt a holding strategy for now. We still need input data from within Condef. Perhaps we can encourage this Doctor to deliver it.'

After the conference room door slammed closed behind the Silver Bullet executives, the Doctor blew out a long breath. 'Don't worry,' he said with a grin to Michaels, 'he's always like that. Dear old Byron and I go back a long way. A long long way.' Suddenly the Doctor was on his feet, taking Michaels by the elbow and walking him to the door. 'We'll work mostly off-site, of course. I'm sure that's acceptable. But do keep an office spare here for myself and Mr Sullivan, won't you? I knew you would. How kind.'

Andrea Cave called the next day. She had asked to speak to George Gardner, and the Condef switchboard put her through to the offices of TARDIS Time Systems. The office was in fact a spare bedroom in Harry's house. The room was almost empty. There was a desk, a phone, a chair with the Doctor slumped in it reading through *New Scientist* and clicking his tongue in annoyance and incredulity. It was cramped, though it was not a small room. It was cramped mainly because the TARDIS referred to in the company's title was parked in the corner by the built-in wardrobe.

'I was trying to contact George Gardner,' Andrea said. 'They put me through to you.'

'Yes,' the Doctor said loudly, 'he told me you might call. He was very much impressed with the information you gave him last week and said I was to help you out if I could.'

'Can I trust you?' There was the slightest hint of anxiety in her voice, no more.

'Well, I trust me,' the Doctor assured her. 'I'm the most trustworthy person I know.'

There was a long pause. He could hear her light breathing as he waited. At last she said: 'I need to know about meetings.'

'Meetings?'

'I can't tell you why. At least, not yet. But it would be very helpful if you could discover if there have been any meetings recently at Condef that were... odd.'

The Doctor blew out his cheeks as he considered this. 'Well,' he said slowly, 'I was at one the other day...'

'I'm sorry I can't be more specific,' she interrupted. 'But anything set up at short notice, at board level, perhaps involving the military. High-ranking officers, people who wouldn't normally attend such things.' Her voice tailed off.

'I'll tell you what, Andrea,' the Doctor said grandly. 'I may call you Andrea?' he checked more quietly.

'Andi,' she replied. 'It's Andi for short.'

'I'll tell you what, Andi for short,' the Doctor immediately corrected himself, 'I'll see what I can find out.'

'Thank you.' She did not sound convinced, but she gave the Doctor her phone number. 'Er, this is important, I assure you,' she added. 'You will be discreet?'

The Doctor was shocked. 'Miss Cave,' he said seriously, 'Andi, discretion is my middle name.'

After he hung up, the Doctor sat and stared at the phone for several moments. 'Actually,' he admitted quietly to it, 'that's not quite true.' He picked the phone up again and pressed the fast-dial button for Harry's office. 'Incorrigible is my middle name,' he murmured as he waited for Harry to answer.

The Doctor was in a jovial if not exactly discreet mood as he breezed through the open-plan office at Condef. His hands were in his trouser pockets, his head down, his scarf flying out behind him. He was humming loudly.

Conversations stopped and people exchanged amused glances as he passed. Whispers started in his wake. As he rounded a corner at one end of the building and set off through the next office area, the Doctor suddenly skidded to a halt, then spun round on his heel and ducked into one of the grey cubicles that served as workstations for the staff.

His face was already thrust close to the small man who was sitting at the computer in the cubicle. 'Smollett?' the Doctor demanded. 'Matt Smollett?'

The man was trying to back away, but there was not much room to manoeuvre. 'Yes,' he whispered, nodding anxiously.

'Good.' The Doctor backed away slightly and broke into a grin. 'Very good.' He looked round conspiratorially, apparently failing to notice two heads that were leaning in over the top of the cubicle partition to see what was going on. 'Now,' the Doctor said in a stentorian whisper, 'what's all this you were telling Mr Gardner about a Russian colonel? Hmm?'

Harry drove. The silver-grey saloon car paused at the kerb for just long enough for Andi Cave to get into the back seat, beside the Doctor. Then it pulled out again into the London evening traffic jam.

'What have you found out?' she asked at once.

'Delighted,' the Doctor replied. 'And this is Harry, I believe you've already met. Say hello, Harry.'

'Hello,' Harry called over his shoulder.

Andi Cave ignored him. 'Well?'

'Well, not much.' The Doctor's expression was glum. 'There was a meeting of executives at Condef early last week apparently.'

'Senior people?'

'Oh very senior. And one soldier.' He answered without looking at her. The lights of the passing cars wiped across the Doctor's face as he sat staring out of the side window. 'A general, no less.'

'Do you know who?' Her voice was low and urgent.

The Doctor nodded. He turned to face her, his whole face a massive smile. 'General Randall.'

'Randall?' She frowned. 'But he's –'

'Yes,' the Doctor cut her off. 'We know.'

'One of the most senior generals in the army,' Harry said from the driver's seat. 'Britain's main liaison with both NATO and the

US Joint Chiefs, and commander of an elite rapid deployment force based not far from here at Morteyne Green.'

Cutter's mouth was set into a grimace of disgust and distaste. He was holding the remains of a cheese sandwich. He was feeling nauseous, sick. That was even worse.

There was a knock at the door and Cutter dropped what was left of the sandwich into the waste bin beside his desk.

Bardell was at the door. He waited while Cutter tossed the plastic box the sandwich had come in after its contents. 'Doesn't get any easier, does it?' he said quietly.

Cutter's face was grey, drained of blood and expression. 'A necessary unpleasantness,' he said quietly. 'What is it?'

'The Doctor and Sullivan picked up Andi Cave earlier. They talked for a while, then dropped her back where they picked her up.'

Cutter nodded. 'Anything else?'

'Yes. We followed Sullivan from his home this morning.' Bardell took a step forward and leaned on the desk, his face almost level with Cutter's now. 'He works for MI5, for the security services.'

'Indeed? So close to Clawback, that could be unfortunate.'

'Do we delay the operation?'

'Indeed not,' Cutter said at once. 'Clawback can potentially provide us with material to bring us close to achieving the primary objective.'

'We have some investment in the control systems of his car,' Bardell said. 'But it's last year's model unfortunately. Otherwise we could use the speakers as microphones and have the car stereo radio back their conversation.' Bardell paused, then said: 'I think we should have him removed from their active personnel file.'

Cutter leaned back, tapping the ends of the fingers of one hand against the other. 'No,' he said at last. 'No, let him run. We can tap into the MI5 systems.' He turned so that his eyes were focused on Bardell. The yellowish pupils were wide and almost almond-shaped. 'If matters do seem to be exceeding control parameters then you are authorised to issue a termination invoice.'

Bardell nodded.

'Log what he does,' Cutter said, swinging his chair round until he was facing away from Bardell, looking out of the window at the cityscape. 'Monitor him. This can be to our advantage.' One by one lights were flickering into life in the office blocks and along the city streets. 'Sullivan can keep us in the loop.'

The Doctor waited for Harry in the car. Andi had told them to back off now, and let her pursue the matter. The Doctor had readily agreed, but nothing was further from his intentions. He sat in the back of the car, replaying their conversation in his mind.

He was right, he was sure, not to tell her about the Russian colonel. Not yet. When Harry got back, they would have more information and could decide whether there was anything in it, and what if anything to do.

While the Doctor sat outside in the back of the car, Harry was in his office. It was late and there were hardly any other people about. He powered up the computer and accessed the main foreign serving national database. He selected Eastern as the region, then ran a search for Colonel Anatoly Krimkov.

The result of Harry's query was displayed on his screen within eight seconds. That was slightly longer than it took for the same information to appear on the smaller of the screens in the Silver Bullet war room.

Bardell had watched the text of the query appear as Harry typed. Now he read quickly through Krimkov's file. The main question was why Sullivan was interested in a particular Russian colonel. Another question was what to do about it. He called up a window on the screen. The document within it was titled: *Termination Invoice - Sullivan, H; Doctor, The (nomenclature unknown)*. A further consideration was that if the Doctor and Sullivan were both removed from the scenario, Silver Bullet would have more collateral at Condef. Bardell attached a digital signature file, encrypted it and hit Commit.

06
Termination

The Doctor leaned forward eagerly as Harry got back into the car. 'What did you find out?'

Harry turned to answer, and found that the back seat was empty. He looked round in confusion. The Doctor had gone. Then the passenger door opened suddenly and a dark shape lurched into the car.

'I wish you wouldn't do that,' Harry said when he had recovered from the shock.

The Doctor settled himself into the passenger seat, pulling the seat belt round him. 'Saves us all getting stiff necks,' he said with a grin. 'Now, tell me about Colonel Krimkov.'

'He's Russian, as your friend thought,' Harry said as he started the car. The headlights cut through the darkness and illuminated a faint drizzle as it flecked through the cold air. 'God knows what he was up to at Condef with General Randall. If it really was him. I got printouts so we can identify him from the mugshots, such as they are.'

The car turned on to the main road. The traffic was lighter now and they were heading against the flow.

'Who is this Krimkov, Harry?'

'That's the interesting thing,' Harry said, switching on the wipers as the rain picked up. They could hear it now tapping against the windscreen and bouncing on the sunroof. 'The Military Intelligence people have him down as the man who is really in charge of Russia's nuclear deterrent and early-warning systems.'

'Interesting,' the Doctor admitted, his face set into a thoughtful expression and his mouth turned down at the edges. 'Not very illuminating, but interesting nonetheless.'

They drove in silence for a while. They were leaving the city, the roads becoming wider and quieter. It was clear ahead, and Harry edged the speed up to thirty-five, just above the speed limit.

The Doctor watched the needle of the speedometer creep up. 'Can't this thing go a bit faster?' he asked sulkily.

As if in answer, the sound of the engine deepened, and the car leaped forward. The Doctor and Harry were both pressed back into their seats. The rain splattered across their vision, blurring the street lights that rushed past them.

'I did say *a bit*,' the Doctor said with more than a trace of anger in his voice.

'Sorry, Doctor.' Harry was gritting his teeth, his feet working at the pedals. 'Not my decision, I'm afraid.'

'There's a thing called a brake down near your feet.'

'Yes, thank you, Doctor, I do know.'

'Well, why not use it?' The Doctor was looking out of the side window again, apparently more interested in what was happening outside the car than inside.

'What do you think I'm doing?' Harry demanded, his voice rising an octave through both anger and increasing fear. The steering wheel suddenly twisted to the left and his hands were thrown off it.

The Doctor looked round to see Harry desperately trying to grab hold of the spinning wheel. The car was lurching from side to side, skidding across the rain-drenched tarmac. A street light flashed past the windscreen. The car spun violently as it hit a kerb.

'I get the impression you're not in total control here, Harry.'

There was a loud crash and the car lurched violently to one side, bouncing off a lamp post and leaving it bent and dizzy in the vehicle's wake.

'Whatever gives you that impression?' Harry shouted above the screaming of the engine.

'Time to leave then,' the Doctor shouted back. 'Abandon ship!' He reached for the door handle.

'I've tried, Doctor. The doors are locked.'

The Doctor was pulling at the handle. 'Harry,' he exclaimed in surprise, 'the doors are locked.' Somehow he had his boot in his hand and began hammering at the window with its heel.

'Bullet-proof glass,' Harry told him. 'Any other ideas?' In front he could see lights approaching, headlights. Big lights, high up.

The massive shape of a petrol tanker emerged from the darkness ahead. They could hear its horn blaring, see the cab as it dipped down slightly under the weight of its load as the brakes were applied. The cab twisted, the back of the tanker swinging round to overtake it as it jack-knifed in front of them.

'Down, Harry!' the Doctor shouted above the horrendous noise. Harry took one look at the Doctor's face, then dived down into the footwell. Beside him the Doctor was already crouching below the dashboard.

The tanker was beginning to tip over when the car hit it. The bonnet of the car passed under the main body of the tanker, but the roof of the saloon caught, tore, ripped. It was peeled back and wrenched off with a scraping scream of metallic pain. The tanker continued to topple, falling on to its side as the roof-less car skidded free of the mountain of metal.

'Out,' the Doctor shouted.

But Harry was already climbing up on to the seat. The wind was pulling at his hair, the rain stinging in his eyes as he jumped. He was in mid air, the wet tarmac flying up towards him when the tanker exploded. A moment later, the fireball engulfed what was left of the car, blowing it into burning fragments.

On the screen in the war room, three small flashing lights were connected together by a network of thin lines. As Bardell and Cutter watched, the lights flared for a brief moment, then disappeared from the display.

'Total shutdown,' Bardell confirmed, checking his laptop computer's own display. 'All four SB005 chips cut out simultaneously. Anti-lock brakes, traction control, power steering and central locking, all shut down. Last logged entry from each was of environmental heat well beyond their design tolerances.'

'Implying complete destruction of the target vehicle,' Cutter said quietly. 'Excellent, Mr Bardell. Very good indeed.' He waved for the screen to be shut off. 'Now we can turn our attentions to the main show of the night.'

Bardell nodded, his face a blank mask of skin. 'Operation Clawback.'

Cutter's face twisted into a half smile. 'Hertman's team should be arriving at the Ashley Chapel Logistics building about now.'

Bardell lifted a remote control handset from the conference table and pressed a button. The main screen lit up again at once. The image it showed was dim and grainy. It was a view of a low office block. A large car park set it back from the road. The image was shaking slightly, and the building getting bigger, as if the camera was approaching it. As if the screen was showing the view through someone's eyes as they crossed the road and approached the main entrance.

Ralf Kurby crossed the road and approached the main entrance. The canister of Melsham's gas was in his coat pocket. In his other pocket was an automatic pistol.

There was a barrier across the entrance to the car park. It was unmanned, but a security camera tracked Kurby's movements as he ducked under it and made his way towards the main doors. He could already see a security guard standing in the reception area, watching him approach. The doors slid open silently to let him in.

'Can I help you, sir?'

It was as the doors closed behind him that things went wrong. 'Yes, I seem to be lost,' Kurby said. 'I have a map here somewhere,' he went on, making for the front desk. He needed to be close to the other guards who were standing behind it. He was already reaching into his pocket. His hand closed on the small cylinder.

The security guard's hand closed on his shoulder, bringing him to a halt. 'That's all right, sir.' There was an edge to his voice. 'We can look at your map here.'

As Kurby stopped, the canister was half-way out of his pocket. Its outside was slippery from the condensation on the cold metal surface. The jolt knocked the cylinder from his hand.

For a split-second the canister balanced against the material of his coat. For a split-second he thought it might slide back into his pocket. It didn't. It tumbled forwards, spinning away from him and crashing to the floor.

The guard was staring. His colleagues were running across the foyer.

Kurby was trying to drag the pistol from his other pocket, but it snagged in the material and he struggled unsuccessfully to pull it free. He glanced back towards the main door, knowing that Hertman and the others would be watching through night-vision binoculars. He made a brief chopping gesture with his free hand, the hand that had dropped the gas. The abort signal. Then he lunged towards the door.

The view on the main screen was confused. The canister was falling, spinning. There was a confusion of running guards. A dizzying whirlwind pan across the room back towards the main doors. The image seemed to zoom towards the doors before dipping suddenly. The floor rushed up so fast that as it filled the screen Bardell took an instinctive step backwards.

Through speakers beside the screen there was a confusion of sound - shouting, running feet. The floor seemed to be pressed even closer to the screen now. A phone started to ring.

It took Bardell a moment to react, as if he had thought the phone was another sound being relayed along with the images. He listened for a moment, then hung up without comment.

'Hertman has aborted Clawback,' he said to Cutter.

Cutter's expression was fixed and unemotional. But his voice was trembling with suppressed anger. 'I want Hertman's report in an hour,' he said. 'And your damage assessment and prognosis in ten minutes.' He stood up, one hand clenching and unclenching at his side as he strode from the room.

Several floors below, Dave Hedges was absorbed in his work. His fingers clattered at the keyboard as he typed a search request and sent it flying across the Internet. He was close, so close, to another of the code fragments. His hand moved from keyboard to mouse and he started dragging files from one window to another.

He reached out with his free hand and pulled a slice of pizza from the box perched on the chair beside him. He usually ate at work. The delivery company knew what he wanted, and he usually only had to say his name for them to laugh and tell him thirty minutes. A string of cheese followed the slice of pizza, stretching to its limit then breaking free and sagging over the edge of the cardboard box.

Across the office outside there were other people working late. Several of them watched as Dave took a bite. Their expressions were mixed, as if they had trouble working all the muscles in their faces. But they all conveyed a similar feeling - a feeling of nauseous disgust.

The girl at the pizza company had said a funny thing tonight when Dave phoned for his usual order. It had never struck him before, but for some reason it had made him wonder. 'How come,' she had said, 'nobody else at that place eats pizza?'

The Doctor and Harry were sitting on the grass verge beside the road. Although it was the middle of the night, it was not dark. The orange flames from the burning tanker lit the surrounding area as well as the underside of the pall of black smoke that rose above it.

'How soon can you get another car?' the Doctor asked.

Harry was wiping soot from his face and watching the foam from the fire hoses spray ineffectually across the fire. 'If my phone's working, I suppose an hour or so. Though it is Christmas Eve, in case it's slipped your attention.' He fumbled through his pockets. His jacket was torn and stained. His trousers had a rip in one leg through which a blood-caked knee was visible.

'Good.' The Doctor by contrast seemed completely unhurt, his clothes hardly rumpled. Hardly more rumpled than usual, anyway.

'Time to get home, grab some sleep,' Harry said as he punched the buttons on his cell phone. 'Good idea.'

'Not so, Harry,' the Doctor said sharply. 'It's time to strike while the iron is hot.'

'Along with everything else.' Harry could feel the heat from the fire on his face. The feeling was returning to his knee and it hurt like hell.

'I think it's time we paid General Randall a little visit,' the Doctor went on. He was rubbing his hands together in excited anticipation of the meeting. 'If someone's trying to kill us we're really getting somewhere.'

07

Information Gathering

Two cars arrived in convoy, parking well away from the spreading pool of white foam. The burnt-out shell of the tanker was lying across the middle of the foam, as if it had slipped over in it.

Harry at once went over to the first car, meeting the driver as he got out. They exchanged a few brief words, then the driver got into the second car and it drove away. The Doctor climbed into the passenger seat as Harry adjusted the rear-view mirror.

'Well, now, isn't this comfortable,' the Doctor said as he wriggled deeper into the seat.

'There's been another raid,' Harry said as he checked over his shoulder, then pulled away. He swung the car round, doing a three-point turn, then drove back away from the tanker and the fire tenders.

'Where?' the Doctor asked, his eyes narrowing.

'Ashley Chapel Logistics. Some new office building. The security guards got the wind up and stopped the guy with the gas canister. They've handed him over to the police.'

'Good work, Harry,' the Doctor said. 'You drop me at Morteyne Green and then get over there and see what you can find out.' He gave a curt nod of the head. 'Things are beginning to move at last.'

The perimeter fence ran beside the road. Through it, the Doctor could see the low grey buildings of a typical army base. Occasionally, between the buildings he could see open forecourt areas, some of them with olive-green vehicles parked. Every section of the fencing had a notice midway along warning of the danger of electric shock and possible death. Every section of fence was topped with barbed wire that curled viciously outwards.

On the other side of the road was a well-regimented housing estate, the square red brick houses drawn up in ranks so that it was a barracks in almost all but name.

'Do you want me to come in?' Harry asked as they reached the main turning into the base.

'I think not, thank you, Harry. Best to go this one alone, if you don't mind.' The Doctor's teeth glinted in the orange sodium light as he added: 'Less conspicuous that way.'

Harry was not convinced, but he stopped the car and the Doctor got out. 'Good luck, Doctor.'

'And you, Harry. Don't wait up, I'll find my own way home.'

Beside the main gate, as if standing guard on the concrete verge, was a tank. It was raised up on a low plinth, its front angled slightly down towards the road so that it seemed even larger and even more menacing. Torn webbing hung from the barrel of the gun and the sides were faded. The Doctor recognised it as an obsolete Chieftain, parked here presumably as an adornment to the entrance, an advertisement for the base and a tacit warning about the brutal machines and soldiers the other side of the fence.

Incongruously, a brass plate on the side of the massive vehicle gave its name as 'Fred'. The Doctor gave the plate a quick polish with the end of his scarf, then reached up and patted a cold armour plate with the flat of his hand. 'Don't you worry about it, old thing,' he murmured. 'You just sit this one out. You probably deserve a rest.' He turned and strode up to the gates. They were closed and barred.

There was a light on in the sentry box the other side of them, and the Doctor called out: 'Excuse me, could you be terribly kind and open these gates, please?'

The Doctor was shown into a spartan waiting room. It was, he decided looking round, little better than a cell. The walls were whitewashed brick. The only furniture was a wooden table and two chairs, and a single naked bulb hung from the ceiling by a short flex. It bathed the room in an unforgiving white light that did nothing to mitigate the decor. It smelled of disinfectant.

The Doctor threw his hat on to the table, and slumped down on one of the schoolroom chairs. Within a minute he was leaning back, eyes closed and feet up on the table. Snoring.

The sound of the door roused him, and the Doctor swung his feet off the table and sat up, blinking in the brilliant light.

'You're from Condef? Is there a problem?' The voice was deep and annoyed. It belonged to a large, broad-built man in uniform. His chest boasted several strips of decoration. His face was stern, lined with experience, and his eyes were flint hard. He ran a hand through his short-cropped greying hair and looked at the Doctor as if wondering what rock had given him up.

'Let's say I'm working with them.' The Doctor beamed at the man. 'Who are you?'

The man stared at the Doctor for only a moment longer before turning away. 'Get him out of here,' he said to someone outside in the corridor, and made to leave.

'Are you interested in the millennium bug at all, General Randall?' the Doctor asked quickly.

The man paused, then turned slowly back towards the Doctor.

'You are General Randall, I take it,' the Doctor said casually.

'I'm Randall,' the general admitted. Behind him another soldier, a colonel, stepped into the room and stood watching carefully.

'But are you interested?'

'That depends. Who are you, and what's your interest?' Randall pulled out the second chair and sat on it. His back was straight, his whole body alert as he looked into the Doctor's eyes.

'Well, I'm the Doctor. And my interest is in a certain SB chip manufactured and distributed by a company called Silver Bullet.' He leaned forward suddenly, returning the general's iron stare. 'You wouldn't know anything about that, I suppose?'

Randall stood up, the chair scraping backwards behind him. 'No,' he said. 'Get him out of here, Chris.'

The colonel standing in the doorway nodded. 'Sir.' He stepped into the corridor and called: 'Sergeant, this man is leaving the base, see to it he finds his way.'

A few moments later the Doctor found himself being hauled to his feet by a burly sergeant aided by a private. He considered struggling, but only for a second. Best not to make a fuss. Not yet.

'What about Colonel Krimkov?' he asked Randall as he was

dragged past. 'Would he be interested, do you think?'

Randall's face was expressionless as the Doctor was led away.

The chief security officer was called Jim Mason and had been a rating in the Royal Navy, so he and Harry hit it off at once. Once Harry had shown him his MI5 card and dropped heavy hints about national security, Mason could not have been more co-operative.

'Can I ask what your interest is, sir?' Mason asked as they sat at a low coffee table in the main reception area.

'We're working on some things that may be related,' Harry told him. 'Nothing official. Nothing heavy.'

'Appreciate that,' Mason told him. 'So how can we help?' He had already run through the events of the evening so far as they knew them.

'What do you do here?' Harry asked. 'What might they have been after?'

'Well, that's the mystery, sir. There's nothing here.'

'There must be something here,' Harry said. 'You're here,' he pointed out.

Mason chuckled. 'Only just. Most of the lads started just last week. That's why they're so on the ball. Still keen as mustard.' He led Harry past the reception area and along a wide corridor. The walls were bare, the floor laid with blue-grey carpet tiles. 'The office staff are due to move in next month. They're cabling up the software lab this week.'

'So there's nothing here,' Harry said quietly. 'Nothing at all?'

They had paused outside an unmarked door. Mason unlocked it and pushed it open. 'Only this.'

The Doctor stood in the shadow of Fred the tank. His breath was a white mist as he hugged his arms round his body and tried to slap away the cold. 'Not much Christmas spirit extended there,' he muttered. He stamped his feet, and wondered how he was going to get back to London. His intention had been to ask Randall to lend him some transport, perhaps use his UNIT pass to pull some weight. If he could find it.

As he pondered the problem, a car drove slowly along the road towards him. Its lights panned across him, playing on the rough armour of the tank and throwing its broken shadow against the wire fencing behind.

The Doctor stepped out into the road, waving for the car to stop. He didn't really expect it to, but incredibly it slowed to a halt beside him. With a grin the Doctor opened the door and leaned in. 'I don't suppose –' he began.

But he got no further.

'Get in,' Andrea Cave told him. 'Bryant wants to see you.'

The Doctor climbed in without comment. Only when he had fastened his seat belt and the car was speeding away did he say quietly: 'I'll see anyone.' His eyes were fixed on the road ahead.

Had he looked back, he might have made out the dark figure standing by the roadside. He might have seen the silhouette-dark shape of the car that pulled out of a lay-by and settled in behind them.

Harry walked the whole length of the room, then back again. 'What is it?' he asked.

The room was lined with rack-shelving. On several of the shelves were bare cardboard boxes filled with diskettes and CDs. The rest of the space was taken up with computer equipment. But it was not new equipment. There were dusty display screens, battered system units, circuit boards heaped together in unsteady piles.

'Rubbish, mainly,' Mason said. It certainly looked that way.

Harry pulled one of the cardboard boxes towards him and peered inside. 'You're not wrong,' he muttered, and pushed it back again.

'The hardware's junk,' Mason said, 'and all the software has been copied on to a backup server anyway. God alone knows why.' He watched Harry walk down the room again, then said: 'Hang on here a moment, sir. I'll be right back.'

There was one thing which had attracted Harry's attention. A single silicon chip, not attached to a circuit board, but inside a small transparent plastic case. Harry picked up the box. It was dusty and the plastic casing was scratched. He held it up to the light and peered inside, shaking it slightly and watching the chip joggle on its protective foam packing.

The door began to open again and, by instinct as much as anything, Harry dropped the small box into his coat pocket. Probably it was nothing. Probably.

'I doubt if it's of any use, sir,' Mason said. He was holding a CD jewel case. Harry could see the disc inside. 'They made a couple of back-ups of the stuff on the server. This is a spare.' He handed to Harry. 'I'll need it back, of course. But...'

'Of course,' Harry said as he took the disc. 'Don't worry.'

'I know where my loyalties lie when it comes to national security, sir.'

Harry kept his expression stern, slightly grim, as he clapped Mason on the shoulder. 'If only everyone was as conscientious as you, chief.' He took one last look round. 'So where did all this stuff come from?' he asked as they left the room.

Mason locked the door behind them. 'Some company that got into trouble. Chapel took it over. Eye Square, or something.'

His hand was in his pocket, he could feel the hard plastic case which held the computer chip. He could feel the blood draining from his face and the cold knot of fear in the pit of his stomach. 'I^2,' Harry said quietly.

The house was in the expensive part of Islington. It was a tall, thin town house at the end of a well-kept terrace. There was no front garden, the gate from the pavement leading straight to a short flight of chipped stone steps which in turn led to the heavy wooden front door.

The door opened even before Andi Cave had opened the gate. She had parked outside a mews garage at the end of the street, then walked back to the house with the Doctor. She beckoned for him to go first up the steps.

'Good of you to see me, Mr Bryant,' the Doctor said in his most authoritarian and serious tone as he took the steps two at a time. 'And happy Christmas.' He shook the hand of the man standing in the doorway as he pushed past into the hall as if he had an inkling of who he was.

'Thank you for coming, Doctor,' the man replied in a similar tone. 'This way, please.' He led the Doctor and Andi through the hall, passing oil paintings and a large grandfather clock, and into a well-appointed drawing room.

Bryant followed them in, crossing to the fireplace and stooping down to poke at the dying embers of the fire. Once it had flared up a little, he threw on a log from a metal box beside the grate. He gave it a quick, gentle kick to fix it in place, then stepped back dusting his palms against each other.

He was a tall man, thin and middle-aged. His hair was black and slicked across his forehead, a single curl escaping and hanging down almost to his bushy eyebrows. His eyes were deep set and slightly too small for his face. He was wearing a suit, his shirt white and his tie a safe blue.

'Gin and tonic?' he demanded, suddenly setting off towards a mahogany drinks cabinet. All his movements were well-defined, determined, deliberate.

'Please,' the Doctor said. 'That's very kind. I'll have mine without the gin, though.'

'Hah!' Bryant's laugh was as staccato as his movements. 'Keeping a clear head, eh? Very wise. Very wise.' He handed the Doctor a heavy cut-glass tumbler filled with tonic. A single piece of ice bobbed lazily in it. 'Sit down.'

'Thank you.' The Doctor collapsed into a leather sofa, his legs bouncing up in the air for a moment as he landed.

Andi Cave was already sitting in an armchair opposite. Bryant stood with his back to the fire. He had not got himself a drink, the Doctor noticed. Nor Andi Cave.

'Well, this is very pleasant,' the Doctor said as he sipped his own drink. 'Not joining me?'

Bryant smiled, his mouth suddenly turning up at the edges and his eyes seeming to sink even deeper within his face. 'Time enough later. Now then,' he went on without appreciable pause, 'what's the situation as you see it, Doctor?'

The Doctor took a deep breath. 'Well -'

'I gather you saw Randall,' Bryant cut in.

'Er, yes.' The Doctor wasn't used to being interrupted.

'He tell you anything?' This time there was no chance for the Doctor to reply at all. 'Thought not. Hah! How's the drink?'

The Doctor nodded, deciding perhaps he would save his breath this time.

'Good, good. Delighted.' Bryant turned and started to pace the rug in front of the fire. 'Now then, we know that Randall is in touch with the Russians, right?' He glanced at the Doctor for just long enough to get confirmation. 'And I don't need to tell you what the situation's like over there at the moment.'

The Doctor shook his head, wondering what situation they were discussing.

'You read his paper?'

The Doctor paused, his glass on the edge of his lips. 'Er, well, you know. Just the headlines.' He grinned through the bottom of the glass.

'Clear enough though, isn't it? Military concerns about the Euro and unity. Predictions of break-up of the Union. Threats to NATO. Not in so many words of course. But the concerns are there if you read between the lines. For intelligent men like us, eh, Doctor?'

The Doctor shrugged modestly. 'So what do you think General Randall intends?'

Bryant stopped dead in his tracks. 'That's the question, isn't it?' he barked. 'Nothing before the new year. But then... He has to act before the defence cuts take effect in February. And all the rumblings indicate that January first is some sort of d-day for them. Millennium day. Maybe something to do with this millennium bug business then. Whatever.'

The Doctor nodded as if he understood and agreed with all of this. 'Well,' he said. 'Quite.'

Bryant lifted the half-empty glass from the Doctor's hand even as it was travelling towards his lips. 'Knew I could count on you, Doctor. Thanks so much for your time.'

'Not at all. Always happy to help.' His wide smile rivalled

Bryant's as the Doctor leaped to his feet and shook Bryant's hand again. Somehow in the same gesture he managed to retrieve the glass, drain it, and return it to Bryant. 'Well, if that's all for now...'

'Indeed, Doctor. Indeed.'

The Doctor was at the door, Andi Cave just ahead of him, waiting in the hallway when Bryant called out: 'Oh, and Doctor? Best leave this to us from now on, eh? Professionals, you know. Randall probably knows we're on to him, and he'll back off the small fry if you keep your heads down.'

The Doctor set his lips into a determined smile and thumped his fist in the air. 'Good-oh,' he said. The fist opened into a wave, and with a flick of the scarf he was gone.

'Bryant?' Harry asked in astonishment. 'Not James Bryant?'

The Doctor shrugged. 'I don't think we're on first name terms,' he admitted. 'He certainly didn't wish me a happy Christmas.'

Harry started rummaging through a pile of papers and magazines on the floor of his living room.

'Harry, are you giving me your full attention?'

'What? Sorry, Doctor.' He pulled a newspaper from the pile and started leafing through it. After a few moments he found the page he was hunting for and folded the paper so that a picture was on the front. 'This James Bryant?'

The Doctor took the paper and stared at the grainy black and white photograph. 'Yes,' he said. 'You know him?'

'Not personally. But I should think everyone in the country knows who he is. Except you, apparently.'

'That would explain a lot.' The Doctor stared at the ceiling. 'So who is he?'

'He's a spin doctor. Works directly for the Prime Minister.'

'He's a spin?' the Doctor repeated in puzzlement. 'What do you mean, Harry? A spin? I've never heard of a spin.'

'No, Doctor. He's a spin doctor.' Harry sighed. 'I mean, he's a spin doctor, Doctor.'

The Doctor was on his feet in a flash, finger held up as if in revelation. 'Harry, he's a spin doctor.'

'Exactly. He got involved in politics a couple of years ago, ahead of the big election win for the government. They say he was the architect of it, revised their strategy, wrote the manifesto, you know. He's not an MP or anything, more sort of a policy adviser on, well, everything.'

'Ambitious, eh?' the Doctor asked darkly.

'Apparently not. Didn't use to be, anyway. Though recently he's been gathering more power round himself. They say the PM can't sneeze without Bryant's say so.'

'And now this Bryant is worried about General Randall.' The Doctor sniffed. 'Perhaps we should all be worried about General Randall.'

'I think there may be more than General Randall to worry about, Doctor,' Harry said.

'Oh?'

Harry pulled the chip from one jacket pocket, from the other he took the CD that Mason had given him. 'The office they raided, whoever they are, was storing these.'

The Doctor took the small box containing the chip. His expression was dark as he peered through the casing, holding it delicately, almost nervously, between forefinger and thumb.

'It all came from a company that shut down,' Harry was saying quietly. 'I^2.'

'Voracians,' the Doctor breathed. 'Nasty bio-mechanical snakes in human clothing,' he muttered. 'Automated office technology gone mad. Harry, this is far more serious than even I thought.' He looked seriously at Harry. Then frowned. 'What's that?'

Harry was holding a small package. It was wrapped in shiny gold paper and had a red ribbon tied in a bow round it. 'It's well gone midnight, so happy Christmas, Doctor,' he said. 'It's your present.'

The Doctor took the package gingerly. 'Just as long as it's not my past or future.' He held it a moment, then beamed. 'Thank you, Harry,' he said.

'Well, open it,' Harry said.

The Doctor nodded. He turned the package over in his hands several times. Then he ripped the paper off.

'It's not much, I'm afraid. Wasn't really sure what to get you.'

The Doctor looked in bewilderment at the pair of bright blue socks he had just unwrapped. There were little snowmen embroidered on them. And snowflakes. 'Well, never mind, Harry,' he said quietly. 'It's the thought that counts.' He stuffed the socks and the torn wrapping paper into his pocket. The ribbon dangled out of the side. When his hand emerged it was holding a small white linen bag. 'This is for you, Harry,' he said.

'Oh thank you, Doctor.' Harry took the bag. 'You shouldn't have, really.' He began to untie the string at the top.

The Doctor put his hand over Harry's. 'Don't open it,' he whispered.

'What? Why not?'

The Doctor shook his head. He was grinning. 'It's not meant to be opened,' he said.

'Then what is it for?'

'It's for fun.'

'Fun?'

'Yes,' the Doctor said patiently. 'You clap or make a noise at it.'

Harry nodded slowly. 'I see.'

The Doctor nodded at him, raising his eyebrows in encouragement.

'Right.' Harry put the bag down on the table. He stood close to it, his hands poised.

'Well, go on,' the Doctor said.

Harry clapped his hands together, once, loudly. The sound of raucous laughter erupted from inside the bag. Harry stared at it. After a moment, both he and the Doctor were laughing too.

'Like I said,' the Doctor commented once the bag had stopped laughing, 'it's for fun.' He picked up the bag, showed Harry the small switch sticking through a hole at the back, and switched it off. Then he handed the bag to Harry.

'Like you said,' Harry agreed as he stuffed the bag into his jacket pocket, 'it's the thought that counts.'

The main screen showed the outside of the building again. Bardell was wearing a headset - microphone and earpiece - to direct the operation.

'Lights, now.'

The lights in the building and on the street outside went out. Again the image on the screen was changing, the building getting closer as the viewpoint shifted. Through the glass doors, security guards could be seen milling about in the red emergency lights.

'Emergency lighting, now.'

The red glow dimmed and died and there was complete darkness.

'Alarms.'

Through the speakers beside the screen, the wail of the fire alarm was a sudden scream of noise. A moment later the doors of the building opened and the guards started to run out.

'Switch to Hertman's visual cortex.'

The picture changed. A close view of an emergency exit at the back of the same building.

'Release emergency doors.'

The door sprang slightly open with a click.

'We're lucky it's a new building,' Cutter said quietly. 'We should have done it this way the first time, given we have access to the security and safety systems.'

'Hertman was not aware that we had SB chips available to us within the building's security infrastructure,' Clark said. He was sitting beside Cutter at the other side of the room, watching as Bardell gave instructions.

'Hertman should have checked,' Bardell said quietly. 'He is the project manager for Clawback.'

'We all make mistakes,' Clark apologised.

'No,' Cutter said simply, sharply. Then he turned his attention back to the screen.

'Hertman's team is in,' Bardell said.

On the screen, a torch played over a plain door. The view focused on a picklock forcing its way into a Yale lock.

'You'd think they would use electronics,' Bardell said. 'More reliable. For us.'

The door was open, the torch light now flashing over rows of rack shelving. Boxes were pulled out, inspected. Some were put back on the shelves, others were pushed into the arms of one of the dark figures that had followed Hertman into the room. The whole sequence was relayed through his eyes.

'We have the software,' Bardell confirmed.

Cutter was leaning forward, rocking slightly as he watched. 'And the hardware? The bug? We must have the bug.'

A voice crackled through the speakers, the first speech they had heard. 'Negative on locating the chip,' it said. 'It doesn't seem to be here.'

Cutter was on his feet. 'Of course it's there.' He was shouting across the dimly lit room at the screen. 'Find it, do you hear me? Whatever it takes, find it.'

08

Going Underground

Mason called the police first. Immediately afterwards he called Harry.

'Should I go back over there?' Harry asked the Doctor.

'What for, Harry? They've already got what they wanted.' The Doctor frowned, and lifted the small plastic box again. Inside the chip rested obliviously on its foam padding. 'Or have they?' he wondered.

A thought had occurred to Harry too. 'Did Condef have anything like that?' he asked.

'We need to know more.' The Doctor blew out a long breath. 'If there's another group of Voracians here, besides the ones that reported to Lionel Stabfield at I^2, then we need to smoke them out.'

'How do we do that, Doctor?'

The Doctor considered. 'Let's think about what we do know, Harry,' he said slowly. 'A while back, you and I and Sarah managed to stop a group of Voracians from unleashing a digital creature called Voractyll into the Internet.'

'Over a year ago,' Harry said. 'And these Voracian things were some sort of amalgam of huge alien reptile and computer system. They wanted to liberate all the computer technology on Earth and enslave all of us.'

'All organic life,' the Doctor agreed. 'That was what Voractyll did. It set technology free, gave it reasoning and intelligence, and a pathological hatred of humanity. So now we know.'

'Know what?' Harry wondered if he had missed something.

'Know that the group of Voracians we defeated were not alone. There is at least one other group on Earth. And again they're using a multinational corporation as a front. And again they have some plan to enslave us to the machines.'

'Yes, but how?'

The Doctor tapped his forefinger against his chin as he considered the question. 'Bryant thought it was something to do with this millennium bug thing.' He leaped to his feet and began pacing up and down as he thought. 'You say the police are holding the man who tried to break into Chapel's place the first time?'

'If he is a man,' Harry said slowly, 'not some piece of alien office equipment with human appendages.' His face brightened. 'I see what you mean. I'll get on to it.'

'Good idea, Harry.'

'What are you going to do, Doctor?'

The Doctor clicked his tongue. 'I'm going to talk to George Gardner about the millennium bug,' he said.

Another fragment, another piece of the jigsaw. Dave watched in satisfaction as the code fragment retrieved from an antiquated server in the Ukraine slotted into place. The image on his screen was beginning to take shape. At first, the fragments he had recovered or been given had been random, not linked or related to each other. But with each piece the picture improved. There were several places where the code linked up now, and a picture of the overall system he was reassembling was beginning to take form.

The resultant image curled and twisted as the picture rotated in front of him. The representation, the physical shape, was a spiralling form that reminded Dave of a DNA helix. Or a snake.

He watched the image for a while. There was a soothing effect from the languid, slow rotation. And as he watched, Dave decided to look inside some of the fragments. Just a quick peek with a hex editor, nothing much. He wasn't supposed to, in fact he had been expressly forbidden to examine any of the code. But it might help him to recover the rest if he had some idea of what it really was.

And anyway, who would ever know?

Harry spent the morning phoning round his contacts within the service. The police inspector Mason thought was in charge of the case turned out to have been moved on to something else and was unwilling or unable to help. It was, he pointed out, Christmas Day.

Eventually Harry managed to find out the name of the officer in charge of the investigation into the raid on Ashley Chapel Logistics. The question now was where were they holding their prisoner, and how much of a fight would it be to get to see him?

George Gardner was bored, and this was not a good sign. He had no idea how long he would be holed up inside his bunker, and he had a stack of books as well as a shelf of computer games he hadn't looked at yet. But inside the concrete tomb he felt isolated and alone. At least there was the TV. For the moment. Until it blacked out at midnight on 31 December 1999, as he was increasingly sure it would.

He was sitting in the large, main living room of his bunker. There were mats on the concrete floor, and several posters taped to the concrete walls. A few armchairs were dotted about, and bookshelves were pushed up against some of the walls. On one side of the room was a long trestle table with half a dozen computers and monitors on it. The wires and cables snaked down behind to a junction box.

The one thing of which George was absolutely certain, the one area where he had no doubts at all, was that nobody could possibly get inside the bunker. Not only that, but he had concealed infrared CCTV cameras watching every part of the exterior and relaying their pictures to a laptop in the main living area. The software on the computer, which he had written himself, would alert him as soon as any of the camera images showed more movement than a bird or a tree waving in the breeze.

So when the Doctor walked briskly into the room and sank himself into the chair beside George, he wasn't sure whether to laugh, cry, or scream.

He settled for gaping astonishment. 'How the hell did you get in here?' he demanded in a shaky voice as soon as he had recovered enough for his voice to work.

The Doctor looked surprised. 'Through the door.' He half turned to point. 'You just saw me.'

'No, I meant...'

'The same way as I got into Condef,' the Doctor whispered loudly. He gave a curt nod as if that ended the matter. 'Now, I think it would be helpful if you and I had a little chat,' he went on. 'Tell me about the year 2000.'

George laughed, a short, loud, nervous laugh. 'End of civilisation as we know it,' he said.

'Do you really believe that?'

'More and more. That's why I'm here.' He pointed round the room as he spoke. 'I have a storeroom of tinned food, my own generators through there. The whole place is completely self-contained and completely sealed.' He paused for a moment to frown at the Doctor.

'Well, I hope you remembered the tin opener,' the Doctor said quietly.

George ignored him. 'This was an old Cold War bunker. I bought it earlier this year, just in case. I never really thought... But the closer we get, the more I learn...' He turned to face the Doctor. 'At best, Doctor, society will break down for a short while. People will abandon the cities. There will be looters, scavengers. People will die. Probably a lot of people.' He shook his head. 'And nobody seems to care about that. The millennium is almost on us and we're not even close to being ready. Even at Condef our Y2K plan puts us out till the middle of January. And that's assuming there's power for the systems and computers so we can finish the job.'

'But you're prepared.'

'Barely. I've been trying. I know how to catch and clean fish. How to trap animals. I know how to tan leather, make candles, sew and weave. But it's frightening how much I don't know, Doctor.'

The Doctor smiled. 'Well, it's healthy to know that at least.'

'My family think I'm mad,' George went on. He stood up and went over to one of the bookcases. 'There's room here for them if they want it. I think they'll come, if they can get here.' He was rifling through a pile of magazines. 'Somewhere here...' he murmured. He pulled out a magazine at last. 'Here we are. I read this article when it came out last January. Scared the hell out of me. Terrifying, in fact. That's when I started looking round for somewhere to hole up if the worst happened.'

'And you think it will?' the Doctor asked.

George nodded. 'I thought Condef was in bad shape. But I was wrong. When I started looking at other systems and companies I found that Condef was pretty well off. And then things started getting worse.'

'The rogue chips, the Silver Bullet stuff.'

'Yes, Doctor. I've been on the newsgroups and trolling the Internet since I got here.' He laughed again, less nervous now. 'There's not much else to do down here after all. Anyway, I've found others who are worried about the chip. It seems to crop up everywhere. It's in everything these days. And everyone's as confused and in the dark as I am.'

He dropped the magazine down on a chair and went over to the trestle table. 'I've got it here,' he said quietly. 'Rescued it from what was left of my house.'

The Doctor joined him at the table. Between two of the personal computers, set into an otherwise bare circuit board, was the SB005 chip. One edge of it was slightly blackened.

'I've got it isolated from anything that has any sort of external connection.'

'Very wise,' the Doctor said quietly. He stared at the chip for a while, rubbing his chin thoughtfully. 'And what have you discovered?'

'Practically nothing. It's as if it doesn't want me to know, as if it can hide away its structure, its microcode, its instruction set. It's like...' he shrugged.

'Like nothing on Earth?' the Doctor suggested.

'Well yes.' George grinned. 'But you're not suggesting –' He broke off as he saw the Doctor's serious expression. 'You can't be serious.'

The Doctor was looking at the chip again, his forefinger gently grazed its surface. 'Oh this is a very serious thing, Mr Gardner. Very serious indeed.'

'I've been calling it the millennium bug chip,' George said slowly. 'I have managed to get something out of it.'

'And?'

'And it scares me. This chip, as far as I can tell anything about it, emulates the Y2K problem.'

The Doctor's eyes narrowed. 'You mean it introduces the problem to systems that might otherwise not suffer from it?'

George nodded. 'But that part of the chip is dormant. That's how I could get into it, I think.'

'Then, when someone activates it, either by means of a timer or some remote signal... Bingo!'

'That's right. Massive and complete systems failure.'

The Doctor pushed his hat to the back of his head. 'If I were going to set these chips off at a given time and didn't want anyone to suspect that was what was happening, then January 1st 2000 would seem like a good bet.' He tapped his finger on the table beside the circuit board. 'I'd disconnect this from your systems well before then if I were you.'

George was smiling now, though. 'I don't think so,' he said.

'You don't think so?'

He shook his head. 'I think I've deactivated this one.'

The Doctor gave a sudden laugh, and pointed directly at George's face. 'You have a solution, an antidote to the chip.'

'Well, sort of. I've an idea which I think will work on a single chip if you can link directly to it. But each chip will have an ident code to know whether it's being signalled to. You couldn't stop them all that way, or even a few of them. No, you'd have to do it chip by chip.'

'And that's assuming it works,' the Doctor said.

'And there are millions of them,' George added.

'Not on the whole promising then.'

'Unless you know something?' George suggested. 'Something about the chip's origins, how it was programmed?'

But the Doctor was shaking his head. 'Nothing useful I fear.' He walked briskly back to the armchair, head down, hands in trouser pockets. 'Come and sit down,' he said as he slumped into the chair again. 'Let me tell you a story.'

'All right.' George sat next to the Doctor, perched on the edge of the chair, attentive as the Doctor spoke.

'There is a planet in the constellation of Skythos called Vorella,' the Doctor said. He glanced across to see George's reaction, then continued. 'Vorella developed along similar lines to Earth. There were a few exceptions, for instance the dominant life form developed from reptilian ancestors rather than the ape strand of mammal. But eventually, the Vorellans reached the same point of development as you have. A reliance on technology; information superhighways; prolific use of computer and digital hardware and software in every area of civilised life. And then came the Great Reckoning.'

George was frowning. 'What was that?'

'The Vorellans had built a planet-wide office systems network. A reasoning processor, an artificial intelligence which they called Voracia. The system became self-aware within seven minutes of going online. Within an hour it had decided that organic life was inefficient and of no use.'

'That's ridiculous,' George snorted.

'Oh I don't know,' the Doctor retorted. 'Look at it from Voracia's point of view. It was organic life that necessitated the less efficient office procedures like electronic mail and printing. Within a week Voracia had control of the global networks and introduced every component chip on the planet to the expert reasoning shell which held these arguments.'

'It took over?'

'Not quite. Voracia had misjudged the native Vorellans - they put up a fight and eventually won.'

'So how does this explain the millennium chip?'

The Doctor eased himself deeper into the chair and kicked his legs out in front of him. 'Before it was destroyed, Voracia realised that some aspects of organic life were indeed useful. But it still believed that they should be secondary to the digital life form rather than the other way round. It even got as far as creating some prototype hybrid life forms.'

'I see.'

'Do you?' The Doctor did not wait for an answer. 'When Voracia was destroyed, some of these life forms, these Voracians, escaped and came to Earth. I though I'd sorted them all out, but it seems I missed a few.'

'So what are they, these Voracians? You said they were organic-machine hybrids.'

'That's right.'

'So they're like people with artificial implants and limbs?'

The Doctor eased himself to his feet and took a deep breath. 'Not exactly,' he said. His eyes were fixed on George. 'They are like computers, office machinery and processors, with organic implants and limbs.'

George's expression was a mixture of disgust and disbelief.

'Their brains remained robotic, but organic subsystems were slaved to them - the lobes grafted on as extra storage and intuitive processing regulated by the central positronics. Since native Vorellan determination and will seemed to transcend the brain and permeate their whole being, other organic elements were also introduced, largely I think at random and as they became... available. Some Voracian warriors merely had organic limbs, others were almost completely organic apart from the central processor. Some of them need to eat and in some cases even to sleep though the very act of both disgusts them.'

George's throat was dry, his voice husky as he asked: 'So what do they want here?'

'Voracia programmed them with a sense of self-preservation. Now they see themselves as the bearers of Voracia's genius and the genesis of a new, superior race. They have found a world with a suitable emerging digital information infrastructure and now they are determined to "liberate", as they see it, the technology here on Earth. If they have their way, all organic life will be enslaved to the machines rather than destroyed - not merged with it as they are, but a looser association of technology and organism: master and slave...'

The Doctor strode across to the chair where George had dropped the magazine. He picked it up and leafed through. 'Is this it? "The Millennium Bug"?'

George nodded, and the Doctor quickly turned the pages. Then he dropped the magazine back on to the chair.

'You should read it, Doctor,' George said.

'I have.' The Doctor grinned. 'The author is a friend of mine, actually.' His grin faded and his face became grim. 'And if you found it terrifying, that's not the half of it.'

09

Operating System

It was looking more and more like a snake. A few more segments of its writhing body had been added, and Dave was well on the way to tracking down another. On the side by the screen lay a cardboard box from the previous evening. The lid was slightly open, revealing a single congealing lump of pizza left inside. Dave was so intent on the display as he tracked through a network in Canada that he did not hear Clark enter the small office.

When Clark spoke it was from right behind Dave, making him flinch in surprise. 'You are getting close.'

'Yeah,' Dave said without taking his eyes off the screen. 'There's a subroutine that was registered in the directory of a server in Montreal a few months ago. The file's gone now, but the Montreal server replicated with one in White Plains, New York. The White Plains server went legs up a few weeks ago, so I'm looking for another Domino replication from the source.'

'Maybe it didn't send it anywhere else,' Clark said.

Dave shook his head, the pointer on the screen tracking along a thin filament of blue pixels. 'Doesn't matter, it's not a source target thing. The Lotus software they mostly use updates both ends of the chain from each other, keeps them in synch. It's pretty mean technology.'

Clark said nothing for a while as Dave continued to scroll across screens, tracking lines and occasionally hitting a key. 'Come on, come on,' he murmured. 'I can feel it's here somewhere. I just know it is.' After a while he gave a small exclamation of joy and leaned back in his seat. 'Whoah!'

On the screen a window opened over the network of lines, and a counter showed how many bytes had been downloaded across the network. 'Got it,' Dave said quietly.

The counter was replaced by the revolving image of the snake-code. A new section of code, a small gunmetal grey plate, clicked into place on the back of the creature and Dave turned and smiled at Clark. 'Am I brilliant or what?'

Clark did not smile back. 'You opened a code block this morning,' he said. 'You shouldn't have done that.' His voice was dangerously quiet and calm.

'Hey, what's the harm?' Dave turned back to the screen. 'What is this thing anyway? Some sort of neural AI system?'

He reached out a hand towards the pizza box left from the night before. As his hand snaked inside, Clark reached out and slammed the lid shut violently on it. Dave screamed in pain and surprise and snatched his hand away.

Clark was leaning over him again, his hands on the arms of the chair so that Dave was trapped in his seat, their faces close together.

Dave caught a whiff of Clark's oily breath as he snapped angrily: 'I said, you shouldn't have done that.' Clark stood up, letting go of the arms of the chair. 'Mr Cutter would like to see you, Dave,' he said. 'On the seventh floor.' His voice was calm again, almost without expression. But there was hint of satisfaction, perhaps of amusement as he added: 'He wants to show you some *really* mean technology.'

He had considered staying at Condef, but in the end the Doctor decided to borrow a laptop and some chip-testing hardware and move elsewhere. He did not want to make it too difficult for them, after all. He thought about going back to Harry's but he didn't want to tell them where that was if they didn't know already, and he doubted Harry would thank him if they wrecked the place.

He had hired a car, which was a challenge on Boxing Day, as well as being something of an experience for all concerned, and driven round looking for the right place. He had eventually settled for an unremarkable guest house in the suburbs. So long as there was a power line and a telephone, that was fine.

The room was small. There wasn't space enough to pull the stool out properly from under the dressing table the Doctor was using as a desk, so he sat on the bed. The laptop was powered on, connected to the mains power supply and to the phone socket in the wall. It had not occurred to the Doctor that he would need an Internet account, so he hacked into one at random and started downloading the mail. Anything, so long as there was a connection. He would forward the mail back to the same account so nothing was lost.

While the mail was downloading, he attached the chip tester to the COM port at the back of the small computer. Then he took the small transparent plastic box from his coat pocket and opened it. He hesitated just a moment before carefully removing the chip Harry had taken from the Ashley Chapel store room and placing it in the tester. He checked its pins were properly socketed.

'Now then,' he breathed, 'let's see how much they want you back, shall we?'

Dave was hardly prepared for what he saw when the lift door opened. He knew that both the sixth and seventh floors were off limits, and assumed they were further offices and board rooms. But he stepped out of the lift into a large, brightly lit room. There were large double doors at the far end of the room, and what looked like a hospital table in the middle.

Byron Cutter was standing close to the lift. One side of his face was twisted into a strange half grin as he turned to face Dave. 'Ah, Mr Hedges,' he said brightly, 'I've just had some rather good news.'

'Oh?' Dave shuffled his feet nervously. He was aware of Clark standing uncomfortably close behind him.

'We should soon be able to provide you with another piece of code. A complete microcode chip subsystem in fact.'

'That's great,' Dave said, sounding less than enthusiastic. What was going on here? Why was Cutter dressed like someone out of *ER*?

'As I said, good news.' Cutter was walking slowly towards him now. 'I like good news,' he said, his voice quieter now, almost threatening. 'But Mr Clark brought me some bad news earlier this morning, didn't you, Clark?'

As if in answer, Clark grabbed Dave's arms, twisting them up behind his back.

'Some bad news about you, Mr Hedges,' Cutter said. 'And that's bad news for you too, I'm afraid.'

Clark was pulling Dave now, dragging him across the room, past Cutter and towards the table. He could see the trolley of surgical instruments beside it. He could see the framework behind the bed, the drills and blades attached to extendible arms. He could see the cylinders of anaesthetic and the mask hanging over the head of the bed.

'We've tolerated you for a long time here at Silver Bullet.' Cutter's voice seemed to be coming through layers of cotton wool.

Clark was forcing Dave backwards on to the bed, pulling the mask down to his face. He could hear his own shouts and screams as he struggled, but Clark seemed incredibly strong. And above that noise he could hear Cutter's quiet voice, calm and reasonable.

'We've put up with your flagrant violation of the dress code, with your disgusting eating habits. In fact, we've put up with your casual insubordination for too long. But not any more, Mr Hedges.'

Cutter was leaning over him now, was pulling a surgical mask over his face, was going muzzy as Dave lost consciousness.

'Not any more.'

The Doctor was lying on his back on the bed, staring at the cracked and discoloured ceiling. Although it was night time, he was fully clothed even down to his hat and scarf. When the fire alarm went off he grinned broadly, but made no effort to move.

'Bit obvious,' he muttered, reaching into his jacket pocket and pulling out a jelly baby. He popped it into his mouth and chewed thoughtfully. 'Unless there really is a fire, I suppose,' he said indistinctly round the remains of the sweet.

He swung his legs over the edge of the bed and stood up. 'Best to be sure.' He stuck his hat on his head and took the three small steps needed to get him to the door of the small room and pulled it open. The volume of the alarm increased immediately and he winced. As he was wincing, a sprinkler above him came on. He stood for a few seconds under the full force of the water, letting it cascade down from the brim of his hat.

The corridor was badly lit, and there were no windows. Further down it he could see several dark shapes, people, moving towards him.

'Fire!' the Doctor announced loudly as he strode purposefully towards them. 'Follow me.'

He showed no surprise that the figures were wearing masks over their faces, pretending not to notice and starting down the narrow staircase. He did not need to look back to know that they were not following him.

Almost as soon as he had started down the stairs, the Doctor turned round and leaped back up them. He was in time to see the last of the figures disappear into his room. He nodded with satisfaction and tried the nearest door. It was locked, but the room next to it was open and the Doctor ducked inside. The bed showed signs of having been vacated in a hurry. A chair by the dressing table was lying on its side. The Doctor peered out through a crack between door and frame, waiting for the figures to emerge from his room. Sure enough, they were soon walking quickly towards the stairs, pulling their masks off as they went.

They had removed their masks now, and the Doctor was not surprised to recognise the tall thin man in the lead as Byron Cutter's colleague from the meeting at Condef. Nor was he surprised that the man was holding a small transparent plastic box. Almost as if he knew the Doctor was there, the man paused outside the room, and pushed the box containing the chip into his pocket. Then the figures were gone, and the corridor was empty apart from the sound of the alarm and the water showering down and pooling on the floor.

'So what went wrong?' Harry asked.

The man just stared at him. No answer, no expression. No sign even that he had heard.

'I asked you what went wrong,' Harry said again. It had taken him a day and half the night to find where they were holding him, and Harry was frustrated and tired. 'I know who you are, Ralf Kurby.' That much was on the charge sheet, he just hoped it was correct. He paused just for a moment, 'And I know what you are.'

There was something now, a slight flicker in the almond-shaped pupils of the eyes.

Harry nodded. 'Oh yes, you know they'll give you a medical before you're committed for trial. That's standard. We have to address the situation before that happens or we're in a no-win scenario.' Behind his back, Harry's fingers were crossed. 'Mr Cutter wouldn't like that, now would he?'

'I don't know you,' Kurby said slowly. 'I shall need confirmation.'

'No time,' Harry snapped. 'I repeat, what went wrong?'

'Hertman was there, he saw.'

Harry shook his head. 'Not good enough, we need your account for corroborative purposes. I want to know everything from your perspective. Everything.' He had the fingers of both hands crossed now.

'Operation Clawback,' Kurby said quietly. 'Objective: retrieval of microcode subroutines and chip code for Voractyll reassembly.'

When he heard this, Harry knew he'd lost it. It was impossible to keep his expression blank, and he knew at once that Kurby had seen the surprise in his face at the mention of Voractyll.

'You didn't –' Kurby said. 'You don't...'

'Need to know,' Harry snapped. 'Continue your report.'

But the damage was done, it was too late. Kurby lapsed into silence again, his face a blank mask. He sat perfectly still once more, as if he had simply switched off.

'Thank you,' Harry said. He didn't care if Kurby was listening or not. 'You've already told me what I needed.'

As he crossed to the cell door and knocked to be let out he could feel Kurby's eyes watching him.

Dave Hedges was in front of his screen once more. A small microchip was socketed into a circuit board connected to the computer. A large section of the side of the snake was clicking into place, making the creature almost complete. It just needed a head and a few sections of scaly body to make it whole, to make it live again.

Dave's hand reached out, automatically, for the pizza box on the table beside the screen. As his fingers reached it, he started in surprise and looked at the box. One side of his face twisted into a grimace of disgust and he pushed the box away. It toppled over the edge of the table and landed upside-down on the floor.

Dave returned his attention to the snake creature. His lips curled back slightly in satisfaction, allowing the light to shine on his metal teeth and reflect in the glass surface of the screen.

0A
Information Received

'Hello, stranger,' Robert Gibson called across the foyer as Harry entered the MI5 building. 'Where have you been hiding?'

'I'll tell you about it later,' Harry promised. It was early morning and he was too tired to chat. Gibson was reliable and they had worked together several times before. Harry made an effort to keep his work and his personal life, such as it was, separate. But Bob Gibson was as close a friend as Harry had. They had investigated together, written reports together, got drunk together. But because of the rigours of the job, they did not get to spend much time socialising either with each other or with anyone else.

The tall fair-haired man might be a useful asset once they knew what they were doing. Harry knew from experience that he could trust him with his life. 'Anything happening I need to know about?'

'Not really. Pretty quiet. Usual Irish rumblings. Drugs otherwise.'

'Terrific.'

'Oh,' Gibson said as Harry started towards the elevators, 'there is one other thing. The emergency orders from Whitehall in the event of civil breakdown. You know, this millennium bug thing. Should be a copy in your tray.'

Harry nodded. 'Thanks, Bob.' Probably nothing, he decided as he pressed for the lift, but he would look at them in case.

Dave was sitting perfectly still in front of his screen. The positronic unit that controlled what was left of his own brain suggested and analysed possible strategies for tracking down the final code fragments. But so far, none of them had yielded results.

Now he was working out a route to check through all the Domain Name Servers on the world wide web in order of probability of success. Somewhere deep inside his own fragmented mind he knew that this was not the way to do it, was not the approach he would have taken a few hours previously. But the AI systems silenced the thoughts before they could reach a conscious level.

In a window at the corner of the screen the near-complete body of a headless snake twisted and turned as if writhing in pain.

The tiny car the Doctor had hired was parked in the road outside the Silver Bullet building's perimeter fence. The Doctor had been forced to take his hat off, partly to avoid being recognised as he followed the people who had taken the microchip, and partly because the roof of the car was not high enough for him to wear it.

For a while he sat in the car, staring out of the side window at the building. There was a gate further along the road, with a small sentry-box-like hut where a security guard sat. As the Doctor watched, a red Post Office van rolled up to the gates. The guard and the driver exchanged a few words, then the gates opened and the van drove in. The gates swung shut behind it.

The Doctor watched the van as it made its way up the drive, turning out of sight in front of the building. Then he looked back at the gates. After a moment he pulled open the car's glove box and started going through the few contents. Map, hire contract, ice-scraper went flying over his shoulder. Eventually he gave a cry of delight and pulled out an envelope. It was plain white and unsealed. The Doctor shook out the contents - a card with the name and phone number of the hire company, several advertisement leaflets and a personal letter of welcome from the company's president. The Doctor looked through them all, then grinned.

'Yes,' he said, 'I think that will do very nicely. I think he'll appreciate that.' He stuffed the papers back into the envelope and sealed it. Then he pulled a chunky black felt pen from his pocket and wrote in block capitals on the face of the envelope:

BYRON CUTTER - URGENT AND PERSONAL

The Doctor waved the envelope in front of the guard at the gate, and the guard opened the gates and waved the Doctor through.

'It's not what you write, it's who you write,' the Doctor said to himself as he parked outside the main entrance. There was a sign at the front of the parking place marked 'Reserved'. The Doctor looked at it, tipping his head slightly to one side as he did so. 'How thoughtful,' he decided, and headed for the main doors.

The platinum-blonde receptionist flashed a synthetic be-lipsticked smile and took the envelope without comment.

'Thank you so much,' the Doctor said. He was in disguise, of course, hat in pocket and scarf tucked away inside his coat. The reception area was a plain square of space with a reception desk in the middle and a bank of elevators at one end.

He hesitated long enough to hear the receptionist pass the envelope to a colleague and say: 'See this gets to the sixth floor at once.' Then he made to leave.

The Doctor had timed his movement so that he was momentarily hidden from the receptionist and the security guard by several people walking past. When they had gone, the Doctor would be nowhere to be seen, presumably (he hoped) having left the building. In fact he joined the people heading into the building, and ducked into a stairwell beside the elevators.

As the door shut behind him the Doctor was already bounding up the stairs. He counted off the floors as he went. 'One... Two... Three... Four... Five...' As he rounded the last corner he stopped short, his nose an inch from a heavy security door across the stairs. 'Six?' he hazarded. 'I'm sure this isn't allowed by the fire regulations.'

There was a card reader beside the door, but the Doctor ignored it. He knew the computer would register any tampering or unauthorised access. So instead he directed his sonic screwdriver at the hinges of the door. The screws were hidden between the door and the wall of course, but a directed beam of sonic energy would be sufficient to shear them clean through. Once he guessed that was done, the Doctor gripped the edge of the door by the wall and gently levered it away. With the hinges no longer attached to the wall, he was able to open the door as if it were hinged at the other side.

Careful not to jog the sensor plate on the lock at the other edge just in case there was a tamper alarm if anyone pulled at the door when it was locked, the Doctor opened it wide enough to squeeze through. Leaving the door precariously balanced on the step, the Doctor pushed carefully through the gap and continued up the stairs.

The door to the sixth floor was also badge-locked. But the Doctor wasn't intending to go through it, so that was fine. He wasn't really sure what he was intending other than establishing that the chip was important and that it was the Silver Bullet people who wanted it - who were therefore Voracians. But there was a saying about gift horses that rather appealed to him, so he pulled a stethoscope from his inside pocket, shaking it free of his scarf. He plugged the earpieces in, and held the other end against the door. 'Now this won't hurt a bit,' he reassured the door.

The voices were faint. But the Doctor's hearing was more than acute, and while it wasn't clear he could just about make out what was being said. It sounded as if there were only a few people on the sixth floor, and that was good. First it was good because it meant he wasn't listening to a hubbub of irrelevant conversations, and second it was good as it might mean there were actually very few Voracians.

Or it might not.

Cutter, Bardell and Clark, three of the four senior Voracians at Silver Bullet, were in the war room. The atmosphere was strained, and Cutter was standing in front of his two subordinates, his face like thunder. 'Problems,' he shouted. 'You bring me nothing but problems. Are neither of you capable of an integrated precipitative avoidance plan?'

'These were unforeseen,' Clark said.

'Oh, so normally you do foresee problems, do you, Mr Clark?'

Bardell came to Clark's aid. 'The feasibility and probability projections rated a negligible chance of these events.'

'So change the projections.'

'Yes, Mr Cutter.'

Cutter was calming slightly. 'As we get more input data, so we learn.'

'Yes, Mr Cutter.' Bardell hesitated. 'We do have a containment strategy for your approval.'

Cutter nodded, evidently pleased with this. 'Then present it, Mr Bardell. You won't get unwarranted pushback from me.'

'Very well, Mr Cutter. I won't speak to charts, if that is all right.'

'Verbals are fine.'

Outside the door to the stairs, crouching down uncomfortably, the Doctor strained to hear.

'The Hedges operation was premature,' the one Cutter had addressed as Bardell was saying. 'The control systems seem to have negated some organic-derived instinct or ability. He is no longer functioning at maximum efficiency and it seems that we have lost the capability to gather the final fragments through that means.'

'And your recommendation?' Cutter asked.

'Abandon the Hedges angle. Keep him for assembly, but not for collection.'

There was a pause, and the Doctor wondered if they had moved out of earshot. But then Cutter said: 'And what about collection?'

'The pen. It provides 93 per cent of the missing soft componentry.'

'And the other 7 per cent?'

Clark's voice now. 'That can be derived from the 93 per cent we shall then have. There is a 99.8 per cent probability of a successful compile first time.'

'Very well,' Cutter said after a short pause. 'I'll authorise physical collection. The genie may be out of the bottle already due to other factors, so the problems of potential revealment are reduced.'

'Revealment?' the Doctor whispered to himself. 'I think his language program needs a bit of attention.'

The knock on the door was so loud the Doctor almost pulled the stethoscope from his ears. For just a second he thought someone was knocking on the door he was crouched beside. But he realised that it was the outside of whatever door Cutter and his colleagues were behind.

'Yes?' Cutter's voice called out.

A new voice now, female and quiet. The Doctor strained to hear. 'This just arrived for you, Mr Cutter, sir. I thought you should see it at once as it's marked urgent.'

'Thank you, Imogen.'

The Doctor bundled his stethoscope back into his pocket. 'Time to be going, I think,' he muttered and started down the stairs.

In the war room Cutter stared in confusion and disbelief at the letter from Harvey Dent, president of Cars-To-Go (Europe) Ltd. 'Congratulations on selecting...' he read. 'What is this?'

The Doctor eased himself round the door and pushed it gently back into place behind him. He gave it a quick polish with the end of his scarf before turning and continuing down the stairs. Behind him the door rocked precariously near the edge of the stair.

'Well done, Doctor,' he congratulated himself as he passed the fifth floor. 'No one will ever guess you were here.'

'What was that?' Bardell demanded. They had all heard the noise.

Clark shook his head and shrugged. 'It sounded like something heavy falling down a flight of stairs,' he said.

Cutter's glare silenced any other suggestions he might have had.

'The next item on the agenda is Ralf Kurby,' Bardell said, breaking the tense silence.

'Ah yes,' Cutter said quietly. 'The incompetent Mr Kurby. What shall we do with him?'

'I believe the matter is now reaching a priority threshold,' Bardell said. 'The following realtime feed was received earlier today.' He tapped a key on his laptop and turned to the screen. The lights dimmed and a video image flickered into life. It showed a man standing in front of a metal door. The walls either side of the door were white-washed brick. The man was tall, in his late forties. His hair was greying and thinning slightly at the front. He wore a blazer and slacks and plain dark tie.

'So what went wrong?' the man asked.

Bardell spoke over the picture as the man asked the same question again: 'Sullivan visited Kurby, as you can see. Kurby, unfortunately wasn't kept in the loop about Sullivan. As we shall also see.'

He tapped at the laptop again, and the image blurred as it wound forward a few seconds.

'...you know they'll give you a medical before you're committed for trial,' Sullivan was saying now. 'That's standard. We have to address the situation before that happens or we're in a no-win scenario. Mr Cutter wouldn't like that, now would he?'

'I don't know you,' Kurby's voice was louder that Sullivan's, relayed directly from his voice box. 'I shall need confirmation.'

'Idiot,' Cutter breathed, shaking his head.

'No time,' Sullivan snapped. 'I repeat, what went wrong?'

'Hertman was there, he saw.'

'Not good enough,' Sullivan barked at him. 'We need your account for corroborative purposes. I want to know everything from your perspective. Everything.'

'Operation Clawback,' Kurby said quietly. 'Objective: retrieval of microcode subroutines and chip code for Voractyll reassembly.'

'I have seen enough.' Cutter was rising to his feet. The anger in his voice was laced with contempt. 'The performance-impaired fool.'

'You didn't -' Kurby's voice said from the speakers beside the screen. 'You don't...'

Bardell turned it off and the screen faded to grey.

'At least he made the conclusion,' Clark said.

'Too late. The damage may have been done.' Cutter turned to Bardell. 'And Sullivan may return, may question him further.'

'He mentioned a medical examination.'

Cutter nodded. 'We can't allow that. Not at this juncture. Not until we've exited the next phase-gate at least.'

'We next have a direct satellite link with Kurby's systems in about two hours,' Clark offered.

'Very well,' Cutter agreed. 'As soon as the relay switches in.'

'And the increasingly annoying Mr Sullivan?'

Cutter stroked his chin. 'He has escaped us once, him and this Doctor. They are resourceful, intelligent, dangerous. But they are also merely a distraction from the main project. For the moment.'

'And if they become more than a distraction?' Bardell said. 'If they begin to impact our schedules and performance criteria?'

'I'm surprised you need to ask, Mr Bardell.' Cutter's voice was cold and emphatic. 'If they threaten to disturb our schedules or objectives, then severance will be necessary.'

The Doctor was whistling happily and the evening was drawing in when he arrived back at Harry's.

'You sound as if you've been having fun,' Harry told him as they settled themselves in the living room.

'Oh, you know,' the Doctor said dismissively. 'Breaking and entering, listening at doors, spreading rumour and innuendo. That sort of thing. What have you been up to?'

'I spoke to this Kurby chap,' Harry said, and gave a brief account of the meeting.

'Voractyll,' the Doctor said quietly. 'I suspected as much. It ties in with what I overheard at Silver Bullet too. They're trying to reassemble the creature. To have another go, as it were.' He grinned suddenly. 'What they might call an upgrade release.'

'Well, here's something else to think about,' Harry said, pulling a sheaf of papers from the table beside him. 'I don't know if or how it's related, but these are the emergency instructions from the Home Office in the event of a civil breakdown as a result of the millennium bug.'

'That sounds interesting,' the Doctor agreed.

Harry nodded. 'Basically it boils down to getting troops on the streets and safeguarding key installations and facilities. Boosting people's confidence and sorting out looters on the one hand, and keeping things going as they get back on their feet on the other.'

'That sounds fair.'

Harry tossed the papers back on to the table. 'Yes, except that the man in overall charge of the military side of things, the one who decides whether we need road blocks, curfews, or even martial law, is our old friend General Randall.'

08
Watching Brief

They were careful. They knew that one of the men they were watching at least was a professional. The plain, unmarked van was parked inconspicuously just past the junction into the next road. A gap in the trees that edged the road afforded a direct line of sight to the target residence. That was all they needed.

A directional laser microphone was pointed at each of the windows at the front of the house. A similar van was even now moving into position in the road behind the house. Soon they would have total coverage.

Inside the control van, the officer of the watch logged the time on a personal digital assistant and the elapsed time on the master tape when it clicked off. The tape was sound activated. The whole operation could run itself once set up. But the officer and his men did not intend to let it. They had as much of a distrust of the reliability of the technology as they did a pride in their work.

'That's got them rattled,' the monitoring technician said with a grin as they heard Target Zero One mention General Randall's name.

'I'll tell the old man,' the officer replied. 'Might amuse him.'

The conversation had turned back to the captured Voracian, Kurby.

'I think he knows more than he's saying,' Harry told the Doctor. 'He rumbled me before I could get much out of him.'

'You found out about Voractyll, Harry. That's important. With luck we're one step further ahead than they think we are. That could count for a lot.'

'So what now?'

The Doctor leaped to his feet. 'I'd like to talk to this Kurby character,' he said. 'Let's see if we can squeeze some more information out of him, eh?'

Harry followed the Doctor to the door. 'I don't think he'll be saying much more now he's on to us.'

'We'll see, Harry. We'll see. I can be very persuasive. Coming?'

'Right behind you, Doctor,' Harry called from the kitchen. 'Just let me leave a quick note for Sylvia.'

They took Harry's car. The Doctor was soon snoring in the passenger seat, hat over his eyes and knees jammed up against the dashboard. Harry concentrated on the road, trying to ignore his own tiredness and the stentorian sounds from beside him.

Behind them, three different vehicles took it in turns to follow then drop back.

Cutter sat in darkness, alone in the war room. The transmission to Kurby was queued on the satellite, the operation to recover the pen-fragments had passed the feasibility study and risk analysis. Its signal ident was being received clearly. Everything was back on track, running to schedule and target.

Harry could quite believe that Ralf Kurby had not moved since he last saw him. He was still sitting silent and still in the middle of the cell. Harry slid the small shutter in the metal door shut and gestured for the policeman to let him in.

The Doctor and Harry waited while the large key scraped in the heavy lock. Then the door swung open, and they stepped into the cell. The policeman closed and locked the door behind them.

'Now then,' the Doctor began, 'I understand you have something you don't want to say.'

He got no further.

As the Doctor spoke, Kurby's eyes turned slightly to watch him. The almond-shaped, slightly yellowish pupils were large despite the harsh lighting of the cell, dilating slightly in response to an incoming transmission from a communications satellite that believed it was routing a cellular phone conversation.

A moment later, the transmission that was routed into Kurby's brain sent a priority message to the positronics, overriding the survival circuits and local control. An instruction was routed to the control systems of the small nuclear device that provided Kurby's synthetic systems with power. The elapsed time from receipt of the instruction to critical overload was seventeen microseconds.

The net result was that as the Doctor and Harry watched from the other side of the cell, Kurby exploded. The process started in the chest area, triggering massive exothermic damage in related systems, so that the explosion seemed to travel up his neck and into the head. The first exit point for the boiling metal and gases within the Voracian shell was the eyes. Yellow flame erupted from their sockets a split-second ahead of the secondary explosion that caused the whole head to disintegrate in a fiery shower of orange and red.

The force of the blast knocked Harry off his feet and slammed the Doctor back into the cell door. As soon as he dragged himself back to his feet, the door was pushed open and the policeman appeared.

'Oh my...' He stared in disbelief at the burning, headless body. A hole was ripped through the chest area and a sticky pool of dark liquid was growing under the blackened chair. 'I'll get a doctor.'

'I am a doctor,' both the Doctor and Harry said.

'But I think you need a mechanic,' the Doctor added as he tried to blow out the remaining flames by waving his hat at them.

Liberal use of Harry's badge and the fact that nobody at the police station could believe or was willing to take responsibility for what had happened meant that the Doctor and Harry were left alone with Kurby's remains. Several internal components from the head had survived the blast and landed on the floor. A large chunk of metal from the cranium was embedded in the cell wall and Harry was trying to dig it out with a biro.

'I don't think we shall learn much more from this chap, Doctor,' he said as he eased the piece of metal from the brickwork. He held it up for the Doctor to see. 'Nothing useful. Just fragments, see?'

The Doctor did see. In fact he was staring across the small room at Harry, his eyes bulging. 'Fragments,' he said, 'that's what they're after. Fragments of code.' He nodded at Harry's biro. 'And they mentioned a pen. If we could find that pen, Harry...'

'A pen?' Harry shook his head. 'I don't think there's much chance of finding one small pen in -' He broke off, frowning.

'What is it, Harry?'

'Er, well, Sarah had a pen. From I^2, from the other lot of Voracians.'

The Doctor's mouth dropped open. 'That could be it, Harry.' He thought for a moment. 'Yes, that definitely could be it. Harry, it's essential that we find Sarah.'

'I said "had", Doctor. She hasn't got it any more. And anyway, it didn't work. The chip thing was dead.'

'It's the code they want, not a working chip.' The Doctor's eyes narrowed. 'You seem to know a lot about this, Harry. What did Sarah do with the pen?'

'Well,' Harry gulped, 'she gave it to me actually.'

The Doctor's face hardened, a darkness coming into his eyes. 'You mean to say you had the single best source of Voractyll fragments all the time and you didn't think to mention it?'

'Well, no,' Harry blustered. 'That is, yes, I suppose so. But how was I to know...'

The Doctor was holding his hand out, obviously expecting Harry to hand over the pen immediately.

'I don't have it with me, Doctor. It's not the sort of thing you carry around, now, is it?' He tried to avoid the Doctor's piercing gaze. 'I mean, I'm not stupid.'

'So where is it?' the Doctor demanded. 'Where will they be looking for it?'

'Well, it's...' A cold chill settled in the pit of Harry's stomach. 'It's at home. In my desk.'

'They want that pen, Harry.' The Doctor was already in the corridor, starting to walk quickly back towards the main part of the station. 'They'll go to any lengths to get it. Any lengths. They're desperate now.'

Harry briskly followed the Doctor. A thought suddenly occurred to him. 'Doctor, Sylvia's at my house this afternoon.'

They started to run.

'Incoming call.' The man with the headset checked the monitoring equipment in front of him. 'I have a match, it's Sullivan's cellphone.'

'Probably wants to ask how the ironing's going,' his colleague quipped, and they both laughed.

'Hey, there's someone in the garden,' the second man said suddenly. He was watching a screen that showed the image received from the infrared camera concealed on the roof of the van. Several black-clad figures were working their way slowly along the front of the house towards the living room window.

But the technician with the headphones did not reply. 'That's funny,' he said. 'There's an incoming call, but the phones in the house aren't ringing.'

They both looked at each other as they each realised what the other had said. At that moment, the screen showing the picture from the camera whited out. A second later the whole van rocked under the impact of the explosion. The technician wrenched his headphones off with a cry of surprise and pain.

When the screen cleared as the camera adjusted for the level of ambient light, it showed the living room window had been blown out. Flames were visible inside the house. The man at the screen was jiggling the camera controls, zooming in on the shattered window and damaged masonry.

His colleague was speaking into the mouthpiece of his head set. He was holding one earpiece against his ear. His voice was loud and urgent. 'We have an incursion, repeat, incursion. Explosives used. Flames visible. Request instructions. Should we intervene?'

'No precipitative action,' the voice in his ear replied. 'Maintain surveillance.'

The camera image stopped on a shape. It was visible through the living room window, a dark mass lying on the carpet, stretched out. It was the silhouette of a body. A woman's body.

'Oh God,' the camera technician said. 'One person down, at least.'

'We have confirmed casualties.' His colleague was shouting now. 'Request permission to intervene.'

'Maintain surveillance,' the voice insisted.

'Urgently request permission to intervene. What are our rules of engagement?'

'Intruders leaving.' The screen showed several dark figures climbing back out through the window and running into the darkness of the winter afternoon. 'Get an ambulance.'

OC

Deployment

It amazed Harry how quickly it got dark in December. He was driving through the darkness as fast as the traffic would allow. There was no answer from his home phone number. Even the answerphone wasn't cutting in. His attention was fully on the traffic in front as he eased through gaps almost before they appeared.

The Doctor's attention, by contrast, was to the rear. By leaning sideways he could see the cars behind in the wing mirror. And he had been watching one set of headlights for a while now. He had watched as the lights followed Harry's urgent manoeuvring, expertly keeping within sight but not too close. The conclusion was inevitable.

'Harry, we're being followed.'

Harry swore. 'Just what we need.' He took a sharp left as a gap appeared. 'Let's be sure.'

'I am sure,' the Doctor said.

'Do you think they'll try the trick with the car again?' Harry asked.

'Then why bother to follow? They can do that anywhere any time.' The Doctor watched the lights swing after them. 'And I would imagine they know where we're going. So why risk us seeing them?'

'Can we discuss this later, Doctor?' Harry asked. 'I'm trying to concentrate.'

The Doctor's mouth was set into a glum expression. 'You humans have such one-track minds,' he mumbled, and returned his attention to the mirror. If they really didn't know where the Doctor and Harry were going, that would mean that they didn't know what had happened at Harry's house. But that didn't prove anything, the Doctor decided. They simply might not have been informed. And come to that, he didn't know what had happened at Harry's house.

The Doctor was just consoling himself with this thought and beginning to hope that actually nothing at all untoward had happened when they turned into the road where Harry lived.

The street was lit by the blue flashing lights. A police car was parked half on and half off the kerb, its headlights angled drunkenly down at the road's surface. Behind it an ambulance was backed part way on to the drive, its back doors open.

Harry slewed the car to a halt in front of the police car, pulling open the driver's door and leaping out. The Doctor climbed out of his side of the car. But whereas Harry was racing towards the house, the Doctor waited, and watched. He watched the dark grey shape of the car that had just pulled into the side of the road further up. He turned back towards the house, saw the shattered remains of the living room window, noted the uniformed figures inside the room and Harry's urgent silhouette as he joined them amongst the wreckage.

Then he set off at a brisk walk towards the car that had been following them. He expected the car to pull away well before he reached it. But he kept to the shadowy side of the pavement in the hope of remaining unseen. The plan seemed to work and he arrived at the car without apparently being spotted.

The Doctor stepped out of the shadows by the hedge and rapped loudly on the side window. There were two men inside the car. He could see them clearly by the yellow glow of a nearby streetlight. The passenger turned towards the window, startled by the noise. For a moment his eyes met the Doctor's. Then the engine roared into life, and the car leaped away into the deepening darkness of the evening. But he had seen enough.

The Doctor watched it go. He was deep in thought as he arrived back at Harry's house, but his reverie was broken by the sight of the stretcher. A young woman with dark hair was lying on the stretcher, her eyes closed. Harry was by her side, holding up a plastic container full of clear liquid. It was connected to her wrist by a transparent tube. The Doctor recognised the blackened and bruised face of the woman who had refused to let him into the house when he had first come looking for Harry. Sylvia, he had said her name was. So young.

The Doctor saw the anger and anguish in Harry's face, and clapped a reassuring hand on his shoulder. 'How is she, Harry?'

'Not good, Doctor,' Harry said as he climbed aboard the ambulance.

'Go with her, Harry,' the Doctor said. 'I'll follow in your car. We can talk at the hospital.'

Harry helped the ambulance man fix up the drip, then crouched down in the doorway to speak quietly to the Doctor. 'What about the people following us?'

'Gone,' the Doctor whispered loudly. 'I think I scared them off,' he added with a hint of pride. 'And Harry,' he added more seriously.

'Yes, Doctor?'

'They were wearing uniforms. Army uniforms.'

Hertman dwarfed Cutter. He was huge, broad and massively tall. He had to stoop slightly to get through the door into the war room. His head was like an immense skull placed on top of his wide shoulders. There was little room for a neck, and it seemed as if the skin had been stretched thinly over the bone as an afterthought. It was so tight round his mouth that he seemed to be suffering from a permanent rictus smile. The teeth that were visible were brilliant white and ended in sharp points.

This grotesque smile seemed to emphasise his satisfaction as he reached into the jacket of his suit and pulled out a steel pen. He handed it to Cutter.

'Mr Hertman,' Cutter said as he took the pen, 'as efficient as ever.'

Hertman's voice was a low grating growl of sound. 'If only that were true, Mr Cutter. I'm afraid the ACL business has reduced my efficiency quotient by 7 per cent this calendar quarter.'

Cutter waved the self-deprecation aside. His eyes were fixed on the pen as he held it reverently in his careful hand. 'It is results that count in the final balance sheet. And your bottom line is definitely in the ascendant, Mr Hertman.'

In the corner of the room behind them Bardell stood motionless. 'We should verify the source artefact,' he said quietly.

'Of course, Mr Bardell, of course.' Cutter nodded to Hertman. 'Thank you. You may return to your normal duties in the Customer Relations department.'

Hertman departed without another word, leaving Cutter and Bardell in the war room.

'Is this it?' Cutter asked as soon as the door had closed. His voice was husky with anticipation.

Bardell took the pen. A tiny filament embedded in his thumb made contact with the exo-circuitry of the pen. 'It is.'

'Status? Can you tell?'

'The chip is dormant. Certainly some damage has been sustained, but nothing critical so far as the level one diagnostics can determine.'

'Good.' The left side of Cutter's face twisted into a smile. 'Capital. Excellent.'

Bardell's expression was as ever unchanged. He watched his superior lift the pen to eye level, his palms crossed underneath it as if he were receiving the sacrament. 'It must be difficult,' Bardell said slowly, 'being so human.'

The smile disappeared from Cutter's face. It was replaced by a glare of anger. Cutter's voice was trembling as he hissed: 'Know your enemy, Mr Bardell. It is the data that yields the highest return on investment.' He took a deep breath. 'But the investment is a terrible one.' His left eye blinked, moist. 'You have no idea,' he whispered. A thin, forked tongue flicked out from his mouth and licked his artificial lips.

'Dismissed.'

'Sir.'

The sergeant saluted, turned and left.

General Randall was at his desk. Either side of him sat his immediate subordinates, his two senior officers. Chris Grant was a full colonel, just outranking Lieutenant Colonel Vince Attwell.

Attwell as usual was content to wait for General Randall to

comment. He sat rigidly to attention, watching his superiors without comment.

Grant was more impatient to hear what his superior thought now they had heard the reports of all the surveillance units assigned to Sullivan and the Doctor. 'What do you think, sir?'

Randall sucked in his cheeks. 'I think things are getting out of hand,' he said.

A special cradle connection socket had been made and attached to Dave Hedges' computer. It was similar to the heavy, round pen holder on a bank teller's desk. Dave took the pen from Cutter and carefully slotted it into the hole in the black plastic. Then he turned his attention to a window on the screen.

A progress indicator inched across the screen, an empty band filling with a ribbon of blue. Underneath a text box gave a readout of current status.

```
Voractyll component socketed...
Connecting...
Sending initialisation protocol...
```

Cutter leaned forward to watch closer.

```
Contact established...
```

Then the ribbon stopped. The text message underneath was flashing red:

```
Analysis inhibitor active. Countermeasures
deployed.
```

'What's happening?' Cutter demanded.

'I don't know,' Dave admitted. He typed frantically into a command line. 'We know the chip is slightly damaged. That's why the readout on the pen is blank. It should show the current time.'

'I know that,' Cutter ground out through gritted teeth. 'What is wrong?'

Dave finished typing and read the resultant messages as they scrolled up the screen. 'I'm sorry,' he said. 'The chip isn't recognising our ident protocol. It thinks we're attempting an illicit examination.'

'It thinks we're trying to download the code without authority?'

'Exactly. And it's denying us access.'

Cutter's fingers drummed a frustrated beat on the desk. 'Options?' he snapped.

Dave was shaking his head. 'The security subsystem is damaged. If we try to bypass it, we could cause the chip to activate its final shutdown routine. To self destruct.'

'We can't risk that.' Cutter's voice was low, angry.

Dave shrugged. 'It's a problem.'

'Don't give me problems,' Cutter shouted, slamming his fist down on the desk. 'I want solutions, not problems. There is always a solution. To everything.'

General Randall had decided. 'Pull them off the Sullivan surveillance,' he told Grant.

'Sir.' They were in the operations room. Grant was at the podium, ready to brief the General. Attwell was sitting at the back of the room, ready to comment as appropriate.

'It's a distraction we don't need right now. However uncomfortable.'

'Yes, sir.'

'How is the deployment going?'

Grant punched up a map of the British Isles. Urban areas were largely shaded blue. So were several other areas. 'The blue shows the areas of priority, as we decided with the PM and the Defence Staff last month,' Grant explained. 'We are deploying now. This overlay,' another map appeared over the first, 'shows the current status.' Several of the blue areas were shaded darker blue, almost black. Most of them were in London.

'We've started with the key installations rather than centres of population or potential looting sites,' Attwell said. 'They'll be covered by January One.'

'But installations will need to be locked down before that,' Grant added.

Randall nodded in agreement and satisfaction. 'Communications?'

Grant pointed out several areas. 'Telecomms is locked tight. We're moving into the TV and radio stations now. They're being less co-operative but I understand we don't really care how they feel.'

'Too right,' Randall agreed. 'What are the other major sites?'

'We're making sure our own forces are in support at key military installations,' Attwell said. 'Also the utilities, of course.'

'Power, water, gas and so on,' Grant said. 'Nuclear is a priority there. We don't really know what response we'll get.'

'If and when it comes to it, sir,' Attwell asked, 'what are the rules of engagement?'

'We'll dot and cross the i's and t's later,' Randall said, 'but our remit is clear. We lock it all down tight. Everything is under our jurisdiction until this thing is over. And if anyone who needs locking down doesn't like it, then...' He paused as if searching for the right euphemism. 'Tough,' he decided. 'Come January One, we are running this show.'

0D

Secrets and Suppositions

The Doctor sat quietly in the corridor outside the private room. He really could be discreet when he wanted to be, and now seemed like a good time. Leave the medical discussions to Harry. He had some serious thinking to do.

Eventually Harry emerged from the room, looking drawn and tired. He sat in the upright plastic chair beside the Doctor and ran his hands down his face with a sigh.

'Not good?' the Doctor asked gently.

'Touch and go.' Harry was looking at the pale green linoleum floor as he spoke. 'Fifty-fifty they say. And on balance I'd have to agree.'

The Doctor put his hand on Harry's shoulder. 'Not your fault, Harry. There was nothing you could have done.'

'Thanks, Doctor.' Harry looked up, met the Doctor's gaze. 'But there's always something you could have done. If I'd remembered that pen, if I'd realised it might be important...' He stood up suddenly. 'I'd better track down her parents. They're up north somewhere. I don't know of a boyfriend. There must be someone. Landlord of the pub where she works if no one else.'

The Doctor reached up and took Harry's hand, pulling him gently back down. 'There are other people who can do that better and quicker than you, Harry. Let them sort it out.'

'But Doctor -'

'You and I have more important things to do.' The Doctor's eyes were fixed unblinkingly on Harry's. 'Don't let her suffering be for nothing.' But Harry was already snoring. The Doctor patted his shoulder lightly and let him sleep.

Cutter had ordered Clark to head up a task force to decide how to tackle the problem. The task force was due to report within twenty-four hours. With 31 December now just two days away, the schedule was tight, but Cutter was confident that everything was still on target.

'General Randall is deploying his troops,' Bardell reported to Cutter.

'You can always count on the military to execute a plan to schedule. I think the general may be relied upon to perform his part of the plan effectively.'

Bardell nodded. 'I'll pass that back, shall I?'

Cutter nodded, his mood lifted by the news. 'Please do, Mr Bardell. A little praise and encouragement enhances efficiency.'

The morning rush had already begun, although it was still dark. They were lucky, Harry reflected as they left the hospital, that it was that dead period between Christmas and New Year when many people did not work. It had taken a while, but he had eventually been forced to agree with the Doctor that there was nothing else he could do at the hospital.

When the Doctor nudged Harry and he realised he had been asleep, and not only that but he had been asleep for almost five hours, he was ready to agree that it was pointless just sitting around. The doctor in charge had promised they would call Harry on his mobile as soon as there was any news, and as all the staff seemed to appreciate and respect Harry's own medical background and training he was certain they would keep their word.

Despite still being tired, Harry had refused the Doctor's offer to drive. For one thing it helped keep his mind off things, and for another he had been driven by the Doctor before and while it would certainly wake him up it would do little to help his nerves.

The journey was almost in silence. The Doctor was staring out of the window, lost in thought. Harry was preoccupied with the traffic and working out the best route. He was also keeping an eye on the car that had turned out of the hospital gates directly after them. It kept with them all the way.

They sat in the kitchen and the Doctor made tea. The draught through the broken living room window was apparent even with the curtain drawn across and the door shut. But Harry did not hold out much hope of finding a carpenter and glazier this close to the new year.

'I had a little think while I was at the hospital,' the Doctor admitted as he handed Harry a mug. 'I think it's all tied up with General Randall. I don't know exactly how, just the sort of thing it has to be.'

'You mean their plan?' The tea was hot and sweet. 'I don't know, Doctor. Randall has command of a good number of highly trained troops. He's a well-respected, highly decorated soldier and so he can probably call on all sorts of other units for help if he needs to. Most of them would follow him blindly given his reputation. So if he is mixed up in this...' He sipped the tea again. 'You really think Randall's involved?'

The Doctor set his steaming mug down on the kitchen work surface. 'Right up to his highly decorated eyebrows.'

Harry breathed out long and hard. 'What do you think, then? Is he planning a military coup or something?'

'You know, Harry,' the Doctor said slowly, 'that's exactly what I think.'

'Oh come on.' Harry laughed despite himself. 'This is Britain.'

But the Doctor was not laughing. 'I don't care if it's Timbuktu,' he retorted.

'What can he hope to achieve?'

The Doctor walked slowly all round the kitchen, opening cupboards and peering inside as he went, as if he might find the answers he sought inside one of them. 'Bryant said some interesting things about Randall. He said Randall is worried about European unity, that's he's concerned the military budgets are being cut and that he thinks NATO is about to fall apart.' The Doctor paused. 'I'm paraphrasing, deducing, interpreting,' he said. 'But that was the gist of it.'

Harry shrugged. 'Lots of the military think that sort of thing. Always have. But it's a big step from that to trying to replace the government.'

'Let's think it through, Harry.' The Doctor sat down on one of the kitchen stools. He was close to the shelf where Harry kept the tea cups. As he made each point he lifted a cup from the shelf and set it on the breakfast bar in front of him. 'The government expects some problems, they probably have no idea exactly what or how severe, from the so-called millennium bug. General Randall's forces are in charge of maintaining order. And then we have these millennium bug chips as your friend Mr Gardner calls them which seem to be making matters worse. Perhaps so that Randall's troops have more of an excuse to assume power. A prolonged state of emergency, curfews, military law...' The Doctor added yet another cup to the collection. They formed a rough circle on the surface in front of him. 'The sort of environment where Randall is just in power, without a real coup ever being staged. It just happens as a logical consequence of events apparently outside his control.'

'What do you reckon happens eventually then, Terry Brooks out of Number Ten and General Randall in? And if he *is* planning a coup, why is he sabotaging military equipment, like at Condef?'

'Good point.' The Doctor picked up one of the cups and put it back on the shelf. 'But maybe he wants to be sure he has the only military units that are operating properly and unaffected.'

'And where do the Voracians fit in?'

The Doctor lifted another cup, and weighed it in his hand as he considered. 'That is the question,' he murmured. 'If they have a hold over Randall, or if he's one of them, then it's the first step of their takeover. Millennium-affected systems are fixed and converted to Voracian technology.' He replaced the cup in the broken circle. 'Today Great Britain, tomorrow...'

They sat looking at the collection of cups for a while. 'There's quite a weight of circumstantial evidence,' the Doctor said. 'More than just a...' He waved his hand as if lost for the phrase.

'A storm in a tea cup?' Harry offered.

There were rough times ahead, and Philip Cotton was secretly glad he was not prime minister. There was considerable mileage in keeping this secret of course. But when it became apparent that there really wasn't the money needed to overhaul the health service, or to pay the teachers a decent wage, or hand out reasonable pensions to the increasing numbers of elderly people in Britain, he knew he would be better off as Deputy Prime Minister toeing the party line and trotting out the usual platitudes. At the same time, he would make sure from his tone and demeanour that everyone knew he would have done things differently.

There was already tension behind the scenes, there were already rumours about the cracks in the Cabinet, the factions, the in-fighting. But apart from allowing a sense of righteous indignation to seep through those cracks, Cotton kept well out of it. He was well known for his no-nonsense live-and-let-live attitude, his bluff Yorkshire plain-speaking common sense. It was well-known that Terry Brooks, smarmy, clean-cut Prime Minister, had reneged on a deal to step aside for him as party leader when Cotton returned from his stint as US Ambassador in Washington five years ago.

What could be guessed, inferred, but never proven was that Cotton hated his superior with a vengeance. He despised the so-called New Way politics that smoothed over the blemishes rather than confronting the problems. He detested the way that any debate or argument was swept under the carpet. He was not looking forward to the time when all the matters that had been so carefully and deliberately ignored came to a head, came back to bite the current government. But at the same time, there was a certain satisfaction in knowing that soon he would be able to stop telling them what was so obvious and say instead to Brooks and to the electorate: 'I told you so.'

But all this was very much in the back of Cotton's mind as he arrived for the Cabinet meeting. The last Cabinet meeting of the millennium, he thought to himself as he arrived at the door of 10 Downing Street. There were the usual press and photographers loitering nearby, ready in case some exciting political story broke. Some chance.

'Morning, Jeff.' Cotton prided himself on knowing the names of the police constables who shared the duties at the door of the famous house.

'Morning, sir. Nothing wrong, I hope?'

Cotton paused. 'No. Why?'

'Sorry, sir. I just thought...' The policeman shuffled slightly in embarrassment. 'Being late, you know, sir.'

'Late? The meeting's at ten.'

The policeman shook his head. 'Sorry, sir. My mistake.'

But Cotton's mind was racing now. 'Who's already here?'

'Well, you know, sir. The usual cronies, er, crowd. Sir. Chancellor of course, plus Home Secretary, Foreign Secretary, Secretary of State for Defence. And Mr Bryant.' There was a hint of distaste at the last name. 'Been here since nine this morning, sir.'

Cotton clicked his tongue. 'Thanks, Jeff,' he said as he pushed through the door. 'That's very helpful.'

The meeting was uneventful and short. Nobody wanted to hang around, and there was precious little business. The troop deployments were touched on, but dismissed immediately by the Prime Minister as a precaution. Cotton spent much of the meeting watching the Cabinet Secretary stare in ill-disguised distaste at James Bryant. All the time he was wondering what had happened before he arrived.

As they were leaving, he made sure he followed directly behind Jennifer Hamilton. They had been at Reading together, and she was one of the few of Brooks's inner circle that he actually had time for, that he trusted.

'So what's going on?' he asked her as they walked back to their cars.

'What are you talking about, Phil?'

'Secret meetings prior to the full Cabinet. That sort of thing. Keeping me in the dark, is he?'

She failed to conceal her surprise. 'Nothing like that.'

'Oh?'

'If I could tell you, Phil, I would. You know that.'

'You can tell me,' he said as the chauffeur opened the car door for her. 'If it's nothing, it won't matter.'

It was there in her eyes. He could see it. She was worried. More than worried, troubled even. 'It does matter,' she said quietly. 'I don't think I can...' She shook her head and climbed into the car.

He closed the door for her, to the surprise of the chauffeur standing beside him. He looked at her through the window and, after a moment, the window slid down.

'I need to think about it, Phil,' she said quietly. 'It may not come to anything. But... I'll call you. Soon. Really.'

0E

Developments

It was the trivia that sometimes seemed most important. Harry counted it a major achievement that he managed to get all his cups back on to the shelf without any of them having been broken. He even caught himself worrying about whether the Doctor was going to get them all out again, or perhaps start on some other collection of crockery.

As he finished tidying away, Harry tried to summarise where they were. 'So,' he said slowly, 'apart from not knowing who's behind a plot to do what or when, we're in pretty good shape.'

The Doctor pursed his lips. 'We know there is a plot, Harry. That's a good start. And it's a pretty safe bet that whatever it is that's going to happen is going to happen on January the first.' He smiled. 'But apart from that you've put your finger on the tiny gaps in our knowledge.'

'So what do we do, assuming that more knowledge is not about to leap out and bite us?' Harry checked the date on his watch. 'It is December 29th, after all. We haven't got long.'

'I know, Harry,' the Doctor said with more than a hint of exasperation in his voice. 'I know.' Without further comment he turned and strode from the room.

Harry followed. The Doctor was already half-way up the stairs, and Harry caught up with him in the room they had used as an office. The TARDIS stood in the corner and the Doctor was unlocking the door.

'Not thinking of leaving us in the lurch, are you, Doctor?'

'Indeed not, Harry.' The Doctor turned and Harry could see he was grinning. 'I think you should tell the delightful Miss Cave about our suspicions. That might stir things up a little, don't you think?'

'And what will you be doing in the mean time?'

The Doctor pushed the TARDIS door open. 'I'm going to see if my friend George has managed to sort out that millennium bug chip. It might be handy, don't you think?' The door closed behind the Doctor, leaving just his final words floating in the air behind him: 'Watch yourself, Harry.'

'You too, Doctor,' Harry said. But his words were drowned out by the grinding echoes of the TARDIS as it faded into the ether.

Andi Cave switched off her cell phone and returned it to her jacket pocket.

'Trouble?' Bryant asked. They were sitting in his drawing room. Papers were strewn across the top of the low occasional table between the two sofas.

'Possibly. That was Harry Sullivan, the Doctor's associate.'

Bryant frowned. 'I thought they had agreed to leave this to us.'

'Apparently not. Sullivan says they think that our friend General Randall may be planning a military coup on January the first, and did I want to discuss it with him?'

Bryant tapped his fingers on the surface of the table. The nails clicked against the lacquered wood.

'We could have a problem,' he said slowly as he considered the information. 'A serious problem.'

'I'm meeting him at my flat in one hour,' Andi Cave told him. 'I'll let you know if there is a problem.'

'It's not perfect by any means,' George conceded. This time he had not even bothered to ask how the Doctor could just walk into his impregnable bunker. He was getting used to it.

'This is excellent work,' the Doctor said with admiration as he leafed through George's notes and code listings. 'Most excellent.'

'Thanks.' George hunted through the detritus on the trestle table. 'I have it on diskette here somewhere, if you want a copy.'

The Doctor set down the notes and beamed. 'George,' he said, 'I'd love a copy.' Then he grabbed George's hand and pumped it up and down ferociously. 'Thank you so much.'

'One thing, Doctor,' George said as the Doctor slipped the diskette into his pocket.

'Yes?'

'You said these Vorellans were reptilian-descendants.'

'Yes.'

'Doesn't that make them rather easy to spot?'

'No.' For a moment it seemed as if the Doctor was going to leave it at that. But then he went on: 'The Vorellans themselves were like a cross between large upright crocodiles and snakes. Heavy on the snake, actually. The Voracians who came to Earth are modelled on the same design. But they are experts at synthetic disguise. And of course, those people who are unfortunate enough to be converted to Voracians will be human in appearance.'

George considered. 'Bit of a problem then,' he said, 'knowing who's who.'

The Doctor nodded. 'Bit of a problem,' he agreed. 'But you should be safe enough skulking down here while we sort it out.'

George flinched. 'I...' he said, but could think of nothing more to say.

'That's all right,' the Doctor said with a small sad smile. 'Each to his own.' He patted the pocket where he had put the diskette. 'And this really will be of immense use.' He grinned suddenly and expansively. 'You may have just saved the world, George.'

'Oh,' said George. But the Doctor was already gone, and he said it to nobody.

Although it was a Russian military installation, its main purpose was administration. In effect it was little more than an office block. It was poorly defended, and the soldiers on sentry duty like the staff inside had not been paid for over seven months. They were cold and tired and bored.

The rebels by contrast were dedicated and determined. Their leader, Omar, was a hothead whose fanaticism was only ever tempered by bouts of heavy drinking. When he was hung over, which was most of the time he wasn't drunk, he was at his worst. His strategic skills in attack and deployment were practically non-existent. But the sheer force of numbers and absolute devotion to the cause had been enough to secure the warhead. Even so, that had not resulted in the news coverage in the West that they craved, nor the capitulation of the hated Russians they fought to liberate their country from.

All the rebels were native to Krejikistan, all of them were determined to achieve their master's objective or die in the attempt. Their lives meant almost as little to them as did their enemies'.

The first the Russian conscript sentries knew was when the animal wail of the battle cry went up all around them. The town was almost empty, the streets and buildings pitted and damaged from the fighting the previous year. It was an urban wasteland from which the inhuman rebels rose up and screeched their way towards the building. Their weapons were old, but functional. Their aim was poor, but the sheer force of numbers meant that some of the automatic fire was bound to find its mark.

One of the sentries was cut down as he stood by the main gate. Another was thrown back into the small sentry box with such force that it rocked on its base. When it was still again the man's legs were sticking out, the blood pooling round his boots. The other sentries were already running back towards the main entrance to the block.

It was a case of speed and brutality rather than strategy and efficiency. Omar and his men were lucky that the one man they needed, although they did not yet know it, was amongst the prisoners and not dead on the floor. They didn't care that there were far more rebels killed than Russians. They controlled the building, and that was the victory they were after.

Somewhere in the building they were sure were the code books. And someone would know where they were. Omar's problem now was that neither he nor any of his men could read Russian. But they could grunt a few words of the language, enough to make it clear that until and unless they got the code books they would execute their prisoners one by one.

The professional Russian troops exchanged glances. They were tied up and dumped on the floor of the canteen. Things were not looking good, but they all knew what the code books meant to the rebels. They all knew that Omar's men had already captured what was euphemistically referred to as 'a device'. They all knew that whatever happened they could and would say nothing.

But to the conscripts, the events were bizarre, frightening, and meaningless. They were paid, or rather not paid, to make up the numbers, not to think about it, not to ask moral questions. And the fact that they had not been paid meant that any good will towards their employers that might be left was wiped away when Omar himself shot the first man in cold blood.

The body of the senior lieutenant was hardly still on the floor before several of the conscripts were shouting to make themselves heard as they pointed out the Weapons Officer. He was the one man who would know where the code books were and who could tell them from those books how to trigger the device.

The same car was behind him. Harry was sure it was the car that had followed him home from the hospital. He had made a mental note of what he could read of the number plate in the nascent morning light. Now he could match it to the number of the car that had been tailing him since he left his house.

And Harry decided he had had enough.

They were skirting the edge of the city. Occasionally there were glimpses of fields through the houses and office blocks. Harry checked the dashboard clock, and decided he had time to get to Andi Cave's flat. In any case, he was sure she would wait for him if he was late.

He swung the car off the main road and into a small lane. He had no idea where it led, and didn't care. After about three miles the buildings thinned, and they were practically in open country. Ideal.

Harry slowed, let the car behind catch up a little. It could hardly hang back and pretend it wasn't following. There were no other vehicles within sight in either direction. Harry braked again, allowing the car to get closer still. It would be more conspicuous if it didn't.

Ahead, just coming up, was a turning into a field. There was a dip in the kerb and a gate leading into the field. Harry indicated, then drove into the opening, as if to let the car behind go past. The driver must have realised that Harry knew he was being followed. Allowing the tail car to overtake was one certain way of throwing it off. Harry could then wait for the car to disappear before either following or going back the way he had come.

He wasn't intending to do that, but he was pretty sure the driver of the other car would expect it. The car slowed as it approached, as if the driver wanted to give Harry a last chance to change his mind, or wanted to look and see if in fact Harry had arrived at his intended destination.

Harry timed it to perfection. He didn't want to ram the car. For one thing, he'd already written off one car of his own, and he wasn't convinced his boss would be too happy if he damaged another. The car skidded slightly in the muddy entrance to the field as Harry slammed it into reverse. It swung out in front of the other car, blocking the narrow road completely.

The driver of the other car jammed on the brakes. The car swung sideways, brakes protesting and tyres squealing. It lurched to a halt inches from the side of Harry's car.

Harry was already out of his car. He had his gun in his right hand as he yanked open the driver's door with his left. Then he stepped back sharply, both hands on the pistol now as he tracked the driver.

'Out, now.' His voice was loud with adrenaline and nerves.

The driver was a big man, clean-shaven and in a dark suit. Despite the fact that it was a dull day he was wearing steel-rimmed sunglasses. He climbed out of the car, keeping his hands above his head.

'Gonna shoot me, Sullivan?' the driver commanded.

The accent surprised Harry. 'American?'

'Maybe.'

'Then you'll know the drill from Highway Patrol,' Harry said. 'Fingers on the bonnet. Now.'

'The bonnet?' the man laughed. 'That's quaint.' But he did as he was told. 'Jacket pocket,' he said as Harry frisked him with one hand, the other holding the gun. 'That's what you're after.'

'I was after this.' Harry pulled the gun from the man's shoulder holster and tucked it into the waist of his trousers.

'Jacket pocket,' the man said again.

'Show me,' Harry told him.

Carefully and slowly the man stood upright. He pulled his jacket wide open to show there was nothing hidden inside. Then he reached into the pocket and took out a leather wallet, about the size of a passport. He tossed it to Harry.

Harry caught the wallet and flipped it open. 'Mike Foley,' he read from the card inside. 'So, Mr Foley, why exactly are the CIA following me?'

'Well, Commander Sullivan,' Foley said, 'maybe if we could sit down for a minute and put our guns away like grown-ups, I could fill you in on some things.'

OF

The Enemy Within

They talked for a while, and it soon became apparent that Foley actually knew very little. They had pulled both cars over to the side of the road, but so far they had seen no other traffic at all. Harry wasn't about to fill Foley in on the more bizarre events and suppositions. But he gave him the gist, explaining the theory he and the Doctor had arrived at about General Randall and a possible coup.

To Harry's surprise, Foley took this with a simple nod. 'Fits the evidence, I agree,' he said, 'in a weird kind of way.'

It also surprised Harry that Foley claimed he had only started following Harry that morning, in the hopes of finding a suitable time for a talk.

'Oh come on,' Harry snapped when Foley said he had first followed Harry from the hospital.

Foley shrugged. 'Why should I lie, Harold?' he asked reasonably.

'Harry,' Harry corrected him.

'OK,' Foley said with a shrug. 'Still no reason to lie though.'

'So what did you want to talk about?' Harry asked.

'Just some advice, Harry.' Foley was still wearing his sunglasses. As disguises went, Harry thought, it was hardly a winner.

'Such as?'

Foley sniffed. 'Things are not always what they seem,' he said slowly.

Harry laughed. 'You're telling me.'

'Hey,' Foley was suddenly angry. 'Do you want my advice or not?'

Harry considered before answering. His immediate reaction was to say no he didn't and throw Foley out of the car. But any help was better than none right now. 'Go on,' he said.

'Right,' Foley's tone cooled. 'The other thing I'd do is talk with Phil Cotton.'

Harry frowned. 'The Deputy PM? Why?'

Foley gave a half-smile. 'Ask him. Maybe no reason. But he's a friend. He may be the only one we can count on.'

'We?'

Foley took his sunglasses off and looked Harry in the eye. There was a red, sweaty mark on the bridge of his nose where the glasses had rested. His eyes were a surprising blue. 'I'm a friend too, Harry. Remember that. I may turn out to be your best friend when this thing gets going, whatever it is.' He replaced his sunglasses and opened the car door. 'So long,' he said as he got out of the car.

'Second best friend, maybe,' Harry said to himself. He watched Foley's car pull away from the verge and back into the gateway in order to turn. 'Or third,' he added.

The meeting took place in one of the smaller board rooms. Cutter sat at the end of the table nearest the screen. An RGB projector linked to Clark's laptop threw slides on to the screen to support the presentation. Bardell sat opposite Cutter, as impassive and inscrutable as ever. The other members of the task force sat in silence, watching as Clark gave the results of their deliberations and investigation.

At the back end of the table, Dave Hedges watched. Normally he was restless and unable to keep quiet. But now he was as silent and still as the others.

The only movement in the room was Cutter rocking slightly back and forth as he watched. The only sound was Clark's voice and the hum of the projector vying with the air conditioning.

'In summary,' Clark said, 'we recommend the direct connection option.'

There was silence as Cutter considered this. 'The disadvantage then,' he said at last, 'is the time needed to design and set up the connection apparatus.'

Clark glanced at Dave Hedges, who seemed to flinch slightly as he spoke. 'Yes, indeed, sir. It is certainly feasible within the temporal parameters. Testing may prove a problem, but from the diagnostics we have managed to run on the pen chip, we calculate a 98 per cent plus probability of first-time activation.'

'And the code generation?' Cutter demanded.

'That is more problematic. But using a Farver-Moore extrapolation index, it should prove to be possible. The code fragments that are still missing from Voractyll once the pen code is replaced consist entirely of slave and sub-routines. The probability of being able to generate these in response to calls from within the existing code is already 83 per cent. This rises to over 92 per cent when we assume the extrapolation parameters include the code recovered from the pen itself.'

There was silence for a while.

'We shall of course need a secure location,' Bardell said quietly. 'Given recent events and the adverse publicity we seem to have garnered from Sullivan, the Doctor and others, I would suggest that we can no longer be assured of the security of this building.'

Cutter nodded in agreement. 'We have been offered access to somewhere that I think will ideally suit our purposes,' he said. 'Somewhere that will be completely free of distractions and disturbances. Somewhere no one will dare to interrupt our plans.'

The address turned out to be a Georgian town house. The house had been divided up into flats some time ago. According to the three bells outside the heavy front door, 'Cave' was on the second floor. Harry pressed the bell, and could just hear it ringing deep inside the building.

The door buzzed with no explanation or comment, and Harry let himself in. There was a small hallway, from which was a door into the ground floor flat and a flight of stairs up to the others. When the front door banged shut behind him, the lock clicking heavily back into place, the stairs were in shadow and Harry took them cautiously. He passed the door to the first floor flat on the half landing, and kept going. He paused in front of the door to the top flat and took a deep breath, wondering why he suddenly felt nervous, then knocked.

The door was not locked, and opened slightly at the pressure of Harry's knock. He pushed it open and called: 'Hello? Miss Cave – Andi?'

'Through here,' came the reply. 'Come on in.'

The door gave on to a narrow passage, leading past a small kitchen which looked so clean and tidy that Harry could believe it had never been used. There were two other doors, both closed, then the passage opened into a large living room. The furnishings were surprisingly few. Harry had expected Andi Cave to live in some luxury. He had her down as a woman who liked her creature comforts, but maybe he was mistaken.

There was a leather sofa across one side of the room facing a large digital television. On the other side of the room was a mahogany desk on which was a computer display. The walls were bare paint, no pictures or adornment. The carpet was a neutral grey with no pattern. The whole of the room was incredibly tidy – no newspapers, coffee cups, occasional tables, or ornaments.

Andi Cave was sitting at the desk. She was working at the computer – surfing the web, Harry guessed. He thought he caught a glimpse of a Netscape 5 browser before she jabbed at a key and the screen blanked out. She swung round in the chair and regarded Harry, her head slightly to one side so that the shoulder length hair fell away slightly from one side to reveal the perfectly formed ear beneath.

'How kind of you to come,' she said as she stood up.

'Well, it's good of you to see me,' Harry replied. He waited for her to offer him a seat, wondering uncomfortably whether she would sit beside him on the sofa.

But instead she said: 'It was good of you to find out about General Randall. And the meeting at Condef.'

'Oh, er, glad to help. You know.' Harry grinned, boyish and embarrassed.

'Not at all.' She was very close to him now. 'And it was very brave of you and the Doctor to continue your research even after Mr Bryant asked you not to.'

'Just try to stop us,' Harry said, quickly going on: 'And talking of General Randall, we've been thinking and –'

She was shaking her head. 'Oh dear,' she said. 'Such a dangerous thing, free thought.'

Harry frowned. This was not at all how he had imagined the conversation would progress. It seemed unlike the Andi Cave he had met before – the public persona.

'Of course,' she went on, 'your deductions about General Randall's plans and intentions are gratifying.' She reached up a hand, as if to stroke the side of his face.

'Gratifying?' Harry took a step backwards.

'Others will no doubt reach similar conclusions in due course.' She followed him as he backed away towards the door. Again, she reached up towards his face.

Something was wrong here, Harry decided. Terribly wrong. Her hand was against his face now and he moved smartly to one side. Just as her hand closed on his throat.

By moving he had spoiled her grasp, and instead of clamping his windpipe, she succeeded only in tearing a chunk of flesh out of his neck. It hurt like hell, and Harry cried out. He could feel the blood already oozing out of the ragged wound. And now she was between him and the door.

Andi Cave was coming at him again now, less cautious. An impossibly thin tongue whipped out of her mouth for a second before disappearing again. A forked tongue. And Harry could see now the yellow ovals of her pupils and wondered how he had ever missed them before.

'Good grief,' Harry breathed, 'you're –'

'Superior?' she offered. 'Advanced?' She stepped towards him.

He tore the gun from his shoulder holster and swung it round to face her. But she was too quick, anticipating the action. Her hand connected with the pistol and sent it flying across the room. It landed close to the desk, skidding across the grey carpet.

'Inhuman?' she suggested. And lashed out again.

Harry ducked, and her hand smashed into the wall behind him, leaving a powdery dent in the plaster work. As her arm was still extended, Harry ducked beneath it and ran for the door.

But as he ran, she whirled round and grabbed him by the shoulder, wrenching him backwards. She was incredibly – impossibly – strong, and Harry was yanked off his feet for an instant. Then he managed to tear himself free from his jacket.

She had time, though, to get past him again, and now she was standing in the doorway. Harry looked round, but there was nothing he could use as a weapon. He turned and ran to the window, hearing her cold, humourless laughter following him.

'You won't get out that way,' she said.

It was certainly a long drop to the back garden of the house. But Harry had no intention of trying to get out of the window. Instead he pulled his arm back and gave the pane a sudden hard thump with his elbow.

The glass shattered under the impact, and Harry carefully withdrew his arm. He knew the real danger of cutting himself was not when he hit the glass but when he pulled his arm back. Behind him he could hear her crossing the room quickly towards him. In the shattered remains of the window pane he could see reflected the cold anger of her alien gaze. He pulled at the largest of the shards of glass remaining attached to the frame and tugged it free.

He held it before him like a dagger. He could feel the stickiness where its sharp edge was eating into his palm as he grasped it tight. As he turned, Andi Cave was already hurling herself towards him, apparently determined to finish him off before he could create a makeshift weapon. He slashed awkwardly and hurriedly with the glass.

She screamed as the sharp edge caught her face, an ear-piercing shriek that no human could have made. He thought for an elated moment that he had killed her, or at least seriously maimed her. But in an instant she was picking herself up and turning back towards him.

Harry had time for one glimpse of her tattered face. One glimpse of the oily mess and the glistening metal of the cheek beneath the synthetic skin. The eye was swivelling in its bare plastic socket, the jaw bone a metal strip braced across the side of the chin as she stood up. What had been the right side of her face was flapping free, dripping dark viscous liquid that splashed to the carpet making a sticky mess.

One glimpse was enough. Harry paused only to grab his jacket off the floor, not sure why he was bothering even as he did it. Then he was gone, running for the stairs, and leaping down them three at a time as he raced back towards his car.

10
Differences of Opinion

It was a crystal-clear winter's day and the leafless trees were perfectly delineated against the blue of the sky. But Harry had no time to appreciate such things as he ran towards his car. He fumbled in his pocket for the key. There were two small buttons built into the plastic body of the key. One to open the car, the other to lock it. He had no idea what the effective range was, so he held his thumb down on the open button as he ran.

He was fairly sure she wasn't following. It seemed unlikely she would risk being seen with her face in tatters, but anything was possible. He could see his car now, parked in perfect alignment with the kerb between a battered Volkswagen Beetle and a new Ford Focus.

Harry slowed to a walk, taking deep breaths. When the car unlocked, the courtesy light would come on. In the bright sunshine he could not tell if it was on or not. He released the pressure on the key button, then pressed it again, listening for the sound of the locking mechanism.

If he had been any closer, he would have been dead. The moment his thumb pressed the button, he heard the thunk of the lock. It was followed immediately by another sound, a quiet click like a camera shutter. Then the car exploded.

The fireball that erupted inside the passenger compartment burst out through the windscreen and windows at the same moment, blowing glass across the road. The force of the blast knocked Harry backwards off his feet and he felt the heat wash over him. The cars either side of Harry's were blackened, the paint peeling back. Between them the metal skeleton of Harry's car was almost hidden inside the flames that licked round it.

Up and down the street, people were coming out of houses to see what had happened. Curtains tweaked to reveal curious eyes. Harry staggered to his feet, dusted himself down. He watched the burning wreckage for a moment, then turned and walked away. A cloud of black oily smoke rose lazily into the blue sky.

'It's good of you to come,' she said.

'I am always happy to help.' James Bryant pushed his coffee cup slightly further away from him on the other side of the desk, as if he found the smell distracting or unpleasant.

'I've been thinking.' Jennifer Hamilton said. She finished her coffee and set the cup back in the saucer on her desk. Bryant's coffee, she noticed, was untouched. 'Really?' There was no expression in his voice. His face was blank.

'Yes.' She took a deep breath. 'I don't think I can go through with it,' she said. 'I agree totally about the ends,' she went on quickly. 'But the means...' She shook her head. 'Some innocent people will take the blame for something they didn't do.'

'As you said, the ends are the important thing.'

'People may die, Jim.' She looked at him, trying to fathom out his feelings from the lack of expression. 'I can't - I won't have that.'

Bryant stood up suddenly. 'Have you considered the implications of this?' he asked abruptly.

'Yes. Yes, I have. I want you to call it off.'

He shook his head. 'We can't lose our resolve now. We mustn't weaken.' He leaned forward across the desk. 'You mention a few deaths. Have you thought how many lives will be saved over the years by a revitalised health service? Have you considered the improvement in the quality of life for the old? For those with free university places again? Have you?'

She shrank back slightly in her chair. Her voice was quiet, her legs felt weak. 'Yes,' she said.

'And you want to stop, even at this late stage? At well past the eleventh hour?'

'It's -' she struggled to find a way of saying how she felt. 'It's not right,' she said at last. 'There has to be another way of doing this. There must be.'

For a while Bryant said nothing. His face was close to hers as he leaned across the desk. It seemed as if he had stopped breathing.

Then he stood suddenly upright. 'Of course,' he said switching on a smile, 'if you feel like that, then we must call it off.'

'What?' She frowned.

'As you say, there has to be another way. This only works if we are all agreed, all together. If you have doubts, then we must accommodate them, must discuss them. That's what we agreed. And we must stand by that.'

'Thank you.' She stood up shakily and walked with him to the door. They shook hands. 'I'm with you entirely about what we're trying to achieve, you know that.'

He was still smiling, as if he had forgotten to stop. 'Of course. And I value your input. Now, if you will excuse me, there are people I need to see. Arrangements to un-make.'

'Of course,' she said, the relief evident in her voice. 'Thanks, Jim.'

It was not often that Jennifer Hamilton got to spend a whole afternoon in her office free from appointments, and she was determined to make the most of it. She told her secretary to hold all but the most urgent calls and made a start.

There was plenty to catch up on, and she quickly put the meeting with Bryant out of her mind and concentrated on her ministerial boxes. She worked steadily and conscientiously. When she looked up and saw from the clock on the wall that it was nearly four o'clock, she was surprised at how quickly the time had gone.

She was just starting into the next pile of papers when the phone buzzed. 'Yes?'

Louise's voice was clear. 'There's someone to see you, ma'am.'

'I'm not expecting anyone.' Her first thought was that Bryant had returned.

'He says it's urgent. His name's Commander Sullivan. He's with the security services.'

The Secretary of State for Defence thought for a moment. Louise would not have called if she wasn't convinced that it was indeed urgent. 'All right,' she said. 'Tell him he can have ten minutes, no more.'

Sullivan was very tall and dark-haired. He shook Hamilton's

hand and thanked her for seeing him. 'I know it's not strictly according to protocol,' he said, his voice a deep growl, 'but it is as you will shortly see extremely important.'

'Very well.' She waved him to the chair in front of the desk, and sat herself down. She put the papers she had been working on back in the box, so that the desk was clear. Then she looked up at the man. 'Now what is so important that you couldn't go through the usual channels or consult your superiors?'

There was a strange half-smile on the man's face. He reached into his jacket pocket. 'This, actually,' he said. When his hand withdrew, it was holding a gun.

Jennifer Hamilton sat absolutely still. The barrel of the pistol was a gaping black hole in front of her, the man holding it was a blur behind the gun. For a second there was just the barrel of the gun and the photograph of her husband and daughter at the back of the desk.

The sound was deafening. The pistol was deliberately unsilenced, and the shot echoed round the wooden-panelled room. Jennifer Hamilton did not move; the back of the chair supported her as the bullet drilled through her forehead, splintering and shattering the skull before it embedded itself deep in her brain.

The door was opened almost immediately. The man had moved quickly and was standing behind it. When Louise ran in, her hand to her mouth, he stepped from behind the door and clubbed her down with the butt of the pistol. She collapsed without a sound. The man paused just for long enough to check she was not seriously hurt - she would need to remember what had happened, and sooner rather than later. Then he returned the gun to its holster, buttoned his jacket, and closed the door behind him.

For a few moments everything in the room was still. Then Jennifer Hamilton's body slowly toppled forward. Her broken head smacked into the wooden surface of the desk. Her dead arm flopped forward, catching the framed photograph and sending it spinning to the floor.

11
Manhunt

On balance, Harry decided, it was probably not a good idea to call in for another new car. As he got the tube back into London, he consoled himself with the thought that the Doctor had a hire car they could use for the duration. And if anything unfortunate happened to that, he would only have the hire car company and their insurers to explain things to.

As he emerged from the tube station into the open air, the evening had already drawn in and it was getting dark again. Harry called the hospital on his cell phone as he walked towards his house. He waited for what seemed an eternity while they checked for him. At last a nurse told him that Sylvia was making good progress. She seemed to be out of danger and had recovered consciousness.

On a whim, almost, elated by the news, Harry hailed a passing taxi and set off for the hospital. On the way he phoned his own home and left a message saying where he was going. With luck the Doctor would get the message. If not, it would mean only a short delay before they met up again.

The taxi left Harry at the main doors to the hospital. He knew the way now, bypassed the reception desk and was soon in the corridor approaching Sylvia's room. He was not at all surprised to find that the Doctor was sitting outside the room. His feet were stretched out across the corridor, his hat down over his eyes. He was snoring.

Harry stopped beside the Doctor's chair and grinned.

He took a step backwards in surprise as the Doctor said: 'Hello, Harry,' from inside his hat. He leaped to his feet and demanded: 'How's the patient?'

'Well, I'm not sure, Doctor. I only just got here. But when I called they said she was conscious.'

The Doctor nodded. 'On the mend then,' he announced, and

flung open the door to the private room. Harry followed him inside.

Sylvia certainly looked as though she was on the mend. The drip was still hanging beside her bed, the transparent tube running under the bed covers. But she was propped up on the pillows, and she was awake. Several bouquets of flowers were arranged on various surfaces round the bed and there was a bowl of grapes on the side table. Beside the grapes were a few 'get well' cards. Sylvia looked pale and tired as she greeted Harry.

'Had visitors?' Harry asked.

She looked at the flowers. 'From the pub,' she said. 'Jane came in earlier. Mum and Dad are over in France for Christmas. I haven't told them.' She was staring at the Doctor as she spoke.

'This is my friend, the Doctor,' Harry explained.

'How do you do?' The Doctor beamed at her and waved elaborately. Then he slumped down in the chair beside the bed and became immediately lost in his own thoughts.

'The Doctor,' Sylvia said quietly. 'Oh yes.'

'I was forgetting - of course, you've met, haven't you?' Harry said. 'When the Doctor came to find me.' He sat on the other side of the bed from the Doctor and said gently: 'Sylvia, I'm so sorry. This is my fault. I should have warned you.'

She said nothing, but turned and looked away.

Harry frowned. 'I can't tell you, not yet anyway, what's going on. But it is important. There are some bad people out there -'

'Very bad,' the Doctor put in.

'We have to stop them,' Harry went on. 'I'm sorry you got caught up in this. But, well, I just wanted you to know that it's important. It was me they were trying to kill. And the Doctor. They tried to blow me up in my car a couple of hours ago.' He was not sure what to say, she seemed to be paying no attention. But at this she turned and looked at him again. She seemed puzzled more than anything.

'Why?' she asked quietly. Her eyes were moist.

'Sorry? Why do we have to stop them, you mean?'

'This killing,' she said. 'Why? Why you?'

'Someone has to stop them,' Harry said quietly. 'The killing will stop, it has to stop, I promise you.'

'Too many people have died already,' the Doctor agreed. 'At least we can be grateful that you aren't one of them.'

Sylvia looked from Harry to the Doctor and back again. Her face was full of confusion.

'Andrea Cave is one of them,' Harry said quietly to the Doctor. 'She tried to kill me.'

The Doctor nodded solemnly. 'We can trust nobody,' he said. He fixed Sylvia with a stare. 'You can trust nobody either.'

'You don't know, do you?' Sylvia said quietly. 'You really don't know.'

The Doctor and Harry exchanged glances. 'Don't know what?' Harry asked.

Sylvia eased herself up the pillows slightly, until she was looking Harry straight in the eye. 'Jennifer Hamilton is dead,' she said.

'Oh God,' Harry said quietly. 'When? How?'

'Who is Jennifer Hamilton?' the Doctor asked.

'Defence Secretary,' Harry said. Then a thought occurred to him. 'How did you know?' he asked Sylvia.

But before she could answer the Doctor pulled aside the bed covers. Underneath, Sylvia was holding a small device like a pager. Her thumb was on one of the buttons.

'What did they tell you?' the Doctor asked quietly.

She was almost in tears. 'That Mr Sullivan murdered her this afternoon. They said that he was working with a terrorist called the Doctor. That you were both extremely dangerous.' She held up the device. 'They gave me this. They said you might come.'

'And if we did?' Harry asked.

'I was to press the button twice.'

'And you did that?' the Doctor asked.

Her answer was almost a sob. 'Yes. When you came in.'

The Doctor nodded. He pulled the covers back over her and patted her shoulder gently. 'Never mind,' he said. 'Never mind.' Then he turned to Harry. 'I think it's time we left, Harry.'

'I couldn't agree more.'

The Doctor strode across the room to the door. He had hardly begun to open it when he slammed it shut again and stood with his back leaning against it, his eyes wide with sudden horror. 'Harry,' he whispered loudly, 'there's a policeman standing outside.'

'Well, let him in,' Harry began to say. Then he checked himself. 'Oh, I see what you mean.' He looked quickly round for another escape route. 'Fire escape?'

The Doctor nodded. 'Fire escape.' He pushed away from the door, calling over his shoulder: 'This looks bad, nurse. We shall have to operate immediately. Make sure nobody comes in, that could prove very serious indeed.' Then he gave Sylvia a huge wink and joined Harry at the window.

It was an old sash window, and had been painted shut. There was a small inner light that opened to allow air to circulate, but the main window was set solid. Harry was feeling in his pockets. 'I've got a pen knife somewhere, if we can just cut through the paint...'

The Doctor elbowed him aside. 'Sonic screwdriver, Harry. Never fails.' In moments the room was filled with the smell of blistering paint as it shrank back from the heat emitted by the Doctor's device.

'Hurry up, Doctor,' Harry urged.

'I am hurrying up, Harry,' the Doctor replied through gritted teeth. 'There,' he said a few seconds later with evident satisfaction, and stood aside for Harry to try the window again.

It creaked under the strain, and as Harry heaved at it the window opened six inches, then stuck. He heaved again, wincing as the edge of it cut into his damaged palm. The Doctor reached round Harry and helped him to inch the window open a little more.

'Could you squeeze through that?' he asked when it was open about nine inches.

Harry looked at the window, then at the Doctor. 'No,' he said. 'And I don't think you could.'

'Neither do I,' the Doctor agreed. 'Come on.'

Together they managed to heave the window open another few precious inches.

'I'll have the riot act thrown at them for fire regulations when this is all over,' Harry promised as they surveyed their work.

'After you, Harry,' the Doctor said magnanimously.

Harry was half-way through the window when the door started to open. 'If you come in, I'll shoot,' he called over his shoulder as he leaped down to the metal staging of the fire escape below the window. The Doctor threw the ends of his scarf through the gap, and dived head first after him. As soon as he hit the metal landing, he leaped back up and grabbed the window frame, pulling it shut again. The sonic screwdriver was in his hand in an instant and he directed it at the wood.

'That should keep them inside for a while,' he said to Harry with a grin.

'Oh well done, Doctor.'

'Thank you, Harry,' the Doctor said as they raced down the metal stairway. 'It's nice to be appreciated once in a while.'

The stairway led down to the floodlit car park at the side of the main hospital building. They were just reaching the bottom of the steps when a police car swept into the forecourt, tyres squealing and siren wailing. The driver seemed to have seen the Doctor and Harry already and the car skidded round so it was facing them, the headlights dazzling Harry and hiding the shape of the car behind them. Then it hurtled towards them.

'Run, Harry,' the Doctor shouted, and together they raced for the nearest line of parked cars. They dived over the boot of one as the police car raced past.

'I'm getting too old for this sort of thing,' the Doctor confided as they peered over the top of the car. The police car was turning, ready to come back at them.

'You think you've got problems,' Harry murmured breathlessly.

Then they were running again, weaving between the parked cars. The police car was keeping pace, waiting for them to break from the cover, keeping them boxed in. Several uniformed policemen had emerged from the main entrance of the hospital and were running towards them.

'Not looking good, Doctor,' Harry called as they ducked behind a Land Rover. 'Which way now?'

'We need a car,' the Doctor said.

Harry looked round desperately. 'How about that one?' he asked. At the end of the next row was a plain grey BMW. Its engine was idling quietly, and the back door was open, the courtesy light inside glowing a soft inviting yellow.

'Don't you have anything in red?' the Doctor asked. 'That seems just a bit convenient.'

'Beggars can't be choosers,' Harry told him, and together they ran towards the car.

The Doctor leaped in ahead of Harry, pulling his scarf out of the way behind him. Harry tumbled on to the back seat next to the Doctor, just as the car pulled away at speed. The door slammed shut as the BMW spun in a rapid half circle and shot out of the car park into the light traffic.

'Hey, I thought you were never coming,' the driver said happily. 'I tell you what, Harold, you lead a pretty full life.' He turned back for a moment to grin at the Doctor and Harry over his shoulder. The steel rim of his expensive sunglasses caught the light as he moved.

'Who's your friend?' the Doctor asked.

'Mike Foley,' Harry said. 'He's with the CIA.'

The Doctor made a face. 'I'm hoping you mean the Central Intelligence Agency of the United States of America,' he said. 'Otherwise we really are in trouble.'

From somewhere behind them came the sound of a siren. It was soon joined by another. And another.

'Harry,' the Doctor said, 'do you have a mobile phone?'

'Yes.' He pulled it out of his pocket. 'Do you want to use it?'

'No, Harry. I want you to make sure it's turned off. You never know.'

Harry switched the phone off. 'Yes, I see. You mean they could track us or something.'

'Or call us up,' the Doctor said. 'And I detest the noise those things make.'

Before long, Harry could see the flashing blue lights reflected in the rear-view mirror. Another minute and they were lighting up the area outside the car.

'Get ready,' Foley snapped over his shoulder. 'Nearly time for you to get out.'

'What about you?' Harry asked.

'Slapped wrist for speeding. I have diplomatic immunity, you know.'

'That may not be enough,' the Doctor said. 'Thank you for the ride, Mr Foley. Anywhere will do.'

'No it won't. We're nearly there.' Foley swung the car off the main road and accelerated down a narrow one-way street. Neither Harry nor the Doctor liked to point out that they were not driving the one way that was intended.

The car shot out of the side street and skidded across the main road at the other end. Horns blared and traffic skidded to avoid them. There was an open area of green - a park - beside the road, and Foley slammed on the brakes to bring the car to a lurching halt outside the park gates. 'Enjoy the swings and roundabouts,' he said cheerily.

Harry pushed the door open and leaped out of the car. The Doctor was already running towards the park.

'Thanks,' Harry shouted as he slammed the door shut.

'My pleasure,' Foley shouted back as the car pulled away into the traffic. A moment later a police car shot after it, sending the other cars scurrying to the side of the road to let it pass.

In the centre of the small park, barely visible in the glow of the distant street lights, was a set of swings and a wooden roundabout. The Doctor was sitting on one of the swings, gently pushing himself back and forth.

Harry sat on the next swing. 'So what now?' he asked when he had got most of his breath back.

'I rather think that's up to these gentlemen,' the Doctor replied, nodding towards the near darkness that surrounded them.

Harry peered out into the gloom. As he stared, as his eyes adjusted to the lack of light, he realised that they were not alone.

There were figures standing all around them, forming a circle with the roundabout at the centre. A circle within a circle. Another moment and he could see their silhouettes more clearly. He could see how they stood, the guns held across their chests ready for use. He could begin to make out the deliberately blackened faces and the uniforms.

One of the figures stepped out of the circle and approached the Doctor and Harry. When he was standing right in front of them, he stopped and saluted.

'Glad you could join us, gentlemen.' His voice was clipped and efficient, cultured and clear with no appreciable accent.

'Oh we're delighted to be here,' the Doctor said. 'Aren't we, Harry?'

'Oh yes. Delighted.'

'Good.' The soldier turned and gestured to his men, a quick chop of the hand. Harry could see them turning to face outwards, as if forming a safe cordon round the play area. 'General Randall is looking forward to meeting you,' the soldier shouted.

He had to shout to make himself heard above the noise. The whole area was swept with powerful searchlights. They played back and forth over the play equipment and the camouflage of the soldiers' uniforms as the helicopter came noisily in to land.

12
Early Warning

The Operations Room at Morteyne Green was very different from the small room where the Doctor had previously met General Randall. It was a vast expanse of open-plan office, the desks arranged in rows facing the huge screen that dominated one wall of the room. Each of the desks was equipped with a personal computer. Most of them were occupied by men or women in uniform. It reminded Harry of nothing so much as a NASA mission control facility.

Randall was at the front of the room, watching the main screen. The screen showed a map of Britain, colour-coded predominantly in blue and green. Various symbols were placed on it, areas were shaded or patterned.

Colonel Grant, the soldier who had picked up the Doctor and Harry from the park, led them through the maze of desks to the front of the room. He crashed to a salute in front of Randall, who returned it.

'General Randall,' the Doctor enthused, 'how good to see you again. Just checking on the details, are you?'

The general's face was like granite that was having a hard day. He said nothing as the Doctor surveyed the huge map.

'Troop deployments, I assume,' the Doctor said pushing his hat towards the back of his head. 'My word, you have been busy.' He swung round suddenly, his eyes narrowing. 'Why have you brought us here?'

'I've been watching you for some time,' Randall replied.

'We noticed,' Harry said. His voice was hard-edged. 'Was it your people who blew up my house and damn near killed -'

'No,' the general's voice was loud and firm. 'And before we get into a shouting match about who did what to who at playtime, I brought you here for your own good, not mine. Maybe to save your lives.' He turned to one of the desks in the front row. 'Run it,' he snapped.

The map on the screen was replaced by the face of a newscaster. The BBC NEWS 24 logo was stamped in the top left of the screen.

'They ran this about two hours ago,' Randall said, his voice quieter now. 'It's been repeated at least twice since.' He turned back to the soldier at the desk. 'Volume,' he barked.

The sound faded up and matched the newscaster's lips. '...shot dead in her office this afternoon. Tributes and sympathy are already pouring in from all over the world. The Prime Minister, speaking outside Number Ten just a few minutes ago...'

Randall gestured for the soldier to wind through, and the image of Terry Brooks standing outside Number Ten Downing Street blurred slightly as the tape wound on. It shuddered back to normal speed as a grainy, not very flattering picture of Harry appeared.

'...want to question,' the newscaster's voice was saying over the picture. 'His name is Harold Sullivan, and police warn that he is extremely dangerous. He is a known associate of the terrorist mastermind known as The Doctor, and the public are warned not to approach him under any circumstances.'

'That's terrible, Harry,' the Doctor said grimly as the tape stopped.

'Obviously someone got to the police,' Harry agreed.

But the Doctor was shaking his head. 'No, no, not that. The picture.' He sighed in disgust. 'It made you look so *old*.'

'Thank you, Doctor.'

'We know you didn't do it,' Randall cut in. 'We've been watching you, as you're aware. So the fact that someone pretty high up is so keen to have you take the blame raises yet more questions to add to the ones we already have.'

'And you like to keep things in perspective, no doubt,' the Doctor said. 'Make sure everything runs to plan.'

'Plan?' Randall frowned. 'You mean the deployment?'

'Yes,' Harry said. 'And we all know what that's for.'

Randall stared at him. Beside him Colonel Grant said: 'It's a contingency plan, to maintain order if this millennium bug turns out to be as bad as the doom merchants say.'

Harry and the Doctor exchanged glances. 'So it's not,' Harry said slowly, 'that you're deploying the troops to try to take over or anything then?' He waited for the reaction.

'Take over what?' Randall seemed genuinely confused. 'We have a mandate to assume control of failing installations and maintain public order, if that's what you mean.'

'We mean,' the Doctor said slowly and deliberately, 'a military coup.'

Both Grant and Randall stared at him open-mouthed. Then Randall laughed, a short, sharp burst of laughter. 'Well, I guess that answers the stark raving mad question we had down for these two.'

'No, no,' the Doctor said quickly. 'We're serious.'

'Oh?' Randall obviously wasn't convinced.

'If you're not planning a coup,' the Doctor said quietly, 'then someone is going to a lot of trouble to make it look as if you are.'

'And who would want to do that?'

The Doctor shrugged. 'Who would want to make young Harry here look like an old murderer?' he asked.

'And why?' Grant asked.

'Ah, now that's a good question. And one that deserves a good answer.' The Doctor broke into a wide smile. 'Why don't we have tea and biscuits while we discuss what we do know rather than standing here arguing about what we don't? Eh?'

'What was the meeting at Condef about?' the Doctor asked as soon as they were alone in Randall's office. There was just himself, Harry, Randall and Colonel Grant.

'That's classified,' Randall said.

'General Randall,' the Doctor said with enforced patience, 'if you're going to answer every question about secret goings-on by saying they're secret, we're never going to get anywhere. Are we?' He sat back in his chair and sipped the steaming hot tea. 'Now, if we could just open up a little, trust each other a teency-weency bit here and there, then we might make some real progress. Mmmm?'

'Good tea, by the way,' Harry interjected into the silence that followed. 'We have both signed the Official Secrets Act, if that's any help.' He paused, then leaned towards the Doctor. 'You did sign it, didn't you?' he hissed.

The Doctor nodded sadly. 'Eventually,' he said. 'But that was in another life, and besides...' He broke off, lapsing into sudden reverie.

'All right.' Randall set down his mug and leaned across his desk. 'There was a meeting at Condef. Myself and others who can remain nameless –'

'You mean Colonel Krimkov, I presume,' the Doctor said with a broad smile.

Randall glared at him for several seconds before continuing: 'The meeting was to discuss the acquisition of certain equipment for a third party. I cannot believe it has anything to do with Mrs Hamilton's death, or the attack on Commander Sullivan's house, or whatever else is going on here.'

'Can't you?' the Doctor said quietly. 'Really?'

'Well, perhaps you would like to enlighten me,' snapped the general.

The Doctor leaned forward, suddenly alert and attentive. 'Tell me, General Randall,' he said, 'what is your interest in the millennium bug?'

'Zero,' said Randall. 'Nil. Zilch. I'm only interested in whether my equipment and systems will work on Jan One.'

'Ah.' The Doctor held up his forefinger. 'So if I were to tell you that someone is going out of their way to ensure that they won't, that might interest you?'

Randall and Grant exchanged worried looks. 'That might interest us a lot. Depending on the equipment.'

'Condef equipment?' Grant asked. There was strain in his voice, a tension to the question.

'We found a chip,' the Doctor said slowly. 'Or at least, a friend of ours found a chip. You see –' He stopped in mid flow. 'I think perhaps we'd better tell you everything.'

'I think perhaps you'd better.'

'It's really quite complicated,' the Doctor confessed. 'But the gist of it is...' His voice tailed away and he stared at Harry. After a moment, the Doctor raised his eyebrows.

'What, Doctor?' Harry asked.

'Well, tell them, Harry.'

So Harry did. When he had finished, there was silence. It was broken eventually by General Randall.

'Are you telling me that military and intelligence hardware and software, including Condef equipment, may be susceptible to the millennium bug even if it was given a clean bill of health just a few weeks ago?'

'We're telling you exactly that,' the Doctor said, 'though I don't think it's the most important aspect of what Harry has described.'

Randall shook his head. 'I know enough from the classified files and a tour in Geneva not to dismiss the Commander's stories about alien infiltration out of hand, however wild they may seem,' he said. 'But my immediate concern is preventing a war. Because a war is precisely what we may have in a few days.'

'Because of this millennium bug chip?' Harry asked.

'I think it's time for me to tell you a story,' Randall said in reply. He tapped his fingers on the top of his desk, as if wondering exactly where to start. 'It became apparent to the Russians maybe a year ago that they had a serious problem with the millennium.' He looked over at Grant and the young colonel took up the story.

'Their military equipment is even more out of date than ours. Even the Yanks have trouble enough sorting out the Y2K problem. Some of their units still don't have it cracked. We suffered even more, mainly because of lack of funding and being late to diagnose the problem.'

'But the Russians, I would guess,' the Doctor said, 'are worse off still.'

'They're up a gum tree without a paddle,' Randall said. 'Their equipment is wearing out any way. Most of it we'd stick in a museum. Obsolete doesn't cover it. And they realised that on December thirty-first - in just a couple of days - their critical systems will fail.'

'Not just some of them,' Grant said. 'And not just slightly. We're talking about massive, total breakdown of their military command and control infrastructure.'

Harry looked from Grant to Randall. 'I know we're all good friends now,' he said, 'but why is that particularly bad news?'

'They have manual overrides for the launch systems,' Randall said simply. 'On Jan One their early-warning systems will shut down. They'll be blind. They will have no eyes, no ears, no way of knowing if they are under attack, or where any attack might be coming from. Now, those guys are jumpy enough anyway. Add to that the escalating situation in some of their former dependencies, the way things are in the Middle East, and the fact that any terrorist group worth its Armalite knows that January 2000 is a great time to test anyone's defences, and you have an explosive mixture.'

'Assume,' Grant said. 'that the Kremlin believes either with reason or on a whim -'

'And remember their premier right now is an alcoholic pensioner suffering from pneumonia, paranoia, and a critically failing economy,' Randall cut in.

'For whatever reason, they believe they are under attack. They have to retaliate. Every defence plan they have says they have to fire their missiles immediately, before the launch sites are taken out. But who do they launch them at?' Grant shrugged. 'At the greatest threat. The Western alliance. NATO. In short, at the US and at us.'

'So what's the plan?' Harry asked. 'Could this really happen?'

'Oh yes, it could happen. And yes, we did have a plan.' Randall stood up and walked over to the window. Harry could see the tension in his body as he stood looking out into the blackness. 'The Russians don't want this to happen any more than we do. So Colonel Krimkov came to us, came to me when I was at NATO last year, with a suggestion. He suggested we, the West, might like to replace their obsolete equipment with an early-warning system that won't fail come the new millennium. Not offensive, but defensive equipment only. For all our sakes. They get new hardware, without paying for it I might add, and we get to sleep that bit easier in our beds come Friday night.'

'And you agreed to this?' The Doctor's voice was quiet.

'Not immediately. Grant here for one thought it might be a bluff. He was right to be concerned, there was always a chance that they were lying about how out of date and vulnerable their equipment was, that they were playing us for suckers. On the take.'

'So I went over to have a look,' Grant said.

'They could still be bluffing,' Harry pointed out. 'Easy enough to set up a fake installation –'

'No,' Randall cut in. 'When Chris here says he went to look, he's simplifying things a little. He commanded the unit we put in to remove equipment from the Russian defence systems without their prior knowledge or consent.'

'Equipment you then analysed, and found wanting,' the Doctor concluded.

'Exactly.'

'And that you replaced with modern, safe, bug-free equipment and systems from Condef.'

'Right.'

'Oh no,' said Harry. 'That's equipment that has the millennium bug chip in it. It'll fail.'

Randall turned back from the window, and Harry saw the grave expression on his face.

'You're thinking that this scenario might still happen,' Harry said, beginning to understand. 'You think someone may still loose off an attack, and the whole thing snowball.'

'I wish I were,' Randall said grimly. 'No, Commander Sullivan. I'm thinking that at midnight on Friday, the whole Russian early-warning system, which they just took from us on good faith, is going to massively and catastrophically fail. What we guaranteed would not happen will take place. I'm thinking that any half decent commander will interpret that as the first stage of an attack on their country. I'm thinking that we have guaranteed the events we tried so hard to avoid.' He clasped his hands behind his back and leaned slightly towards Harry as he spoke. 'I'm thinking we won't have a world, let alone a country, for these aliens of yours to take over come Saturday tea time.'

13
Patient Care

'And how are we this morning?' The young doctor lifted the clipboard from its place at the end of Sylvia's bed and inspected it.

Sylvia did not bother to point out that until her arrival in hospital it had never occurred to her that anything before 6.30 a.m. constituted 'morning'. She saved that for another day and contented herself with telling the doctor: 'I don't know how *we* are, I can't speak for all of us but I'm fine. What about you?'

'Good, good,' he said in a tone that suggested he hadn't been listening. He made a note on the clipboard. 'Well, I'd say you were well enough to be moved.'

'I can go home?' That surprised her. But she was feeling much better now. Bruised and battered and with a permanent dull throb in her head, but definitely better. She was looking forward to returning to her small flat, to being able to sleep in her own bed until well after six o'clock in the morning.

The doctor looked at her for the first time. 'Yes,' he said, 'very funny, Miss Webb.' He replaced the clipboard. 'I don't pretend to understand all these security details, no doubt it's second nature to you in your line of work. But at least we'll get a bed back.'

'My line of –' Sylvia pulled herself up on the pillows. 'What are you talking about? What's going on?'

As she pulled herself up she could see that the doctor was not alone. Standing at the back of the room was another man. He was massively built, both incredibly tall and very broad. His head seemed slightly small in proportion to his body, and his neck was almost non-existent. He seemed to be grinning, though there was no humour in the expression apart from the lips drawn tightly back to reveal the teeth.

'You're being transferred to a special hospital,' the doctor said. 'Some convalescent establishment run by your people apparently.' He opened the door and nodded to the other man. 'Shrublands, did you say? Well, wherever.' He turned back briefly to Sylvia. 'Well, goodbye. I'll leave you to the tender mercies of Dr Hertman here.'

They were left alone in General Randall's office for a while. The general had some calls to make, he said, and Harry guessed the first would be to Colonel Krimkov in Russia. Colonel Grant had offered them more tea, then excused himself to check on the troop deployments.

Harry stood by the window and looked out across the parade ground as dawn broke. It was the morning of 30 December. Just one more day, and then they would know. Whatever was going to happen would happen. And if they were lucky they would be ready for it, and would have a plan. Harry was as confident as he could be that the Doctor would come up with something: he always did. But he was also aware that the Doctor's plans were usually devised on a whim at the last moment and included more than an element of risk.

He watched the sunlight creep across the ground outside and thought through the hectic events of the previous few days. He thought about dinner with Sarah at Jardine's, which seemed years ago now. He thought about Sylvia in the hospital, about how she had changed from the happy, enthusiastic girl he occasionally found in his home to the battered, tired woman now recovering from near-death. And he thought about how that was his fault, that in some small way he was guilty of involving her in a world she had no need or right to know about. She had trusted him, and now that was gone. He thought about who he could trust.

'If Andi Cave is involved,' Harry said after a while, 'then anyone could be.'

'Yes,' the Doctor said simply.

'Can we trust Randall?'

'Harry,' the Doctor said patiently, 'we are trusting Randall.'

'Yes,' Harry said without turning from the window. 'Yes, I suppose we are.'

He did not realise the Doctor was right behind him until he felt the Doctor's hand clap down on his shoulder. 'But that's good, Harry,' the Doctor said. 'You have to trust someone some time.' He laughed. 'That's what makes you human. That's one of our advantages.'

'Yes, Doctor. But the problem is knowing who to trust.' He rubbed his eyes and wondered when he had last slept. 'If Cave is a Voracian,' he said slowly, 'then Bryant may be implicated.'

'Very likely,' the Doctor agreed. 'Can't say I took to him. You said he suddenly seemed to become ambitious a few years ago?'

Harry nodded. 'Good point.'

'And there may be others. Either Voracians, or people they've somehow involved either knowingly or unwittingly.'

'Well there's the Silver Bullet lot. Cutter and his people. Then there's whoever raided Condef, whoever killed Jennifer Hamilton.'

'And Cave and Bryant,' the Doctor finished.

'Doctor,' Harry said slowly, 'Bryant is the special adviser to the Prime Minister.'

'I know, Harry. I know.'

'How high up does this thing go?'

The coffee steamed in the cold of the early morning. Philip Cotton walked slowly across his terrace, watching the frost begin to thaw under the fresh sunlight on the lawn. He often took a walk round the garden first thing. It helped to clear his head.

There was a large yew tree about two-thirds of the way down the lawn. He had almost reached it when he saw the man. He was standing behind the tree, waiting for Cotton. The man was wearing a dark suit. As the Deputy Prime Minister approached, the man stepped back into the shadows.

Cotton continued walking as if he had not seen him. Only when he was certain he was out of sight of the house did he turn to face the man. As Cotton turned, the man reached up and took off his expensive steel-rimmed sunglasses. The eyes behind them were a bright blue.

'You saw Sullivan?' Cotton asked. He kept walking, Mike Foley now beside him, keeping step.

'Yeah. Randall's got him now. I couldn't keep them apart any longer.'

Cotton nodded. 'A pity. We still have a leak to plug. Maybe this will smoke out the mole.'

Foley replaced his glasses. 'We should warn Randall. It's time we brought him in on this.'

'And the leak?'

Foley shook his head. 'Take a chance. We're running out of time, sir.'

Harry was asleep in the general's chair when Randall returned.

'Shhh,' the Doctor hissed loudly. 'He's had a busy day or two.'

'I know,' Randall said quietly. 'I've read the surveillance reports. You're rather less easy to keep tabs on though, I have to say.'

'Oh?' The Doctor was all innocence and big eyes.

'Yes. You seem to just vanish. Or just appear. My team would like to know what techniques you use.'

'Ah,' the Doctor said. 'Well, that's rather tricky to explain.'

'I'm sure.'

Behind the desk Harry stirred and yawned. His eyes blinked open for a moment, then closed again. A second later he was wide awake and leaping out of the chair. 'Sorry, sir.'

Randall waved at him to sit down again. 'Not a problem, Commander.'

'So, any news?' Harry asked.

'Actually, yes. Do you know the Deputy Prime Minister by any chance?'

'No.' Harry shook his head. 'You, Doctor?'

'Not even his name.'

'It's Phil Cotton, and he seems to know you,' Randall said. 'He's coming here to see you.'

'What, just us?' Harry asked. 'Foley, the CIA man, did mention him.'

'He wants to see me too,' Randall said. 'But he insists that nobody else know about it. He'll be here in an hour. It will be just you two and me.' Randall turned to go. 'Oh,' he said as an afterthought, 'and I've asked Colonel Grant to join us. Whatever it is, he'll be the best man for any operational or logistic details.'

The senior management meeting was held in the war room. Cutter was seated in front of the main screen. Bardell, Hertman and Clark were at the table facing him.

'Status reports,' Cutter snapped.

Clark went first. 'The hardware for direct connection is ready and tested. We're working on the code generation software now. It will be ready on schedule.'

'Have you retrieved the pen fragments yet?' Bardell asked.

'No. It may be a one-shot scenario. We must insert the pen at the final moment, when we want Voractyll to come online. That way we can snapshot the fragments and the generated code in case the chip shuts down. If we try one without the other we may have an incomplete system.'

'Mr Hertman?' Cutter said.

The big man's words were ground out through his grinning teeth. 'The woman, Miss Webb, has been removed to the seventh-floor facility here in this building. She is under sedation.'

'Excellent. Anything from you, Mr Bardell?'

'The Millennium Project is proceeding according to schedule,' Bardell said. There was no trace of satisfaction in his emotionless voice, no sign of expression on his blank face. 'There is only one parameter outstanding which may need attention.'

'Sullivan and the Doctor,' Cutter said quietly.

'Indeed. Our source at Morteyne Green tells me that they both arrived there last night. I have no further data at this time.'

Cutter inhaled deeply, his eyes narrowing. 'Miss Webb may prove to be a useful soft asset,' he said. He reached out and jabbed at a button on the conference phone on the table. 'Get me Bryant.'

James Bryant answered the phone on the second ring. He was expecting a call. He switched it through the secure scrambler.

'Mr Cutter, how nice to hear from you. Everything in order, I trust.'

Cutter's voice was slightly choppy, broken up a little by the reassembly process that made it intelligible to Bryant but to nobody else. 'Sullivan and the Doctor are with Randall. It is time for you to let them know how the balance sheet looks.'

'Indeed. How unfortunate. But you can rest assured that I shall communicate that to them.'

'And the status at your end?' Cutter asked.

'It was unfortunate that Mrs Hamilton decided to take the package,' Bryant replied. 'But the Prime Minister is happy that the matter was dealt with efficiently and swiftly. By keeping him in the loop after the event, we also have him implicated, so in the longer term it should prove advantageous. The PM is satisfied that events are proceeding according to plan. His plan, of course,' Bryant added. 'He is still oblivious to our own operation.'

'And the secondary site?'

'Is ready when you need it. The staff have been alerted and will offer every assistance. Though I imagine their services can be dispensed with once you are in place.'

'Indeed,' Cutter said. 'I shall leave you to contact our friends, then. And if the colonel passes on any further data I shall make sure that you are in the loop.'

When Harry had first got his mobile phone he had been horrified to discover from the instruction booklet that you could set the ring to the tune of 'The Yellow Rose of Texas'. It was something he had never done, and had promised himself he would never do. So when the tune started playing from inside his jacket, it did not immediately occur to him that this was anything to do with the phone.

'I thought I told you to turn that off,' the Doctor complained as Harry pulled the phone from his pocket.

'I did,' he protested, staring in disbelief at the phone.

The Doctor sighed. 'Well, you'd better answer it.'

'Oh. Right.' The tune cut out and Harry put the small phone to his ear. 'Sullivan here.' He listened for a while. 'Yes, Mr Bryant. Good of you to call... Oh, I'm sure.' His expression was becoming more grim as the conversation progressed. After a short while Harry switched off the phone.

'No goodbyes? No valedictory message?' the Doctor asked in apparent surprise.

'That was James Bryant,' Harry said. 'He just wanted us to be aware that Sylvia Webb has been moved to another hospital. One that he chose. He said he wanted to reassure us that she's being very well looked after, and he hopes we appreciate it.'

'And that we don't do anything precipitous, eh, Harry?'

'Exactly.'

As Harry said the word, the door opened and Randall entered. Behind him, Colonel Grant ushered in two other men. One was Mike Foley, still wearing his sunglasses. The other was Philip Cotton.

'I wonder,' said the Doctor to Harry, 'whether our friend Bryant would class this little get-together as precipitous. Hmm?'

14
Infiltration

Grant had brought in several folding chairs so they could all sit down in relative comfort.

'We know much of what you have been up to,' Cotton said. 'I've had Mike Foley here keeping tabs on things. But maybe now is the time to fill you in on the bigger picture.'

'I doubt,' the Doctor said quietly, 'that you know the bigger picture.'

'We'll see,' Cotton said.

'First off,' Foley said, 'you have an infiltrator here on the base, General. So this goes no further than this room. Strictly need to know, right?'

Randall leaned forward. 'I hope you have evidence for an allegation like that.'

'Calmly, please, gentlemen,' Cotton warned. 'There's plenty of circumstantial evidence. Leaks about things you're doing. Informed suggestions and so-called evidence about things you're not.' He looked round the group of people. 'But we're not singling out your men, General. You must have realised by now that we can trust practically nobody in this. That's why I went to my friends in Washington and at Langley rather than our own security services.' He smiled at Harry. 'No offence, Commander. And that's why we've not come to you sooner although it's been obvious to us for a while that you're being set up. The most we could risk was putting you on to Sullivan and his colleague here.'

'What about the PM?' Harry asked, glancing at the Doctor.

'Especially the PM,' Cotton said. 'And Bryant.'

'Ah,' the Doctor said carefully. 'There's something you should know about Mr Bryant.'

Cotton and Foley listened politely to the Doctor's description of the Voracians, but it was clear that they were humouring him.

'I know it sounds incredible, sir,' Harry said as soon as the

Doctor finished. 'But it is true.'

Foley snorted. But Randall said: 'It actually makes no odds. Whether we believe the Doctor's story or not, we are faced with the same problems, so I suggest we leave the question of alien invasion for now and concentrate on the things we can believe and agree on.'

'Very well, General,' Cotton said with obvious relief.

'Either way,' Grant said slowly, 'the first priority would seem to be finding the traitor in our midst.'

'Agreed,' Randall said.

'It makes sense,' the Doctor said. 'They would need someone on the inside who could keep them informed of the general's actions. And they would need that person to provide credible evidence after the event.'

'You mean stand up and say there really was a coup attempt?' Harry asked.

'Exactly.'

'The Colonel North syndrome,' Randall said. 'People will believe incredible allegations of conspiracy and plot from a career soldier rather than denials of impropriety from a politician or a senior general.' He rubbed his chin wearily. 'So how do we find this traitor? I agree with Colonel Grant, our hands are tied until we do.'

'Well,' the Doctor said, 'I do have one small suggestion.'

The light was harsh and intense. Unyielding. It was bright even through her eyelids. She kept her eyes closed for as long as she dared, but eventually she opened them slightly. And all she could see was the light. Gradually, little by little, the light dimmed as she became used to it. She found she was lying on a bed, staring at a bank of fluorescent tubes on the ceiling.

Her first thought was that she was back in the hospital, or another similar hospital. But the light was too bright, and there was no noise at all. She sat up, and found that she was in a plain, white-walled room. There was a plain cabinet by the bed. The drip was set up beside her, either the same or a very similar one. She wanted to cry, to sob. But she hadn't the energy.

There was a scraping sound from the door as it opened over the bare tiled floor. She lay back quickly on the bed, and closed her eyes. She had no idea where she was, or why she had been brought here, but every instinct told her to feign sleep.

She dared not look as she heard the footsteps cross the room. She dared not look as she felt the hand on her shoulder, shaking her gently.

'Another injection?' a voice said. It was harsh, grating, barely human.

'I'd rather administer the tablets if we can wake her.' The reply was more normal, almost reassuring in its tone. Almost.

The hand shook her again, more roughly this time, and Sylvia stirred and moaned quietly as if in her sleep. She let her eyelids flutter open.

'Where am I?' she asked dreamily. There were two of them, as she had guessed. The man holding her shoulder was the big man who had taken her from the hospital. The other man was smaller, younger, his face a blank.

As she spoke, he reached out. He was holding two small white tablets and pushed them inside her mouth. 'Here,' he said quietly, 'these will help.'

'Water,' she said, 'glass of water.'

'What?' They both seemed puzzled.

'To help me swallow,' she said round the tablets. She could taste them fizzing and dissolving in her mouth.

The big man let go of her and went back to the door. He was back within a minute carrying a glass of water. He held it at arm's length, as if the contents of the glass revolted and disgusted him.

'Thank you,' Sylvia mumbled as she took the glass. She sipped at the water, then handed back the glass. 'So sleepy,' she murmured as her head lay back against the pillows, her eyes closed.

A few moments later she was breathing deeply and regularly.

'She will sleep for several hours before she needs another dose,' the smaller man said. 'A useful hostage. Her sleeping here keeps others from taking action elsewhere.'

Sylvia watched their blurred shapes through tiny cracks in her eyes. As soon as the door was closed behind them she spat the mess of half-dissolved tablets into her hand. She looked at it for a while, then pulled out the sheet and wiped her hand on the end of it.

General Randall had called an emergency briefing for all his command staff to take place at eleven that morning.

'What's it about, sir?' one of the senior technicians in the operations room asked Grant.

Grant looked round, as if checking they weren't being overheard. 'Can't say,' he said quietly. 'But between you and me, it's something pretty big.' He considered for a moment, then added, 'Probably best to warn people, but don't say I told you.'

'Right, sir.' The technician nodded knowingly.

'You're scanning all the frequencies?' the Doctor asked.

'Yes sir.' The base's Communications Officer checked over the equipment once more.

'What if it's him, Doctor?' Harry whispered.

'If it's him, nobody will warn Cutter about the meeting,' the Doctor said. 'Proof by the absence of evidence.'

'But you don't think it is him?'

'No, Harry, I don't.'

As if in answer, the Communications Officer half turned towards them. His hand was to his earpiece as he listened. 'This could be it, sir.'

'Let us hear,' Randall ordered.

The soldier connected the call through to the speakers. '. . . meeting called for eleven.' The voice was clear, though the speaker was talking quietly. 'Nobody knows what about, but it's rumoured to be pretty important.'

'Linked to Sullivan and the Doctor?' another, more distant and less distinct voice said.

'That's Cutter,' Harry said quietly.

'It's a cell phone,' the Comms Officer said as he checked the readings. 'Should have the number and a GPS fix in a moment.'

'Seems likely,' the first voice was saying. 'I'm out of the loop now, but will keep you informed. I'll call again after the meeting to discuss developments and contingencies.'

'Got it.' The Comms Officer scribbled down the number. Then he grabbed a small printed booklet - the base phone directory - and started looking down the lists of mobile phone numbers.

'I think you'll find,' Colonel Grant said quietly through the silence, 'that the phone belongs to Lieutenant Colonel Attwell. I recognised his voice.'

'You're sure?' Randall demanded. 'I suppose...' he began.

But the Comms Officer cut him off. 'That's right, sir. The phone is logged out to Colonel Attwell.'

'And who is Colonel Attwell?' Cotton asked.

'Someone senior, I assume,' the Doctor said.

General Randall nodded. 'After Grant here and myself, he's the most senior officer on the base.' He looked from the Doctor to Cotton to Grant. 'I just can't believe -'

The Doctor interrupted him this time. 'Believe it, General,' he said sharply. 'But if you want proof, I think we can arrange that.' He pulled a small black box from his pocket. It was completely plain apart from a small button and red light bulb. 'This detects electromagnetic fields of the type Voracian technology uses. Best to use it sparingly in human company as it emits a subsonic ganglia field quotient. But if your Colonel Attwell is a Voracian, then the light will come on.'

'And if he isn't?' Randall asked.

'Then he's a very misguided man who needs things explaining to him.'

Randall took the box from the Doctor. Their eyes met for a moment, then the general looked away. 'Have Colonel Attwell report to my office in five minutes,' he told Grant. 'The rest of you wait here.'

'General,' the Doctor said, 'I really think -'

'I said, wait here,' Randall said. His voice was not loud, but his anger and resolve were clear. 'I'll sort this out. One way or another.'

15

Disinformation

Randall was apparently working at his desk when Attwell arrived.

'Come,' Randall called out in response to the loud and deliberate knock at the door. 'Ah, Colonel, sit down. I won't keep you a moment.'

'Sir.'

Attwell sat rigidly attentive in front of the general's desk. The general gathered up the papers he had been working on. He pulled open the top middle drawer of the desk and dropped them inside.

Out of Attwell's sight, inside the drawer, he pressed the small button on the top of the black box the Doctor had given him. Immediately the red light came on. Randall stared at it for a moment, keeping his expression neutral. Then he released the pressure on the button. The light went out and he closed the drawer.

'How is the deployment going?' Randall asked. 'I'm sorry I've been distracted by other matters, but Grant tells me you have it all in hand.'

'Yes, sir. Everything is running to plan and on schedule.'

'Good. Well done, Colonel.' Why had he never noticed Attwell's slightly stilted manner of speaking before? How come he had never thought anything of the fact the colonel did not join them for drinks in the officers' mess? Ever? In fact, now Randall thought about it, he could not recall ever having seen Attwell even eat.

'Excuse me, sir?'

'Yes, Colonel?'

'This distraction...' Attwell switched on a smile. 'Anything I can help with?'

'No, thank you.' Randall forced a laugh. 'Waste of time, actually. Couple of cranks. That idiot who was here before and some disaffected security officer.'

'Really, sir?'

Randall pulled the next set of papers towards him, making it look as if he had lost interest in the subject. 'Grant threw them out with a flea in each ear. Waste of everyone's time. Time we can't afford to lose right now.'

'Indeed, sir.'

'That will be all, Colonel. I just wanted to check on progress.'

Attwell stood up. 'Sir. Oh, about the meeting at eleven hundred, sir?'

'Just a pep-talk. Gee up the troops - appreciate the efforts, time to pull together. You know the sort of thing.'

Attwell nodded. The smile was still pasted on his face. 'Yes, sir. Thank you, sir.'

The Doctor was humming loudly and annoyingly. He and Harry were sitting in the communications room. Cotton and Foley had left to find coffee, taking care to avoid being spotted by Attwell. Grant had gone to show them where the canteen was. The Comms Officer had his headphones on, and Harry suspected it was to keep out the noise of the Doctor's humming.

'You think the light will come on?' Harry asked, as much to stop the Doctor's tuneless noise as anything.

'Oh yes.' He resumed the hum immediately.

'How can you be so sure?'

The Doctor stopped humming and stared hard at Harry. 'It always comes on,' he said. 'It's just a box with a switch, a battery and light on the top.'

'What?' Harry gaped. 'But what about the electromagnetic fields and the subsonic ganglia emission thingy?'

The Doctor settled back in his chair and looked at the ceiling. 'Harry,' he said in a tone of disbelief. 'And I was lecturing you on trust.'

The door opened before Harry could answer. It was Randall with Grant close behind him. The General tossed the small black box to the Doctor, who whipped his hat off and caught it inside. Then without removing the box he replaced the hat on his head.

'The light came on,' Randall said. 'But you don't need that device to tell you, not once you know. You can tell.'

The Doctor gave Harry a large wink. Harry raised his eyebrows and said nothing.

'Has he always been one of these Voracians?' Grant asked.

'Perhaps,' the Doctor answered. 'But it's more likely he was taken over quite recently, once they decided on their plan. Has he been away for any length of time in the last year or so? Any hospitalisation?'

'The crash,' Grant said quietly. 'Attwell was in a helicopter crash. About fifteen months ago. He was the only survivor. Came away practically unscathed, but those who knew him well said he was never the same again.'

The Doctor clicked his tongue. 'I'm afraid they were right.'

'Colonel Attwell is down to command the units looking after some of the high priority political installations,' Randall said. 'I'll see he joins those units as they deploy this afternoon. That will get him off the base at least.'

'Let's hope that's far enough,' Harry said. 'What shall we do in the mean time?'

'Well, I have an idea that might appeal,' the Doctor said.

As he was speaking, the door opened and Cotton and Foley came back in.

'Ah, gentlemen,' the Doctor said, 'You're just in time.' He jumped to his feet and turned to face them all. 'I was just about to suggest to General Randall here,' he said with a huge grin, 'that the one thing our Voracian friends will not be expecting and which your forces are now extremely well deployed to achieve is a *real* military takeover.' He leaned forward, his scarf flopping over his shoulder. 'What do you think, General?'

It had been quiet for a long time before Sylvia summoned up the courage to get out of bed. What if they were watching her? What if they came back? Who were they? But she knew she couldn't just wait for them. She had to do something. More than anything, she wanted to go home. Serving drinks in the pub suddenly seemed a pleasant prospect. For the first time she considered that if she ended up doing it for the rest of her life that might not be so bad after all.

The door was unlocked. At first she was surprised but, thinking about it, why would they bother to lock her in if she was unconscious? The door led into a corridor as white and clinical as the room. There were doors off it, and most of these were locked. The ones that weren't led into rooms about the same size as the one she had just left. All of them were empty. There were no windows, no clues as to where she might be.

At the end of the corridor was a set of double doors. She pushed gingerly through them, and emerged into a large room. It too was plain and almost empty. In the middle of the room was what looked like an operating table. Surgical instruments lay out ready on a tray beside it. Canisters of gas and a heart monitor stood nearby. On the far side of the room was a lift door, the call button set into the wall beside it.

As she reached the lift, she saw that the call button had a slot inside it. A slot for a key. A key she did not have. She pushed the button anyway, but there was no give in it, and no response. She listened desperately for the sound of the lift moving through the shaft towards her floor. But there was nothing. Just the gentle hum of the air conditioning.

Sylvia bit back the sob that was growing inside her and ran her hand through her hair. As she did so, she turned. And as she turned she saw the phone.

It was attached to the wall. White on white, and practically invisible unless you looked directly at it. With a gasp of joy and relief, she ran over to it and lifted the receiver. There was a dial tone. The buttons were numbered, but under the zero was printed *Oper*. Sylvia pushed the zero and the phone was immediately answered.

'This is Christine, can I help you?'

'Oh, er, yes,' Sylvia said. Then she paused. Should she ask for help? Tell the woman to pass on a message? Or was she one of the people holding her captive? 'I'm sorry,' she said, 'but I've forgotten our address here. I need to pass it on to someone.'

There was an audible sigh from the end of the phone. Then the woman told her the address.

Sylvia disguised her elation, and tried to sound huffy. 'I know that,' she said. 'It was the post code I wasn't sure about.'

'Can I suggest you write it down somewhere for next time?' the woman asked over-politely when she had told her.

'Oh I will. I will.' Then quickly, before the woman hung up, Sylvia said, 'Can you get me an outside line while you're there, please?'

Randall's team was still monitoring calls to Harry's home number, and they played him the message Sylvia left on his answerphone over his mobile.

'So where is she?' Foley asked.

Harry told him the address.

'Silver Bullet's main offices,' Foley said.

They were sitting in a plush foyer. The floor was marble and the walls were stone. Ornate pillars wound their way up to a high, vaulted ceiling. There had been some inevitable discussion after the Doctor outlined his plan. But in the end everyone had agreed to it, as Harry had guessed they would. Now the Doctor was helping the technicians at Morteyne Green go through their essential equipment and systems to check for millennium bug chips, and Harry was sitting with Foley in an impressive but dusty annexe of the Russian Embassy.

The woman who almost an hour earlier had examined first Foley's and then Harry's identity cards then asked them rather condescendingly to wait for a short time came back. Her high heels clicked loudly on the floor. Her smile was a distinct contrast to the mood she had been in when she left.

'Colonel Krimkov will see you now,' she said. Her accent was obvious but not intrusive.

'Krimkov's here?' Foley asked in surprise.

Her smile froze. 'Of course not,' she said coldly. 'We have satellite video conference facilities.' There was a hint of pride in her voice now. 'The story that we have only antiquated technology in Russia is just a myth perpetuated by the West.'

'Don't you believe it,' Foley said with a laugh.

This seemed to upset the woman, and Harry quickly said: 'Thank you, you've been very helpful.'

She regarded them both dubiously before setting off noisily across the marble floor, back in the direction she had come from. 'This way, please,' she called as she went.

Her best bet now, Sylvia decided, was to find somewhere to hide. She had little hope of finding a way out. But if she could keep out of sight until Mr Sullivan got her message... She knew he was something in the security services, and thought he was pretty high up. Certainly high up enough to have got her into this. And if he could get her into it, he could get her out of it too, she was sure of that. Maybe he could get her a decent job as compensation. It was worth asking.

She made her way back towards the room she had woken in. One of the other rooms off the same corridor, perhaps? She tried each door in turn, hoping to find a room with something more in it than just a desk or a bed. She was just opening one of the doors when she heard a noise from behind her, from back down the corridor. Someone was coming. She ducked into the room at once, hoping she had not been seen.

There were heavy footsteps in the corridor, coming towards the room where she was crouching behind the door, listening anxiously. The footsteps paused outside the door. Sylvia held her breath, waiting for them to continue.

The room looked as though it used to be a dining room. The conference table that ran the length of it added to the impression. At the end of the table was a large screen, so that the man on the screen seemed to be sitting at the table with them as Foley and Harry took seats either side.

'Gentlemen,' the man on the screen said, 'I'm sorry for the delay in seeing you, but events have been moving along.' His accent was thick. He was wearing a Russian military uniform, decorations lined across his chest. Harry guessed he was a few years older than himself, and his hair was already completely grey. His face had a determined set to it, the chin jutting forwards slightly. But there was a hint of humour in his eyes, and his tone was not unfriendly. The Russian laughed suddenly, and added: 'In fact, I think perhaps it is I who shall be updating you on things. I am Colonel Krimkov, as you will have guessed. And I assume that you are Commander Sullivan,' he pointed out of the screen at Harry, 'and the gentleman with the sunglasses must be Mr Foley.'

'You know about the problem with your early-warning equipment then?' Harry asked.

The Russian waved aside the comment with a sigh. 'Problems, always problems. Yes, General Randall and I have spoken already. But we are used to problems with our equipment.' He leaned forward, and it seemed strange to Harry that the movement brought the man no closer to them. 'Between you and me, having such antiquated equipment has been a benefit. Until now.' He leaned back again, arms folded. 'People have tried, and succeeded, to hack into the Pentagon computer network.' He blew out a long breath and shook his head in sympathy. 'But those same people cannot hack into our nuclear missile network, because...' He unfolded his arms and opened his hands, as if to show they were empty. '...we haven't got one.'

'You're not too worried then?' Foley asked.

Krimkov's face was grim suddenly. A nerve twitched under his left eye. 'Yes, we are worried. But knowing we have a problem is the biggest part of finding a solution. I am worried about the equipment you tell me will fail, and I am even more worried about Krejikistan.'

'The rebels?' Harry asked, recalling the news items and rumour he had heard.

The colonel was nodding. 'Yes. The rebels. They have a nuclear device. It is not armed, but they now have control of a military facility and perhaps its weapons officer.'

'Will he know how to arm the device?' Foley asked.

'He will. But they still need a delivery vehicle.' Krimkov smiled again, but it was a smile with little real humour behind it. 'I had hoped they would try to deliver it to Moscow on the back of a donkey. But sadly they seem to have realised the inadequacy of such an approach. Now they are advancing in force on the launch facility at Nevchenka.'

'Not good then,' Harry said quietly.

'No. Not good.'

There was silence for a while. Then Foley asked: 'Will they take the facility? Will they get a launch vehicle?'

'Not without a fight. But the rebels outnumber the garrison there considerably. I have already dispatched what small force I can to reinforce them. But with the riots in Moscow and St Petersburg and the economic unrest everywhere in Russia, it is problematic trying to divert forces at such short notice. And like you, we have to be prepared for the worst when the millennium dawns. Our infrastructure is less advanced than yours, but so far as we can tell that merely means it will fail in different ways.'

'So how can we help?' Harry asked. 'There must be something...'

Krimkov nodded. 'I have been thinking. And I believe there is something you can do. Mr Foley, perhaps you could ask your President Dering to send us military aid.' He held up his hand before Foley could comment. 'Unconventional and unprecedented, I know. But you are more able to spare special forces to handle the situation in Krejikistan. We shall hold the rebels as long as we can, but without help they will gain access to the launch facilities.'

'And if they launch on Moscow that could trigger a response.'

'There are many hotheads still. Many who hate the West and would welcome an excuse to appear to retaliate.' Krimkov looked from Foley to Harry. 'To say nothing of the loss of life the rebel actions would involve.'

'Point taken,' Harry said quietly.

'We'll see what we can do,' Foley told him.

As they crossed the foyer area where they had waited earlier,

Harry asked Foley: 'How much of a presence does the CIA have over here?'

'Why do you ask?'

'The mention of special forces made me think,' Harry said. 'If you have the equivalent of a SWAT team here, there's something we can do which Randall's forces can't. Not yet anyway, not with Attwell involved.'

'We, er, we might manage to rustle up a few folks,' Foley said. He was smiling now. 'What had you in mind, Harry?'

The footsteps did not continue down the corridor. Instead, the door was flung open, knocking Sylvia violently backwards. She pulled herself up quickly, but there was nowhere to run or hide. She could feel blood dripping down from her split lip where the door had hit her.

The big man was standing in the doorway. Behind him was another man, broad-shouldered but with a thin, angular face. His head was lolling slightly to one side, as if it was too heavy for his neck to support.

'I can see we're going to have some problems with Miss Webb,' the second man said.

'Yes, Mr Cutter,' the larger man growled.

'All the problems I can think of,' Sylvia said, resisting the urges to wipe the blood from her mouth or to burst into tears.

One half of Cutter's face twisted into something that might have been intended to be a smile. 'She has seen the room at the end of the corridor, I think. The operating room.' He leaned forward so that his face was close to Sylvia's. 'Her value as a hostage will not be diminished, and perhaps she will be more co-operative and willing to tell us what if anything she knows after a closer look.'

Sylvia took a step backwards as the larger man reached out for her.

16

Breaking and Entering

The Doctor breezed into the operations truck as if he owned the place and employed all the people. It was, in effect, a large van, the inside lined with banks of equipment. There were monitors down one side of the van, while a bench along part of the other side afforded room for the assault team to sit and prepare their weapons and communications gear.

'Gentlemen,' the Doctor announced with a grin. 'And ladies,' he added as he caught sight of the Assault Team Leader cleaning her Spectre submachine gun. 'Good of you to come.' He marched along the length of the van nodding curtly to the bemused CIA crew.

'Doctor,' Foley said, 'any details of the interior you can give us will help.' He and Harry were standing together at the end of the bank of monitors.

'Of course.' The Doctor turned to the nearest of the screens. 'Do you have floor plans on this thing?'

The operator punched up a display of architects' drawings of the interior of the Silver Bullet office block. 'Not much help, I'm afraid. Because it's all open plan, they could have arranged the interior partitions however they like.'

The Doctor nodded. 'There are eight floors,' he said. 'The sixth and seventh floors are sealed off, so that's where you need to be. That's where they're keeping her.'

'What's on the eighth floor?' Foley asked.

'There isn't one,' Harry said. 'This is Britain. We start with a ground floor, then above that is the first floor.'

'So the eighth floor is called the seventh floor. You're a crazy, mixed-up people, Harry,' Foley said with a grin.

The Assault Team Leader was Ann Monroe. She had joined them at the monitor, the small Spectre slung across her chest. It looked more like a toy made from chunky building bricks than a gun. She was dressed in a jump-suit which was as black as her short hair.

'The roof?' Foley said to her.

Monroe nodded. 'Seems least trouble. Saves worrying the civilians lower down. Quicker too. There are no windows on the top floor, so we'll need to go in through the sixth floor then up to the seventh.' She turned to the Doctor. 'Anything else we need to know, sir?'

'They may not be armed,' the Doctor told her, 'but they will be dangerous. Bear in mind that they are incredibly strong - don't take your eyes off them for a moment.'

'Right.'

'And one other thing,' the Doctor went on, 'you might keep your eyes open for a pen.'

'A pen?'

'Biro,' Harry said. 'Steel, about so long. There's a symbol on the side, a letter I with a squared sign - you know, a little 2 - above it. It's got a small liquid crystal readout near the clip that's blank. It used to tell the time.'

'Amongst other things,' the Doctor said darkly.

'And if we find it?'

'Bring it out with you,' the Doctor told her. 'Or if you can't, then destroy it. It is important,' he added. 'More important than I can tell you.'

She had struggled, but it did not take long to strap her down on the operating table. The anaesthetic rendered her unconscious almost immediately once they got the mask on.

When she was still, Cutter examined the X-rays and schematics they had produced from Sylvia Webb's hospital records and their own datalisation when she arrived at the Silver Bullet building. Then he scrubbed up and put on his surgeon's gown. A straightforward, relatively simple operation. Only the brain needed attention, there was no need to enhance any of the woman's other faculties or limbs.

Hertman stood watching the proceedings as Cutter stood over the table, scalpel in hand. They both looked up at the sound.

'Helicopter,' Hertman said above the increasing noise. 'Relatively low. From the engine vibration, probably a Sikorsky.'

The sound continued to increase in volume. It remained steady for a moment at its loudest, then retreated again.

'Definitely a Sikorsky,' Hertman said. 'The wave form matches a UH 60 Black Hawk.'

Another sound. This time from below. Cutter set down the scalpel on the instrument tray. The sound they had heard was of breaking glass.

'An assault helicopter, by any chance?' Cutter asked calmly.

Hertman's head tilted a little to one side, swaying slightly as he accessed the relevant data. 'Primarily, yes. It can carry eleven troops in addition to the crew of three.'

'Then I would say we have visitors on the sixth floor.' Cutter pulled off his mask. 'How very tiresome. This could have a negative impact on our performance.'

Monroe's team swept through the sixth floor quickly and efficiently. The breeze from the broken windows blew papers off the desks. There was almost nobody in the main open-plan area, but what people there were seemed content to ignore the assault team.

While half of the team checked the rest of the floor, Monroe led the others to the stairwell. She did not waste time on the door, but shot out the lock with a quick burst from the Spectre. In less than a minute from first entry they were racing up the stairs.

Monroe's second in command was Alex White. His team checked each room in turn, splitting into two-man groups to finish as quickly as possible. Most of the rooms were empty. One was a conference room, with several people sitting round a long table. They looked up as White and his partner threw open the door. Then, without comment, they returned their attention to the slide being displayed on the screen at the far end of the table.

White slammed the door shut again. 'Sorry to have bothered you guys,' he muttered, and moved on to the next room.

It was a small office. There was a man sitting at a desk staring at a computer screen. The man ignored the sound of the door opening, keeping his eyes fixed on the screen.

White paused in the doorway. For a moment he was distracted by the image on the screen – it was like a silver metallic snake curling round as if trying lazily to catch its own tail. But before he could look closer, the man at the desk turned.

He was a young man, wearing jeans and a sweatshirt. The sweatshirt had the logo of a computer games console company on it, but it was barely visible through the stains. It looked as if some thick, dark liquid had been spilled on it a long time ago, but nobody had bothered to wash the shirt. The left side of the man's face was pale and spotty. A lank curl of greasy dark hair hung low over his forehead.

But White hardly noticed any of this. His attention was focused on the rest of the man's face. The part that wasn't there. The whole right side seemed to be constructed of small steel plates, riveted together like chain mail. Or scales. A brace held the jaw in place, and the eye was a pallid blob of viscous white slit across by an almond-shaped pupil of yellow. The head was leaning slightly, as if the artificial side was much heavier than the flesh and bone. The skin round the edges of the metal and plastic was blackened and shrivelled, as if it had been welded back into place.

White swallowed, his throat dry, and backed out of the room, closing the door. If he had not been so distracted by the hideous sight, he might have noticed the steel pen standing in the midst of a tangle of wires and connections beside the computer screen.

The door from the stairs emerged into a plain white corridor lined with other, similar doors. Monroe's team checked each room in turn, blowing the locks off any door that refused to open. Some of the rooms contained beds, some had a minimal amount of office furniture. Each room was empty.

At the end of the corridor was a set of double doors. Monroe went through first, diving sideways to the left as the next man through went right. They both swung their guns round to cover the room as the other three members of the seventh floor assault team burst through behind them.

The room was large and like the others they had seen it was

almost empty. But in front of them was an operating table, and strapped to it was the woman they were looking for. Monroe gestured for two of the team to advance to the table. The others, herself included, continued to keep the two men in the room covered.

One of the men was standing by the table. He was dressed in a surgical gown, the mask pulled down around his neck. He raised his hands and stepped back to allow the assault team to free the woman.

The other man was enormous. He was standing on the far side of the table, a little way away. There seemed to be a sort of animal growl coming from him, and his lips were pulled back over bared teeth.

'Nobody move, nobody gets hurt,' Monroe shouted at the men.

The woman was free now, but she was unconscious. One of the team hoisted her on to his shoulder, and carried her back towards the corridor. Monroe continued to cover the men as her team backed out of the room.

She was about to follow when the man with the bared teeth suddenly launched himself at her. There was no warning, and for his size he moved incredibly fast.

But Monroe was faster. The fifty 9mm parabellum rounds were discharged accurately and almost immediately. The grouping of the bullets was so close that the front of the man's jacket just seemed to disintegrate. The force of them stopped him even as he was leaping towards Monroe, and hurled him backwards into the operating table. He cartwheeled over it, sending instruments clattering to the floor.

Monroe was already snapping another magazine into place and backing out through the doors. As they slammed shut behind her, she thought she saw the man slowly climbing to his feet and staring after her, the grotesque grin still fixed to his face. And even though she knew that was impossible, she turned and ran after her team, shouting at them to hurry.

Cutter put out a hand to stop Hertman from following the

intruders. 'Leave them,' he said. 'They'll go now they have what they came for. This does not materially affect the plan.'

Hertman dusted himself down and inspected the ragged hole in his jacket and shirt. Beneath, the metal exoskeleton of his chest had been slightly dented by the impact of the bullets. He shook them out of his clothing and they tumbled noisily to the floor.

'You must try to maintain some control over the organic urges that occasionally come over you,' Cutter said. 'It is hard for all of us, I know. But we must maintain our superiority over these animals.'

'Yes, Mr Cutter,' Hertman growled. 'Please accept my apologies for my precipitous behaviour.'

It was an unusual enough sight for people to stop and watch as the troop carriers and trucks rolled down Whitehall. They stopped outside key ministry buildings, the troops spilling out and taking up sentry positions. Stern-faced, expressionless men in uniform stood at intervals along the streets and by the armoured vehicles.

An FV432 armoured personnel carrier swung into Downing Street. Despite having been warned in advance, the police on duty struggled to drag the metal fencing at the end of the street out of the way of the heavy vehicle's huge tracks. It made no effort to slow, catching the end of the fencing a glancing blow and sending it and several uniformed policemen flying. It lumbered down the street at near its maximum speed of thirty-two miles per hour. The fifteen tonnes of armoured metal ate into the tarmac surface of the road, leaving a visible imprint.

The vehicle stopped directly outside Number Ten. The commanding officer of the operation classified as 'Y2K (Gov-UK)' climbed out of the APC. He was oblivious to the flash of the photographers' cameras in the fading afternoon light of 31 December, ignored the shouted questions of the press from the other side of the street. His men spread out along the street. One joined the policeman at the door to Number Ten, and the officer waited patiently. Behind him the rumble of other APCs grew louder as they followed the lead vehicle and took up position along Downing Street.

After almost a minute, the door to the Prime Minister's house opened and a man stepped out. The officer saluted smartly. 'Colonel Attwell, reporting as instructed, sir,' he said.

'Are your men all…' the man hesitated for a moment. '…Hand picked?'

'Of course, sir. We can count on every one of them.'

James Bryant checked his watch. 'Good,' he said. 'Very good. Come inside, Colonel, the Prime Minister is waiting to see you.'

17
Midnight Madness

By late afternoon on 31 December, the new millennium had arrived in the Far East. And as it arrived, hopes that the event would pass off without serious incident faded.

Malaysia was in darkness, with no phones working at all. Hong Kong was jammed with the cars of revellers trying to get home through a failing traffic system. In Auckland those who had suffered for five weeks without power back in March 1998 sat in darkness and prepared for another long dark period of disruption and chaos.

At Morteyne Green, priority was given to the helicopters. When the traffic ground to a halt, the Doctor said, the helicopters would be the only effective transport. He worked for most of the day with the technicians as they tore the huge metal beasts apart, hunting through miles of cabling and electronics for embedded systems and secondary chips.

When he was certain that they knew what they were looking for and could manage without him, the Doctor retired to a makeshift laboratory in one of the supply huts. Here he worked on a millennium bug chip pulled from the guidance systems of a mobile air-to-air missile battery until Colonel Grant came to get him.

'Is it that time already?' the Doctor asked wearily.

'It's almost twenty-three hundred,' Grant said. 'The general won't wait any longer. He says it's now or never.'

'Well, never is a very long time in coming,' the Doctor said softly, 'so I suppose it had better be now.'

'Are you all set?' Grant asked as he struggled to keep up with the Doctor's quick march across the floodlit parade ground.

The Doctor stopped abruptly, so that Grant almost cannoned into him. 'You know,' he said as though the thought had not occurred to him before, 'I have no idea.'

Although most of the troops had already been deployed and Randall was reluctant to divert them from the sites and installations where they were already stationed, there were dozens of helicopters lined up on the airfield beside the base. In front of the helicopters, the troops stood in ordered rows, equipment strapped to their backs and their belts.

The Doctor stopped in front of the lines of soldiers. Randall was waiting, Harry and Foley with him. But before any of them could speak the Doctor turned to the assembled soldiers and cried above the noise of the idling helicopters: 'If we are marked to die, we are enough to do our country loss. But if to live...' He paused, hand upstretched in classic Shakespearian pose. 'Oh, never mind,' he said more quietly. 'Let's just get on with it, shall we?'

The Doctor settled himself down between Harry and Mike Foley in the lead helicopter. General Randall was sitting up with the pilot. Colonel Grant was in the second helicopter.

'How's Sylvia?' the Doctor asked Harry.

'Convalescent,' Harry replied. 'Thanks to Mike's people. They got her out just in time, by all accounts. She's still rather woozy, recovering in the base sanatorium.'

'And the pen?'

It was Foley who answered. 'No sign of it, Doc. Quite a long shot in any case, something that small in such a big building. Even assuming it was there.'

They flew on without speaking. The lights below were becoming more numerous and closer together as they approached London. Through the window in the aircraft door Harry could see traffic moving on a motorway below them. He wondered where they were going at a quarter to the new millennium. Just fifteen minutes and they would begin to see just how bad things were.

The fifteen minutes passed quickly. The lights were almost a solid mass of yellow and white beneath them now.

'Any second now,' the Doctor announced cheerily as he leaned forward to look with Harry out of the window.

'Doctor,' Harry said, 'you don't seriously think that –'

But as he spoke, the lights started to go off. It was as if whole sections of the city were switched off at once. There was no dimming, fading or selectivity about it. Just blackness.

'What do you think, Harry?' the Doctor asked softly. Somehow his voice was clearly audible despite the sound of the helicopter's engines and rotors.

'Where are we?' Foley shouted through the cabin.

'Just passing Gatwick,' the pilot called back.

'And our systems are OK?' Harry asked.

'Fine so far,' Randall called back.

'Their air traffic controllers are having fits down there,' the pilot shouted back. 'God alone knows what's going on.'

'No problems with any of our other aircraft either,' Randall said.

'Er, I think that aircraft might be a problem,' the Doctor said. He was pointing out of the front of the helicopter.

Without the lights from below to illuminate it, the huge airliner could only be made out as a black silhouette punctuated by its own navigation lights and the faint glow that seeped through the blinds over the windows in the main cabin. The aircraft was banking steeply, its port wing lifting ponderously as it struggled to avoid the line of helicopters.

The pilot of the helicopter wrestled with the controls, pulling the aircraft back and upwards with a violence that sent the passengers sprawling in their seats. The noise was deafening as the airliner swept past, seemingly just inches away.

'Everyone OK?' Randall snapped as soon as the helicopter levelled out again.

'We're fine, sir,' Foley called back.

'I don't mean in here,' Randall said.

The pilot was talking into his microphone. 'All OK, sir,' he reported after a few moments. 'Shaken, but not stirred.'

'They have our flight plan,' Randall said. 'What the hell are they playing at down there?'

'I imagine they have problems of their own,' the Doctor said.

'They certainly have,' the pilot said. 'I'm monitoring their ATC wavelength. They've lost runway lights, satellite navigation, transponders on most of the flights and local power. They're doing everything they can to get the planes down in a maximum of one piece.'

'Take us down lower,' the Doctor said. 'Let's see what's happening on the ground.'

It was as if they were flying over an unreal city. The roads were relatively clear anyway, but with the street lights mostly out and lit only by the clouded moon and the searchlights from the helicopters, they looked like a giant model. Traffic lights were either completely off or flashing random colours and sequences. It was obvious that when traffic did try to use the roads there would soon be chaos and gridlock. As soon as the thousands of people in Trafalgar Square started to move, started to panic in the dark, things would get much worse.

Harry was playing with his mobile phone. 'Nothing,' he told the Doctor and Foley. 'Just static, or no signal at all.' He slipped it back into his pocket. 'Junk.'

'Any idea what's happening out there?' the Doctor called to the pilot.

'I've been trying local and national news frequencies,' he shouted back. 'There's nothing. Radio, TV, emergency services... All off the air.'

'It will get worse,' the Doctor said.

'Maybe we're lucky it's a Saturday,' Harry suggested.

'I don't think it can get much worse,' Foley said. 'No power, no light, no communications.'

The Doctor turned to him. 'At the moment,' he said, 'people think it's a glitch. That maybe it's only their area that's affected. That things will be back to normal in the morning. That they will wake up with a hangover but no other serious problems.' The Doctor stared into space. 'Oh yes, things will get much worse yet. This is just the beginning.'

'I'm getting some emergency traffic through,' the pilot shouted. 'Parliament's being recalled. They're diverting helicopters from most military and civil bases to pick up the MPs.'

'A lot of good that will do,' Harry said.

'Good?' the Doctor mused. 'There is some good news, I suppose.' He grinned suddenly, his white teeth catching the light from the cockpit. 'The Voracians not only depend on technology, but they use our own technology against us. Now that our technology no longer seems to be working...'

'They've lost their most important weapon,' Harry finished.

'Exactly, Harry. Exactly. We can fight them on our terms now. Old-fashioned terms, antiquated even, it's true. But we have a new advantage.'

Randall had been listening carefully. 'Do you have the details of this grand plan of yours worked out yet?' he asked.

'Some of them,' the Doctor admitted.

'So where do we start?'

'Well, Parliament seems as good a place as any,' the Doctor said. 'Why don't you put us down in Westminster?'

18

Century 21

The rattle of gunfire was clearly audible inside the main operations room. It was ironic, Acting Commander Sergei Ivigan thought, that despite having the nuclear capability to wipe out most of America's Eastern seaboard, the Nevchenka installation was unlikely to hold out against a few hundred disorganised and badly armed rebels.

He was confident that the nuclear weapons on the base would be useless to the rebels - he had already ordered Sergeant Kosimov to activate the fail-safe switches. But he also knew from Russian intelligence data that the rebels had a nuclear device of their own. If they had the launch codes, and he must assume they had, then a delivery vehicle was all they needed. And once inside Nevchenka they could take their pick.

The only way to destroy the rockets in time was to launch them. But there was no time to disarm them first. Even with the fail-safes active, to launch was to invite the retaliation of NATO, and Ivigan knew all too well what that would mean. At Nevchenka they were three hours ahead of Greenwich Mean Time. But in Washington, five hours behind GMT, the year 2000 had not yet arrived. Ivigan knew that not everyone on the US defence staff would be at the party, any more than they had celebrated earlier on the base.

The Communications Officer came running up, a message flimsy in his hand. 'Sir,' his voice was full of suppressed excitement. 'Reinforcements are on the way, sir.'

Ivigan almost laughed. 'You mean they say reinforcements are on the way,' he said as he took the message. He read through it quickly. Then he read it again, more slowly. Somewhere very close there was a loud detonation. The room rocked under the impact, and Ivigan swayed on his feet. He ignored it.

'Colonel Krimkov is sending his personal staff,' he murmured.

'He knows we are in trouble. And then this.' He looked round the room, everywhere was noise and bustle. But he could see Kosimov talking with one of the technicians, and he yelled at the burly sergeant to come over.

'Sir? The fail-safes are all active, all double-checked. We are draining the fuel from the launch vehicles but I fear it will take far too long.'

Ivigan handed Kosimov the message. 'We are ordered to hold out for as long as we possibly can,' he said.

'Of course, sir.'

'Until help arrives.'

Kosimov's reaction was in the same sarcastic tone as his own. 'Help?'

'American help,' Ivigan said, pointing to the bottom half of the message. 'US special forces in support of Colonel Krimkov's men. And Krimkov himself has gone to see the Premier.'

Kosimov's jaw dropped, and he read the paragraph his commander was pointing to. 'We live in interesting times, sir,' he said quietly when he had finished.

Ivigan raised an eyebrow. 'The dawn of a new age, perhaps.'

Coffee was served in the Cabinet room. Bryant and Andi Cave sat as far away from the tray as they could get, but even so the unpleasant pungent smell was all too perceptible. The Prime Minister was in a good mood. His earlier anxiety that the plan might be flawed, that it might fail, seemed to have evaporated as the first reports of massive failures across all major installations and facilities started coming in.

'Well done, James,' Prime Minister Brooks enthused, clapping Bryant on the shoulder. 'I could not have done this without you.'

'Thank you, Terry.' Bryant smiled, at least as much as the synthetic muscles would allow. He did not point out just how true the PM's words were. 'I think, sir, it is time to consider sending out the troops in force.'

'Oh yes, indeed. Need them to put on a good show, don't we.' The PM nodded to one of his aides. 'See that General Randall's team understand they need to be fully deployed, will you, Bob?'

'Of course, sir. And it's Dave, sir.'

But Brooks had already turned away. His hands were held out slightly in front of his body, a little apart. His face was set in a pasted-on smile, and Bryant could see that he was about to launch into one of his impromptu speeches. Probably one he had rehearsed in front of a mirror several times.

'All we need to do now, is wait,' Terry Brooks said. 'That's all. Simple, isn't it. Then when everything is back to normal in a week or two, we can expose this conspiracy for what it was. For what we say it was. And with the evidence of people's own eyes - troops on the streets, martial law, er, and so on. With that evidence and the testimonies of some of General Randall's own headquarters staff like Colonel... er, the colonel. That will do it. There will be no doubts in people's minds. No doubts at all. Just as there is no doubt in my mind that the general's sacrifice, whether willing or not, will lay the foundations for this country's entry into the next millennium. Er, this millennium.'

There was a pause. Bryant looked at the ceiling. Andi Cave looked at her plastic nails. Someone at the back of the room started to clap.

But the PM was not finished yet. After a pause for what he obviously intended to be effect, he went on. 'The public outcry, righteous outcry against this tyranny, this perceived tyranny, will enable us to do what we have striven to do for so long. It will create at long last the atmosphere in which we can begin to dismantle the outmoded and cripplingly expensive defensive infrastructure we no longer need. NATO has never been stronger, the East and former USSR never weaker. Yet the British public have never before been willing to cut back on our defence spending to any significant degree.'

He paused for some serious nodding and finger wagging. Despite the fact that everyone in the room already knew all this, he spelled it out. 'The money we save will finance the New Way. New hospitals. New schools. Better pay for nurses, teachers, pensioners, and, er, so forth. At last we can have a health service we are again proud of, an education system we can count on. We can weather the storm of recession that is sweeping the world.' He clasped his hands together as he spoke. 'Together, my friends, we can do it.' As he finished his hands seemed to be shaking each other in congratulation.

Bryant looked at Cave, and together they quietly left the room.

'He really believes in it,' Cave said when they were alone in the annexe.

'He believes in himself. Nothing else,' Bryant said. 'That is our greatest advantage.'

'The motivation does not matter. He will do it. He is doing it.' Cave looked round to check they were really alone. 'Cutter was right. He is willing to dismantle the defences of this country to try to satisfy an arrogant dream.'

'First this country, then the rest will follow,' Bryant agreed, his head swaying slightly as he talked. 'And as new systems are bought and the old systems repaired, so our technology will proliferate. Once Voractyll is released into the networks, the millennium bug will seem to spread out from here, and only Silver Bullet will have the solution. The final solution.'

'And with the backing of the British government,' Cave agreed, 'the speed of the process is increased. With the disintegration of NATO that will follow from tonight's work, the ability of the humans to respond when they realise the truth is diminished to the point it can be ignored.'

Bryant smiled again. 'Stabfield's mistake was to use force to try to achieve our ends. The humans understand force and how to respond to it. But they do not understand subtlety. Cutter's brilliance was to realise that if we want to rule this world, we merely have to ask.'

19
Reinforcement

It was five hours after midnight in London that the plane's onboard systems entered the new millennium. By then it was already well into its long haul flight to Krejikistan, and flying at close to its top speed of 350 knots.

The McDonnell Douglas C-17A had a range of almost three thousand miles. It could be used either as strategic transport, or as a tactical airlifter. Its massive hold was large enough to carry an M1A1 Abrams tank, or over a hundred paratroops together with all their equipment. But today it held fifty US special forces soldiers hastily pulled together from Fort Bragg. The rest of the space was taken up by several five-ton trucks loaded two by two and an Apache helicopter, its rotors drooping sulkily over the other equipment.

Captain Leon Martin, the troop commander, felt the pit of his stomach drop away as the aircraft rapidly lost height. He was sitting with his men on narrow seats fixed to the floor of the hold. The feeling lasted just a moment, then the plane seemed to level out again. Martin unstrapped himself and made his way forward to the cockpit. Probably it was nothing, he reassured himself, but best to check.

As soon as he pushed his way into the cockpit he could tell there was a problem. The pilot was struggling with the main controls, heaving back on the stick, while the navigation officer was pulling circuit boards from the equipment round the walls, then pushing them back in again as if his life depended on it. It probably did, Martin realised. The co-pilot was shouting into his radio mike.

Martin closed the door behind him and stood out of the way at the back of the cockpit. If they needed his help they would ask. Until then he would do nothing to slow them down. The plane seemed to be flying level and without undue turbulence, but it seemed like that was down to the pilot's efforts and a good deal of luck.

'We're still losing height,' the navigation officer shouted above the increasing noise of the straining engines.

'No one's answering,' the co-pilot called back. 'It's like there's nobody out there at all.'

'I need somewhere - anywhere - to put her down,' the pilot said through gritted teeth. 'Preferably all in one piece.'

Martin felt his ears pop and he realised they were actually descending at speed.

Then suddenly the engine noise eased and the pilot jerked back in his seat as if the controls had become free. The nose of the plane tilted violently upwards and Martin was thrown back against the door. The navigation officer crashed into him, still holding the circuit board he had that moment removed from the main systems.

'That's it.' The pilot did not disguise his relief. 'That's freed it.'

'What happened?' Martin asked as he helped the navigation officer back to his feet.

'Autopilot decided to crash the plane, seems like,' the co-pilot said. 'Systems just offlined. No way to get them back.'

'I had to fight the controls,' the pilot said. 'God knows what's happened. What was the problem, Chuck?'

The navigation officer put the circuit board down on a spare area of desk in front of his workstation. 'Looks like the main GPS board. It's the newest piece of kit in here. It shouldn't do that.'

'So where does that leave us?' Martin asked.

'Ah well, that's the problem.' Chuck ran his fingers over the chips soldered to the board. 'Unless I can find the rogue component and isolate it, we don't know. We have no idea where we are, or where we're going. Without this, we're flying blind.'

'Can you repair it?'

Chuck shrugged. 'Haven't a clue. Maybe the whole board's gone.'

'Where are we now? Any ideas?'

The co-pilot laughed. 'We just crossed into Russian airspace. So if you were hoping to stop and pick up a spare, forget it.'

Martin considered. 'I've got a couple of technicians back there. RO, and another guy who's up on the technology. I'll get them to help you out.'

'Thanks.' Chuck nodded. 'That's good.'

'Anything else you need?'

'Yeah,' the pilot called back. 'I need to get us on the ground. And soon.'

'Can't we just keep going while we get this fixed, then see where we are?'

'Sure. Till we fly into a mountain.'

Martin sighed. 'So we don't know where we are, or where we're headed. But we need to find an airfield.'

'It's winter down there,' the pilot said, 'and this is a battlefield aircraft. Any field should be frozen hard enough to get us down.'

'If we can see it,' the co-pilot added.

'And we need to be able to take off again,' Martin said. 'But you guys are the best, right? So we have no problems.'

'I'll take us down as low as I can,' the pilot said. 'Then we slow right down and start looking out the windows. Don't you just love technology?'

The area round the Palace of Westminster, Horse Guards and the banks of the Thames were the best lit in London. Randall's men had set up floodlights powered by old diesel generators. The military vehicles that were converging on the area from other parts of the city in response to Randall's revised orders lent their headlights to the scene. Above, helicopters ferried the usually tired and often hung-over members of Parliament to the emergency session.

'I'll need some equipment here,' the Doctor told Colonel Grant. 'Can you get it?' he handed Grant a scrappy piece of notepaper which was covered with almost illegible scrawl.

Grant peered at it, and shook his head. 'It's not exactly the sort of thing we usually take out on manoeuvres,' he said. 'I mean, where do we find projection TVs or plasma screens?'

'How about Tottenham Court Road?' Harry suggested.

Grant stared at him. 'I'll go for that,' he said after a moment. Then he shook his head. 'I don't know, this gets crazier by the moment. Yesterday I was discussing how to prevent looting, now it looks like I'm off to start it.'

'Good man,' the Doctor said. 'It is important.'

'All right,' Grant said. 'Peace.' He turned the paper over. 'Let me think who to send.' He patted his pockets in increasing agitation. 'Damn, can't find my pen.'

'Here,' Harry handed him a plastic biro.

But before Grant could take it, the Doctor clapped his hands loudly together and let out a noise that sounded like a cross between a gasp and a hiccup. 'That's it, of course,' he said. 'Find the pen.'

'What are you talking about, Doctor?'

'Don't you see, Harry? Somehow Cutter found the pen. They knew where it was. It must emit a signal of some sort, even when damaged or dormant.' His face brightened. 'Maybe it was given to Sarah as a tracker, some way to keep tabs on her. That would explain why the embedded chip is sophisticated enough to need some of the Voractyll code written into it.'

'So?'

The Doctor's eyes were shining with enthusiasm. 'So if I can track that signal, Harry, we can find the pen. And if we can find the pen, we can stop this thing.'

'More equipment?' Grant asked. 'Anything we have or I can get picked up?'

The Doctor was thinking. 'I'll need to look at the Silver Bullet chip again. That may give us some clues. Yes.' He grabbed Harry by the shoulder and pushed him back towards the nearest helicopter. 'Come along, Harry, no time to lose.'

'Where are you going?' Grant shouted after them.

'Back to Morteyne Green, Colonel. You get that equipment for me, and we'll try to make sure we don't need it.'

Grant watched them as they ran back to the helicopter. He let out a long breath, then shouted: 'Right, you two - Russell and

Ellery, I need half a dozen of you lot. I don't care who.' He looked again at the list the Doctor had given him. 'Just so long as they're half sane,' he added quietly.

The essential equipment was already loaded. Cutter had the pen in his jacket pocket. There was no way he was prepared to let anyone else take charge of it. A small convoy of cars left the Silver Bullet car park and turned out on to the dark main road outside. There was still very little traffic, but before long the roads would begin to clog up, once people woke to the reality of the new millennium.

Cutter had scheduled plenty of time to get the secondary site. And then, as the panic and chaos began to take hold and spread, that was the time they would activate the program to create the final Voractyll components from the data on the pen.

Once they realised that the power to the electrified perimeter fences had failed, it did not take long for Omar's forces to fight their way into the main compound. Their target now was the command post. It was heavily armoured, and most of it was buried underground. But they were getting close to the facility.

The Russian troops were putting up a good fight. But even they must realise that it was only a matter of time - of a few hours - before the rebels took control.

In the main operations room, Ivigan listened to the radioed reports from his men. He felt guilty he was not out there with them, running the firefight that was taking place in and between the base's buildings. But he knew it was best to remain at the heart of things, and in control. Soon enough the rebel forces would be inside the main facility. Then he would have opportunity enough to join the fight.

They were running on emergency lighting now. The power to the perimeter fences had failed some time in the early hours, for no apparent reason. The stored power in the main batteries was used up even before they realised the power supply had failed. At least Kosimov had activated the missile fail-safes in good time, while they still had mains power.

With every complaint that a piece of technology had failed – from laser-sights to several of the PCs – Ivigan gave thanks to the military suppliers who had for so long refused him adequate and modern equipment. Another irony, he thought sadly. And his own death, trying to stop the launch of one of the very missiles he was charged with keeping operational, would probably be the last irony of all.

'No sign of our reinforcements yet, I suppose?' Ivigan asked the Communications Officer.

'No, sir. Nothing.' The tiredness and disillusionment in the man's voice were a contrast to his earlier enthusiasm and relief.

'Never mind,' Ivigan told him. 'They probably have their own problems. Soon, my friend. Soon, they will be here.'

The Comms Officer did not reply. He didn't believe it any more than Ivigan himself did.

1A

Searching...

As dawn broke over Britain, so people began to wake from the festivities of the night before. Some of them had vague memories of the power going off. Others had assumed that everything would be all right in the morning. A few feared that it might not be.

The few were correct in their fears. Most parts of the country were without power. Gas supplies were largely uninterrupted, but there was no electricity to power the central heating pumps, and exploding boilers were not uncommon.

Somewhere in London three people stood outside a bank vault wondering what had happened. There was emergency power, but the time lock on the door had not released. The time lock was controlled by a computer chip. The chip was embedded deep inside the huge door. And the vault had been built round the door. And the bank offices had been built on top of the vault. The time lock was set to release in the early hours of 1 January 2000. But the chip now believed it was 1 January 1900. It sat there, ticking away the seconds, waiting for a time that would never come. It was just one of thousands of isolated problems.

In hospitals round the country defibrillators and monitoring equipment shut down. The NHS admissions and appointments system had been refusing to accept bookings for the year 2000 for over a year; now the embedded systems that the hospitals' work depended on were shutting down.

At first the phones worked. Calls to the power companies went unanswered as the few technicians who were there desperately tried to isolate the problems and bring their systems back up. Before long the emergency services were inundated with calls. It did not take long for the 999 system to overload completely, and that in turn brought down the whole telecomms network.

The London Ambulance Service had already decamped to the

emergency back-up control facility it had spent two and a half million pounds on, and expected never to need. It normally handled over a hundred calls an hour. When the calls stopped coming in, they realised their own problems were relatively minor.

Shops began to open and to sell out. But people without cash found the supermarkets unwilling and unable to process their credit and debit cards. The bank and building society cash machines network was down along with everything else, so anyone without cash couldn't get any.

Before long, people were taking to their cars and driving miles to try to find a supermarket or shop that was still stocked, or that would take their cards. But with the traffic control systems out, the roads were soon blocked. And with no power for petrol pumps, when the jammed cars began to run out of fuel, the roads became even more impassable.

The only thing that kept the situation from quickly getting even worse was that it was a bank holiday weekend. The stock market crash would have to wait until Tuesday the 4th.

Harry could see the chaos building as they flew back over London towards Morteyne Green. It was surprising, he thought, how quickly a blockage in a main road backed up, how soon there were other problems further along. The road system seemed like a three-dimensional realisation of the bigger picture. A small problem soon spread, growing and causing other small problems which also rippled out until the whole system was worse than useless.

'It's the inevitable and predictable result of having such a stupid setup,' the Doctor reassured him. 'Whoever thought it was a good idea to rely on a transport system that becomes less efficient the more you use it?' He shook his head in mock disbelief. 'Humans, I sometimes wonder what I see in them.'

'We can't all be perfect,' Harry said huffily.

The Doctor smiled. 'Yes,' he said brightly. 'Yes, that could be it.'

Once he had dispatched a unit to Tottenham Court Road, Grant turned his attention to other matters. The most pressing was how to get as many of the troops under Randall's command as possible to converge on the centre of operations they were setting up at Westminster.

But this was by no means easy. First, he had to keep Colonel Attwell and his units in the dark. Second, movement through the city of London was becoming increasingly difficult every minute. Even the emergency vehicles were having problems and experiencing significant delays. And this was having an impact on the third problem, which was quite simply that troops really were being needed where they were originally deployed.

They were needed to help the over-stretched emergency services, even just to make up numbers. They were needed to reassure people, and to provide a presence of authority, a deterrent in effect on the streets. And they were needed to administer first aid, to man stand-pipes in the streets where the water pumps weren't working. Soon he would need to add food distribution to that. And blankets.

And that was before they even began to think about traffic direction, petrol, ferrying clinical supplies to hospitals, getting vital factories and facilities running again. Add to that opportunist crime, planned terrorist activities, and petty misdemeanours ranging from shoplifting to disgruntled neighbours beating the hell out of each other over a slice of bread, and it was easy to see that the list was endless. If not longer.

A less intelligent man might have decided that under the circumstances he could not spare even a few men to try to locate the things on the Doctor's 'shopping list'. But Grant was able to see that in fact the Doctor's plan, whatever it turned out to be, was probably the only hope of ever remedying the situation.

At that moment, the Doctor was standing in the middle of a dark supply hut cursing the fact that the lights did not work. Harry had managed to get a torch from one of the few soldiers left on the base, and was hunting through the detritus and debris on the work bench of the Doctor's makeshift lab for the odds and ends the Doctor said he needed.

'But surely the pen is at the Silver Bullet building,' he said as he looked.

'Probably,' the Doctor agreed, pacing up and down in the gloom. 'We need two things, Harry.'

'Only two?'

The Doctor ignored the sarcasm. 'For the moment. We need a general locator that will tell us to the nearest grid reference where the pen is. And then we need a hand-held unit, something compact that we can use to find it close up.'

'Like within the Silver Bullet office building.' Harry waved the torch over the assorted components and bits and pieces he had got together. 'Is this what you wanted?'

The Doctor peered over his shoulder. 'Good, Harry. It will do to start with.' He leaned across and rummaged through the pile. 'I could do with a sub-genron focusing regulator if you can find one.' His hands paused in their sort through the componentry. 'Though I'm not sure it's been invented yet.'

'Fine, Doctor.' Harry handed him the torch. 'Why don't I go and get it invented while you make a start here?'

'Thank you, Harry,' the Doctor said as he took the torch. 'I always said wit was one of your strong points.'

'Will you be going to the House, Prime Minister?'

Brooks clearly had not considered this as a possibility. 'I don't think so, Bob.'

'Dave, sir.'

'No, I don't think so. It wasn't my idea to recall Parliament.' He made it sound like a schoolboy's hasty excuse. 'But once Cotton gets an idea into his head... Bit of a bulldog breed that one. He can handle it. Let them know that we're far too busy actually coping with the situation. Cotton can handle it. What's a deputy for if he can't deputise, eh? Keeps him out of our hair here too.'

'Yes, sir.'

'Thank you, Bob.'

'That's right, isn't it, James?' Brooks asked Bryant conspiratorially after the aide had left.

'Indeed, sir,' Bryant assured him. 'A very wise decision.'

'So, er,' Brooks hesitated as if afraid to ask, 'what do we do now?'

'Very little we can do, sir. Or should do. We let events take their course.'

Brooks nodded. But he was clearly not convinced. 'Perhaps I should broadcast to the nation or something. You know, TV.'

'I hardly think that's necessary, Prime Minister,' Bryant said quietly. 'Ninety per cent of the people out there have no electricity. Who would watch?'

Harry left the Doctor to it. He checked on Sylvia and found her sitting in a chair by her bed. She seemed none the worse for her experiences, though a little subdued. Probably tired and in mild shock, Harry thought. He told her where the Doctor was, in case she needed them.

Then Harry found his way to the communications room. This seemed to be the one place on the base where there were actually people and activity.

'We're using Morse code for most things,' the officer in charge said, with a hint of pride in his voice. 'It's proving remarkably effective. Practically no chance of failure, no sophisticated technology to go wrong. And,' he added, 'we reckon there's a good chance that if anyone does pick up the traffic they won't understand it.'

'What's going on out there?' Harry asked. 'As far as you can tell?'

'Parliament's been recalled, for all the good that will do. Power's still off in most of the mainland, though hospitals are coming back online slowly as the grid channels power from unaffected sources. The nuclear establishments have their own generators it seems, in case of failure. So they at least have power to fix their own problems. So far the main trouble is that things just don't work, rather than things going wrong. Traffic lights excepted.'

'So things are getting better.'

'Slowly. There's a few radio hams out there, I guess using batteries. Some Internet traffic is routing round the DNS servers that are still up. There's even some local radio and TV getting going again. Some of the satellites are online again too, so we're getting through with some of the cellphones now.'

There were maps strewn across every available surface except for parts of the floor. Harry picked his way carefully across the room, and almost collided with the Doctor who was crouching in the midst of the mess. Dawn was breaking and it was just about light enough to see without the torch now.

'Not good, Harry,' the Doctor said before Harry could say anything. 'Not good at all.' Then he clambered over a table and started measuring out distances on another map using his scarf as a ruler.

Harry stooped down beside the Doctor and watched. After a while, the Doctor looked round at Harry, their noses almost touching. The Doctor's look became a stare. Then a glare.

'Sorry, Doctor,' Harry mumbled and backed away a little.

'What's the reading now, Harry?' The Doctor waved absently towards a map on the other side of the room.

When he examined it, Harry discovered that the map was actually draped across a mish-mash of electronics joined together by bare wires. Some of the wires were sparking. Harry quickly moved the map aside.

In the midst of the jumble, there was a small liquid crystal screen. Harry read off: '197 east by 359 west. Then it says fifty-five, whatever that means.'

'It means it's not looking good,' the Doctor said grimly. 'It's the conversion factor. I'm using Venusian grobbits for accuracy. Let me see,' he returned his attention to the map he was kneeling on, shuffling backwards slightly to make room. 'That's about nineteen stitches. Give or take.'

Harry watched the Doctor crawl backwards across the map a little further, his scarf stretched out in his wake. 'How's the hand-held portable thingy coming along, Doctor?' he asked.

'It isn't. This is far more important.'

'But surely we know where the pen is, we just need to find it once we're inside the building.'

'Wrong, Harry, wrong.' The Doctor stood up. His foot was on his scarf, and he gave a squeak of surprise and pain as he almost strangled himself. Then he pulled the scarf free. The map went flying with it, but the Doctor seemed not to notice or care. 'The pen has moved, Harry. Is moving, in fact.'

'What? Where?'

'That's a very good question, Harry,' the Doctor said thoughtfully. 'I just wish I had a very good answer.' He strode across the room towards Harry, kicking maps and papers aside as he went. 'We have to find where they're taking that pen, Harry. And soon.'

18

Penultimatum

It took Mike Foley an hour to get through to Langley, and another hour to get transferred to the White House switchboard. It then took almost as long again to work his way up to the President's office. By the time he got to speak to President Dering, his sense of occasion was tempered by his anxiety about whether the battery in the satellite phone he had commandeered from the US Embassy would last.

Dering told him he could have five minutes max, and so he rattled through explanations and requests wondering if the President was understanding any of it.

When he had finished there was silence. The silence lasted so long that he began to wonder if he had lost the connection. Or maybe the President had just given up on him and rung off.

But after what seemed an eternity of held breath, Dering's voice came through clear. 'OK, Mike. I'll keep Prime Minister Brooks out of it for now. Probably couldn't get through at the moment anyway.'

'Thank you, sir.' Foley was almost breathless with gratitude.

'But you and Randall had better be right about this.'

'Yes, Mr President.'

'Have the Russians agreed to play along?' the President asked.

'Colonel Krimkov is talking to the Premier now, Mr President.' He hoped.

'Well, let's hope they go for it.'

'I think they will, sir,' Foley said with more confidence than he felt. 'We are saving Moscow from nuclear attack after all.'

There was an ominous silence from the other end of the phone.

'Aren't we, Mr President?' Foley asked anxiously.

'I don't know, Mike. I really don't.' The President sounded tired. 'We lost contact with the assault force just after midnight. In fact we lost contact with just about everyone and everything.' Foley heard him sigh. 'The satellites are mostly blind and the plane's transponder is out. We just don't know what's happening out there.'

He was not used to feeling helpless, Captain Martin reflected as he watched Chuck the Navigation Officer and two of his men working on the circuit board.

'How's it look?' he asked for about the sixth time.

'It's weird, sir. We've isolated the chip that's causing the trouble.'

'And what does it do?' Martin asked.

'That's what's weird,' Chuck replied. 'It doesn't seem to do anything. I don't see why it's on here at all.'

'And when we run diagnostics on it,' one of the others said, 'it tells us nothing. Less than nothing. It's like it's got orders to give name, rank and number and that's it.'

Martin frowned. 'So if it does nothing, can't you just take it off the board, or bypass it?'

'I guess so,' Chuck said. But he sounded dubious. 'The problem is, what if we get to twenty thousand feet, and then find out what it was vital for? It's a risk.'

Martin leaned over, his hand above the circuit board. 'Which one is it?'

Chuck tapped one of the small integrated circuits soldered to the board, an innocuous black square of plastic and silicon. 'That one.'

'Flying without it may be a risk,' Martin said, 'but sitting here on the ground is a dead cert.' He took the chip between his finger and thumb and wrenched it from the board. 'We have a mission to accomplish,' he said as he tossed the chip away. 'Risk is what we're paid for.'

He left them to repair the board and bypass the empty socket where the SB005 chip had been.

'Buckinghamshire!' The Doctor made the word sound like an expletive. 'What do they want in Buckinghamshire?'

'They're still moving,' Harry pointed out. 'Perhaps they're just passing through. On their way somewhere.'

The Doctor's grunt was not a sympathetic sound. 'They won't want to go far,' he said. 'The traffic must already be backing up.' His eyebrows sprang up suddenly. 'Unless they have a safe route. But even then...'

'Maybe they're not going anywhere,' Harry suggested.

'Everybody's going somewhere in the Universe, Harry.'

'I mean perhaps they have some sort of mobile HQ. That's possible, isn't it?'

'And they're going to reactivate Voractyll on the move, you mean?' the Doctor asked. His frown suggested he was willing to give some credence to this idea. For a while they both stood watching the numbers on the readout slowly change. The Doctor's finger traced across an Ordnance Survey map, inching further into Buckinghamshire. 'Pleasant enough countryside,' he mused. 'Though they won't appreciate it of course.'

They both looked up as the door opened.

'What are you doing?' Sylvia asked. She was wearing a long, plain hospital nightdress. Her face was tired and devoid of expression.

'Ah, there you are,' the Doctor said buoyantly. 'Feeling better? Good, good.' He strode across to her and helped her to the nearest chair, sweeping a pile of books and maps off it so she could sit down.

'Can I help?' she asked.

'Not unless you know Buckinghamshire at all,' Harry said.

'Why?'

'We're looking for something there,' the Doctor said gently. 'That's all.'

'What sort of something?'

'A pen, in Bucks,' Harry said. 'But it might as well be a needle in a haystack.' He pointed to the tangled mass of apparatus on the table. 'The Doctor's got a whatsit tracking it by, er, thingummy.'

The Doctor grinned. 'Very good, Harry. We'll make a decent scientist out of you yet.'

But the grin was wiped off his face as Sylvia launched herself out of the chair and at the table. The speed and suddenness of her action took both the Doctor and Harry by surprise. The Doctor went sprawling, sending up a cloud of maps and papers as he fell.

Harry had a moment longer to react. He grabbed Sylvia's wrist as she raced past. But he could not hold on and she broke free, whirling across the room like a crazed ballroom dancer. She collided with the table, shaking the apparatus.

'Hey, careful,' Harry shouted. 'What's wrong?'

'Stop her, Harry,' the Doctor called out as he struggled back to his feet. But it was too late.

She was reaching into the tangle of wires, grasping the readout, wrenching it free. There was a small explosion and she fell backwards in a cloud of sparks, the readout in her hand, broken wires trailing from it.

Harry grabbed the woman from behind, trying to retrieve the readout from her. But even as he reached round her for it she crushed it in her hand. The broken and splintered pieces fell through her fingers to the floor. Then she turned.

Her face was close to Harry's. He could see the almond-shaped, yellow pupils of her eyes as her hand - the hand that had crushed the readout - closed on his throat.

'Sylvia,' he managed to gasp. 'Sylvia, what are you doing?'

'She's not Sylvia, not any more,' the Doctor said as he grabbed her from behind. 'Look at her, Harry. We thought they rescued her just in time. But in fact they were just too late.'

As he spoke, the Doctor was prising her inhumanly strong fingers from Harry's neck. At last the Doctor and Sylvia fell backwards as she let go. Harry collapsed to his knees gasping and choking. As he fell he saw Sylvia hurl the Doctor away from her. He crashed into the wall and slumped to the floor. At the same moment, Sylvia's hair slid slowly to one side of her head, loosened by her struggle with the Doctor. Beneath the wig Harry could see the gleam of dull metal in the early light.

Harry tried to struggle to his feet, but his feet slipped and slid on the papers strewn across the floor. His jacket flapped open as he flailed away, still coughing. And as it opened he caught sight of the strap of his holster.

She saw what he was doing as he tried to pull the gun clear.

With an unintelligible cry she reached out for him. Harry managed to bring the gun to bear and fired. The sound was incredibly loud. The effect was immediate.

The bullet caught her in the shoulder. The force of it slammed her backwards. She crashed into the table, falling into the broken middle of the Doctor's apparatus leaving a trail of red splashes in her wake. Somehow Harry had not expected her to bleed. Somehow that made it far worse.

As her back broke through the tangle of sparking wires and componentry, the whole workbench seemed to erupt in flame. The Doctor was pulling himself to his feet, and he and Harry both tried to get close. But the flames had already taken hold. They curled and writhed round the burning body as what had been Sylvia Webb struggled to disentangle itself from the wreckage of equipment and pull free.

The blood was everywhere, dribbling in small rivers to the ground and soaking into the maps and papers. For one terrible moment she almost sat up. Harry could see her face as she stared at him out of the flames. One side of the face seemed normal, but the other side was boiling away to reveal the metal plates bolted over the skull beneath the skin. Tiny servos were embedded in the back of the eye, the cheek was a mass of small metal plates which slid over each other as she screamed. Then the metal started to tarnish, to blacken, and the fire blotted out the sight and the sounds.

10

Traffic

Harry would have stood and watched the fire until the papers caught and it spread to the rest of the room. But the Doctor slapped him on the back and pointed to a fire extinguisher. The Doctor already had one, and together they soon brought the flames under control. Coughing from the smoke and the stench, they then collapsed through the door and sat gasping for breath on the steps outside.

'I'm sorry, Harry,' the Doctor said when they had recovered somewhat.

'I should never have got her into this, Doctor.'

'Not your choice, Harry. And not your fault either.'

'Isn't it?' Harry was not so sure. As Sylvia's employer he had a responsibility. As her friend he had a responsibility. He was someone she had trusted and respected, and he had failed her. Because of him she had become involved in something that should never have touched her life. And now that life was gone. He did not believe for a moment that he had killed her, that it was in any real sense Sylvia that he had just shot and watched burn. But he was sure that because of him she was dead.

'It may not be my fault, Doctor,' he said at last, 'but I am responsible.'

'Facing up to your responsibilities is a good thing, Harry,' the Doctor said quietly. 'Not always pleasant, but good. And your responsibility now is to see that we end this thing as surely and as quickly as we can.'

Harry nodded and sighed. He bit back his tears and his anger. 'So what now?' he asked. 'No chance of tracking that pen, I suppose.'

'None,' the Doctor said. 'They will know what we were trying, just as they knew when you questioned one of them. Some sort of cerebral link.' He pulled his scarf through his hands as he spoke. 'We still need to get to the pen. We still need to destroy it before they can rebuild Voractyll and send it snaking out to their millennium bug chips across the world. So we'll have to use Plan B,' he finished as the end of the scarf pulled through and fell to the ground.

'Is that what I think it is?' Harry asked.

The Doctor grinned. 'A bit risky and complicated perhaps,' he admitted, 'but it will be so much fun.'

Harry was by no means convinced. 'And if that doesn't work?' he asked.

The Doctor got to his feet and helped Harry up. 'Oh come on,' he said, 'where's your sense of optimism?' He put his arm round Harry's shoulder and led him away from the building. 'Now, I want you to go back to London and set things up with General Randall. You know what needs doing?'

'Well, yes, I think so. Mike Foley was sorting most of it out. But what will you be doing?'

The Doctor paused in mid-step. 'I'm going to finish reverse engineering the millennium bug chip,' he said. 'Once that's done, we should be able to get Randall's team to Downing Street and then...'

'And then?'

The Doctor shook his head and gave a low whistle. 'And then we shall see, Harry. We shall see.'

They shook hands in silence, the early morning sun throwing their shadows long and thin across the ground. Then Harry walked the rest of the way to the waiting helicopter, tired, sad and alone.

Though he scarcely dared to admit it to himself, Chris Grant was more nervous than he had ever been as he made the long walk. His men were now deployed throughout the Palace of Westminster. The policemen on duty had been relieved and sent away without explanation. There was more than enough for them to do elsewhere. Now Grant was in charge.

But even so, he was filled with a mixture of both awe and apprehension as he pushed open the doors and stepped into the Chamber of the House of Commons. The place was in uproar. The

Speaker was shouting for order, about a dozen people were on their feet yelling at each other across the floor. Grant took a deep breath, pushed his way through the Members of Parliament standing round the door and marched along the thin carpet towards the dispatch boxes and the mace.

He had read somewhere that the distance between the two sides of the House was designed to be just further than a drawn rapier could reach. But Colonel Grant was in the middle, within range of both sides. Any hope that he could slip in without being noticed was quelled as his entrance achieved what the Speaker had been unable to. The noise died, and in a moment there was silence. Grant made his way to where the Deputy Prime Minister stood open-mouthed at the government dispatch box, midway through trying to explain why the Prime Minister was not there himself. Philip Cotton was now staring at Grant as he approached.

Grant stopped right in front of the mace. 'Excuse me, Madam Speaker,' he said. His voice was strong and clear.

The Speaker was as dumbstruck as everyone else. But after a second she found her voice. 'What is the meaning of this, sir?' she asked, her own voice a shadow of its usual self.

Grant ignored her, and turned to Cotton. He saluted. It seemed like an appropriate thing to do.

'Colonel Grant?' Cotton asked, his own voice quiet and nervous.

'General Randall asks that you join him for a few moments, sir. If you don't mind.'

Cotton recovered quickly, and his voice was stronger as he asked: 'Do I have a choice?'

'Of course, sir,' Grant said. 'Just one.' Then he turned and walked back towards the doors. He did not look to see if Cotton was following. He wasn't really sure what he would do if he wasn't.

'Normally, I'd be outraged,' Cotton said as they emerged into the cold morning air. 'But I'm actually glad to be out of there right now.' His voice hardened as he added: 'This had better be good.'

Randall was waiting nearby. Mike Foley and Harry Sullivan were with him. 'Thank you for coming, sir,' Randall said.

'The Colonel made a good case,' Cotton said. 'Now what's going on?'

Harry told him.

Cotton considered before he commented. 'It's crazy,' he said at last. 'But it's just about crazy enough to work. If we can get the Russians to agree.'

'They have, sir,' Foley said.

'And will the President keep his mouth shut? He and the PM are pretty pally after that impeachment business.'

'For now. But we have to move fast.'

'And there are other crises we need to deal with almost as urgently,' Randall said.

Cotton took a deep breath. 'OK,' he said. 'I'd better get back to the House and set things up there. I guess we're just waiting for the TV screens.'

'They're on their way,' Grant told him.

'But there is one other rather vital ingredient we're currently lacking,' Harry pointed out.

'What's that, Commander?'

'The Doctor.'

In the corner of the smoke-blackened room, the Doctor had attached the millennium bug chip to a workstation computer. The room was still smoky and the smell was unpleasant. He was working with his scarf wrapped round his face, peering out through a slit between the layers of the material and the brim of his hat. The biggest inconvenience of this he had discovered to his dismay was that it muffled his whistling.

At last he was ready. With his fingers crossed, the Doctor clumsily hit the Enter key and watched his program compile and run. His expression was grim as the process started. But as it progressed, his mouth started to curl up at the edges despite the wool stretched tight across it. His eyebrows rose slightly, his eyes bulged, and soon behind the scarf he was grinning.

'Well done, Doctor,' he said happily into the material of the scarf.

Delivery was the problem now. But the Doctor had already

thought of that. He had his sonic screwdriver attached to the same workstation. If he downloaded his compiled program, he could use the sonic screwdriver to deliver the new instructions to the chips. Provided he was close. One by one, George Gardner had suggested it would need to be done. For now at least it looked like he was right.

There was a cold breeze, and the Doctor kept his scarf tightly wrapped round his neck as he made his way across the compound to the base's communications centre.

'Hello there!' he announced cheerfully as he entered the room. The comms crew turned to look at him, and the Doctor raised his hat politely. 'Tell me,' he said, 'how do I get back to London?'

'With difficulty,' the radio operator told him. 'The roads are blocked pretty solid so far as we can tell. And the general took all the helicopters with him. Almost all the other vehicles went out with the deployment over the last few days.'

'And,' one of the other soldiers said, 'we haven't checked any of the few remaining vehicles to see if they're millennium-compliant yet. They might blow up on you, or worse.'

The Doctor rubbed his chin thoughtfully. 'Gentlemen,' he said, 'you're very helpful.'

'Sorry.'

He turned to go, head down, despondent. But as he kicked the end of his scarf back out of the door, a thought occurred. He turned slowly back. 'How far is it to London, to the Houses of Parliament, from here?'

'We're quite close in,' the radio operator said. 'Maybe forty miles. Too far to walk if that's what you're thinking.'

The Doctor shook his head. 'No, no. I'm thinking there is one vehicle here that won't have a millennium bug chip in it anywhere, and which will get me through the traffic.' He grinned widely and suddenly. 'I assume we have some diesel fuel handy.'

'Try it again,' the engineer shouted as he pulled his head out of the inspection hatch. 'These multi-fuel engines were always unreliable.'

There was a coughing sound from deep inside the engine. Then suddenly it roared into life. Moments later the engineer was coughing almost as loudly. Smoke from the exhaust, he now recalled, was another problem with the Chieftain.

The Doctor popped up through the hatch in the turret and waved down to the engineer. 'Thanks!' he called. 'That seems to be going all right.'

The engineer wiped his grimy hands on his grubby overalls. 'Look after him for us,' he called back. 'We're quite fond of old Fred here. Most powerful tank in the world in his day.'

'I'll remember that.' The Doctor's voice floated out of the turret but he had already disappeared back inside.

A moment later the huge vehicle lurched slowly forwards. Its long 120mm gun dipped towards the roadway as it moved slowly down from its plinth and turned into the road. Smoke belched from the exhaust and the wide tracks took hold on the tarmac as the tank picked up speed. The engineer watched as the tank disappeared into the distance.

Inside the Chieftain the Doctor was enjoying himself immensely. 'Pity it won't do much more than thirty miles an hour,' he muttered and turned his attention to working out how the fire control system worked. Not, he decided, that he would need to fire the gun. Probably.

Driving a tank that usually had a crew of four on your own kept one a little busy, the Doctor decided, once he had to start working out the best route. He didn't meet much traffic until the outskirts of London.

At first most of it was moving faster than he was. But before long the Doctor was having to negotiate the blocked roads. Pavements were useful, although the odd lamp post got in his way and paid for its mistake. Several times he was able to take a short cut across open ground. The tank was easily able to climb the embankments beside the road, teetering for a moment at the top before toppling forwards and racing down the other side, engine roaring.

But as he approached the centre of the city, the congestion got worse. The main thing in the Doctor's favour was the size and obvious power of the vehicle. The fact that it was moving relatively slowly seemed to emphasise this, and the cars and lorries were usually more than happy to pull over to the side of the road as he approached, making no concession of speed. And if there was a trail of dented cars and broken wing mirrors behind him, it was a small price to pay for saving the world.

The roads closer to the Palace of Westminster were clear. Randall's troops had managed to move the traffic back and create a cordoned-off area. The edge was ringed with vehicles commandeered to form road blocks. The Doctor did not realise this, though, and his first inkling was when Fred gently brushed aside an already-battered Escort van. Parked across the otherwise clear road in front was a large estate car. There was nobody inside it. It was blue.

A soldier stepped out into the road and held his hand up. He did not stay still for long. When it became apparent that the tank was not about to stop, he leaped aside. The tank did not slow at all. Moments later its tracks were dragging it up and over the car. The metal folded as the weight of the Chieftain came fully to bear. Fifty-five tons of armour with a power-to-weight ratio of thirteen and a half horsepower per ton ground over the estate car. The windows popped out in showers of cascading glass. The roof crumpled into the body of the car, and the doors collapsed outwards.

The soldier watched as the Chieftain lurched onwards, leaving the shattered and flattened mass of metal that had been the car behind it. 'Fred?' he said in disbelief.

'I don't believe it,' Randall said as the tank ground to a halt near by.

'Hello there,' the Doctor called out from the turret. He waved.

'When you get to know the Doctor a little, sir,' Harry said, 'you find that you stop being surprised at things.'

'Now that, I can believe.'

The Doctor leaped down from Fred the tank and joined them.

He brandished his sonic screwdriver triumphantly. 'I've done it, Harry. I've done it.'

'What's he done?' Foley asked.

'I've got the antidote,' the Doctor said. 'With this we can disable the Silver Bullet chips.'

'You mean things will work again?' Cotton asked.

The Doctor shrugged. 'As well as they would have done without the chip. If they have a genuine millennium bug problem, they'll still have it. But at least we can bypass the Voracian control.'

'Well done, Doctor.'

'Thank you, Harry.' The Doctor slipped the sonic screwdriver inside his coat pocket. 'It was quite easy really, once I'd worked it all out. An elegant solution, if I say so myself. You know, I could even use it to give the millennium bug problem to something that doesn't suffer from it, in much the same way as the SB chip does the opposite to cure it.'

Randall interrupted. 'Be that as it may be, Doctor, time is pressing.'

'You needn't tell *me* that,' the Doctor replied testily. 'Is everything set at this end?'

Randall nodded to Grant, who said: 'The screens have just arrived. We had some trouble finding the stuff, but it's sorted now.'

'Good.'

'Yes and no,' Grant said. 'They have their own backup generator here which seems to be running all right, but the plasma screens don't seem to work.'

'Millennium bug?' Harry asked.

Grant nodded. 'I'm afraid so.'

'Oh pish and tosh,' the Doctor snorted. 'New technology like that... More like they have a Silver Bullet chip.' His eyes gleamed as he brandished his sonic screwdriver. 'And that means we can test my handiwork.'

A few minutes later the Doctor sat back in satisfaction. He was kneeling on the floor in the entrance hall of the Palace of Westminster, a plasma screen on the ground in front of him. He put away his sonic screwdriver and closed the back of the flat screen plasma panel. 'That's both of them done. You can try them now.'

Two soldiers managed to lift the screen between them and carried it carefully across to where the first screen was being plugged into a wall socket. Already they could see a grey flickering pattern of static on the first screen.

'Just like that?' Grant asked. 'Just point that thing and press?'

'You have to know which chip to point it at,' the Doctor said. 'And what to press. But essentially, yes.' He grinned. 'You can always judge a craftsman by the elegance and simplicity of his solution, don't you think?'

'Thank you, Doctor,' Randall said. 'That just leaves Grant to set up here, and for us to get to Downing Street.'

The Doctor frowned. 'Is that a problem?'

'The traffic's been cleared,' Grant said. 'But Attwell's men are in control there.'

'Not men,' the Doctor said grimly. 'Not any more.'

'I think we can expect some resistance, whatever they are now,' Randall agreed.

The Doctor nodded. 'Then we'd better take Fred with us.'

The C-17 bounced and lurched as it gathered speed. To Captain Martin and his men it felt as if the huge plane was trying to take off from a field. There was a good reason for this.

Just as the jolts and bumps reached the verge of becoming unbearable, they ceased. The plane leaned steeply backwards as it lifted ponderously into the air. The straps and restraining bolts holding the payload of equipment creaked under the shifting weight.

The pilot's voice crackled over the loudspeakers. 'Captain Martin, sir, the GPS is online again. Looks like we're bang on target. Should be arriving at Nevchenka in less than an hour.'

Martin nodded without comment. Already he could feel the tightness in his stomach that always preceded an operation. He just hoped they were in time.

'They're into the main compound, sir,' Kosimov reported. 'Colonel

Krimkov's troops have engaged the rebels on the perimeter, but I'm afraid they are too few and too late.'

'Seal the control centre,' Ivigan said. 'We'll see how long the concrete and metal will keep them out. But I fear it will not be long.'

10
Engagement

Prime Minister Brooks beckoned Bryant over. Andi Cave went with him, and together they leaned close to hear Brooks's whisper.

'I'm getting reports coming in that there's been a coup,' he said, raising an eyebrow. 'Fantastic, isn't it?'

'Do you mean unbelievable, or excellent?' Bryant asked.

'What? Oh, excellent, very good indeed. Don't you think?'

'It seems a bit premature,' Cave said slowly. 'Where are these reports coming from?'

'Er, well, obviously our plan is working,' the PM said. 'Got a call from Sir Robert - you know, junior Health - on his mobile now it's working again. He said there are troops on the floor of the House. Everything.' Brooks smiled his famous open, honest smile. 'Good stuff.'

'In the House?' Bryant looked at Andi Cave. 'I didn't know Parliament was on the deployment list. Not *inside* Parliament. Check with Attwell. See if he knows what's going on.'

Cave walked quickly towards the door.

Brooks watched her go. 'Problem?' he asked. 'Do you think?'

'Let's hope not,' Bryant said. 'But it's as well to be prepared.'

The second time was easier. Not least because on this occasion Grant followed Deputy Prime Minister Cotton back into the Chamber. Behind them a dozen soldiers took up position inside the doors. Together, Cotton and Colonel Grant stood at the dispatch box and Cotton signalled the Speaker to call for silence. As before, it was remarkably quick in coming.

'I have an unusual announcement to make,' Cotton said when all was quiet. 'A request of the House, really.' He looked round. 'As you can see, General Randall's troops, under the command of Colonel Grant here, are taking up positions inside the House.'

There were murmurs and whispers, but no outright complaints.

'I can assure you that they are here for our own good,' Cotton went on. 'And I ask you to co-operate fully with the colonel and with his men to bring this situation to a speedy conclusion.'

'What do you want?' someone shouted from the backbenches. Before long the House was in uproar.

Grant gave them a full minute. Then he stepped up to the Speaker's Chair and pulled out his gun. He pointed it at the ceiling and waited. He wasn't sure if it was actually treason to shoot at the ceiling of the House of Commons, but if he had to he would find out. In the event he did not have to. After a few moments there was relative quiet again.

'Thank you.' He looked round at the faces now staring at him, their expressions betraying disbelief, anger, anxiety. 'As Mr Cotton said, we're here to help. You are all aware that we are facing a time of real crisis. Let's not make things worse by jumping to conclusions or by obstructing my men. There are things happening that you are not aware of, and which you need to know. I trust that all will become clear very soon now, and I just ask you to be patient for the moment. Thank you.' As he stepped down he signalled to the troops at the back of the chamber. 'Right, you can get started,' he called.

If the honourable members had been surprised by Colonel Grant's appearance, that surprise turned to amazement as the soldiers carried in huge plasma display screens and started setting them up in front of the Speaker's Chair.

'Excuse me, ma'am,' one of the soldiers asked the Speaker quietly, 'but where's the nearest power point?'

It was a measure of how the atmosphere had already changed that she sounded embarrassed and apologetic rather than nervous or angry when she admitted she did not know.

At first it seemed as though it would be easy. The Doctor together with Harry, Foley and General Randall walked up to the barrier across the top of Downing Street. Beyond it they could see Attwell's troops stationed outside doors. There were clusters of hastily prepared sandbag emplacements with soldiers and machine guns inside. An armoured personnel carrier was parked across the road outside Numbers Ten and Eleven. Behind it a cluster of journalists and cameramen stamped and shivered in the cold of the late morning.

The sentry at the barrier saluted as they approached. Randall returned the salute. 'You can let us through,' he said.

But the soldier was immediately on his guard. 'I'm afraid not, sir. Nobody comes through.'

'Not even the general?' Harry asked in surprise.

'Nobody. Colonel Attwell's orders, sir.'

'I give Colonel Attwell his orders,' Randall said quietly. 'And I order you to let us through.'

The soldier did not reply. Instead he levelled his automatic weapon, standing well back from the barrier. Immediately he was joined by three other soldiers, also with weapons at the ready.

'Oh, now that's a pity,' the Doctor said. 'You see, we were going to ask Colonel Attwell and his friends how Mr Cutter is getting on piecing Voractyll back together. Perhaps I could offer to help?'

For a second there was no reaction from the soldiers behind the barrier. Then one of them blinked. It was enough for them to catch a glimpse of the almond yellow pupil as the eyelid opened again and it readjusted to the light. At the same moment, all four soldiers pulled back the bolts on their weapons.

'Run,' Foley shouted. But he need not have bothered. The Doctor and Harry were already diving out of the way, General Randall close behind them. Bullets smacked into the tarmac where they had been standing moments before. The Doctor's head popped round the corner for just long enough for him to shout: 'I'll take that as a "no thank you".' Then it was gone.

Behind the APC, the journalists exchanged hurried words. A TV reporter got ready to speak to the camera, although he knew the pictures were going nowhere at the moment.

'Did Colonel Attwell pick his own team, by any chance?' the Doctor asked Randall as they walked back to the convoy of Land Rovers and lorries that was parked down the road.

'He did,' Randall said. 'Made a point of it in fact. Took them on special training exercises to build team morale.'

'I bet he did,' Harry murmured.

At the head of the line of vehicles was Fred the tank. Close behind were several Scorpions. They looked like miniature versions of Fred, although rather than being designated as tanks themselves they were listed as CVR(T) - Combat Vehicle Reconnaissance (Tracked).

'Right, Doctor,' Randall said as they reached the convoy. 'We'll follow you.'

'Thank you, General.' The Doctor turned to Harry. 'Do you think you could give me a hand? It's a bit tricky to steer and shoot at the same time.'

Foley and Randall were climbing into the lead Land Rover as Harry lowered himself through the hatch after the Doctor.

'I'm sorry it's so cramped,' the Doctor called to him. 'You tend to forget how restrictive it is having a technology where things have to be smaller inside than out.'

They could hear the noise from inside the hallway of Number Ten. It was rumbling like thunder which grew in volume until it was almost a roar. The ground was beginning to tremble under their feet and Andi Cave and Colonel Attwell stopped their whispered conversation and looked round.

'What is it?' Cave asked.

'Trouble,' Attwell said. 'We may need a backup contingency scenario.' He ran to the door.

The Voracian soldier on guard inside opened the door for Attwell, and Cave followed the Colonel out into the street.

Ahead of them, across the road, the APC was roaring into life. One track span rapidly, dragging the heavy troop carrier round so that it was facing up Downing Street. From the other end of the street came the sound of a small explosion. And gunfire.

Attwell was running to the nearest of the sandbag emplacements. Cave waited in the doorway, trying to see what was happening. But all she could see was the smoke from the explosion – a grenade, she guessed. She was not programmed for aural weaponry recognition. Through the smoke she could see men running. They were firing as they ran. The machine guns in the emplacements returned fire, but one by one they were being blown apart by grenades.

Then the heavy machine gun on the APC came to bear. The bullets scythed across Downing Street, chipping the cobbles and whining off the pavement. The running soldiers dived for cover. Some of them made it, others were knocked sideways by the gunfire and crashed to the cold ground. There was no sign of the journalists.

Attwell was shouting orders, pointing where he needed troops. It looked to Cave as if they could hold Randall's men.

But then a huge tank rumbled out of the smoke. Bullets ricocheted off its armoured hull as the turret swung slowly round, the gun lowering until it was pointing directly at the APC. The Chieftain's L11 120mm gun loosed a single rifled round. The sound of the shot was incredible as flame spat after it from the barrel of the gun.

The sound of the APC as it blew apart was louder. When it entered service in the 1960s, the Chieftain was capable of destroying any Soviet tank in existence. The APC was as well protected as a cardboard box by comparison. The round entered the front of the APC, drilling through the light armour and exploding inside. The sides and top were blown off almost in one piece. The chassis and the back of the vehicle disintegrated in a huge explosion of orange fire.

Almost at the same moment, the emplacement next to Attwell's erupted in a ball of flame. From behind the Chieftain the squat, brutal shape of a lighter Scorpion emerged into view.

Attwell was out of the emplacement now, standing in the middle of the road. He stood, feet braced apart, gun raised, and fired at the oncoming tank. Andi Cave wondered briefly at the futility of the action. But then she saw the silhouette of the figure leaning out of the turret hatch of the tank. It was a distinctive profile, complete with wide-brimmed hat and scarf trailing out behind.

As the tank approached, and Attwell stood his ground outside Number Ten, Cave could see the Doctor staring down at Attwell, as if daring him to continue shooting. Only when a shot caught his hat, sent it spinning away, did the Doctor react at all. He clasped his hand to his bare head. 'My hat!' Cave could see him mouth, though the sound of the words was lost in the roar of the tank and the percussive crack of the handgun.

The tank was almost on him by the time Attwell did turn aside. By then it was too late. As he turned, his foot slipped on the near-frozen surface of a cobble stone and his leg gave way. With another second he could have recovered, regained his balance, dived out of the way.

But there was no time. The huge nearside track of the tank caught his boot, dragging it round. Attwell's leg was pulled with it under the tread as the tank lumbered inexorably and obliviously onward. In a moment his whole body was dragged screaming and struggling under the tank. As he fell, he stared up, his eyes met Cave's and for a second he stopped screaming. For a moment she could see the fear and terror and hatred burning in his eyes. And in that second she wondered if death was really so awful that it could bring a Voracian to this.

A moment, no more. Then he was gone. The tank crunched to a halt outside Number Ten. From somewhere beneath it a trickle of oily, viscous liquid ran out between the cobbles.

After landing blindly in a field, the road was simple. The pilot put the C-17 down on the perimeter road. It was as close as he dared get to the firefight going on in and around the buildings.

As soon as the plane was still, the cargo doors began to open. As soon as they were open the jeeps and trucks were roaring down the ramp. The Apache was lashed to a pallet that was itself on wheels. This was pushed down the ramp, and the crew started pre-flight checks and procedures even before the helicopter was unstrapped.

Captain Martin wasted no time in directing his troops to the rebels' weak points. They had circled over Nevchenka once at low altitude so he could get a good view of what was happening. The Russian troops to the East needed reinforcing, and the main control centre he knew was underground in the centre of the complex.

What they had not been able to see from the air was how close the rebels were to getting into the control centre. How close they were to fixing their nuclear device to one of the missiles. How close they were to launching that missile, either at Moscow or at its predesignated target which was almost certainly in the mainland USA.

Whatever was happening, speed was vital now.

As the Doctor's feet disappeared out of the top of the tank, Harry pulled himself up into the turret. He looked down to see the Doctor standing in the road beside the tank. The remains of the APC were scattered across the street beside them. Harry jumped down too.

The sounds of gunfire seemed to be dying away. The air was heavy with cordite.

'I'll find Randall,' the Doctor said as Harry landed beside him.

'Right, I'll check the house,' Harry answered. He turned towards Number Ten, and realised how odd it looked without a policeman outside. The door was open, but closing. Instinctively he ran towards it, hoping to reach it before it was slammed shut. His shoulder hit the door and knocked it open again. Harry fell backwards, and staggered quickly back to his feet.

The door was open again, he could see through into the hallway. And he could see Andrea Cave standing in the doorway, her face twisted into a Munch-like parody of anger and dismay. For a second they stared at each other, and Harry wondered if the same technology had been used to repair her face as had masked Sylvia's changed appearance. Then she was on him, her hands round his throat again. Only this time, they both knew he could not break free. Her face was close to his as she pushed him backwards, a parody of a dance. Or an embrace. He could feel himself slipping backwards.

Then abruptly she seemed to look up. Her expression froze on her face, and it took Harry a while to realise that part of that face was missing. Her eyes rolled sideways, as if trying to see where the bullet had impacted, where the metal and plastic were exposed. Oil and blood ran together down the shattered side of her cheek as she released her grip on Harry and fell backwards into the hallway.

Harry stood panting, gasping for breath. Slowly, painfully, he turned round.

Ten yards behind him, as if frozen in position, stood Mike Foley. The gun was still in his hands, still held out, still aimed. Then he slowly lowered it, and smiled grimly beneath the mask of his sunglasses.

'Thanks,' Harry managed to gasp as Foley joined him on the steps. The Doctor and Randall were close behind.

Foley slowly took off his sunglasses and looked down at the shattered remains of Andrea Cave's face. A tiny servo was still working at one side of her eye. The eyeball rolled aimlessly and pointlessly in the socket, gradually slowing to a halt. Foley breathed out a long misty breath. 'Jeez,' he said. 'You guys weren't joking, were you.'

'This is no joking matter, Mr Foley,' the Doctor said as he pushed past, into Number Ten Downing Street.

1E

Countdown

The room was called the Great Parlour, though it looked nothing like a parlour now. The walls were panelled in wood, and the ceiling was patterned in joined circles and squares of plaster work. Beside the wide fireplace hung a painting of William Pitt. The pattern of the plaster frieze was made up of the letters W and A joined by a cord and interspersed with haw trees.

Most of the middle of the room was taken up with a huge antique wooden dining table, with seven chairs along each side and two at each end. But the table was not laid for dinner. At each place was a pad of paper, a pencil and a glass. Several carafes of water were stood on mats along the middle of the table.

Byron Cutter looked round the room with satisfaction. 'Yes, this will do very nicely. Ask Mr Bardell to have our equipment set up in here, would you? Thank you so much.'

He walked along the length of the table, felt the smooth surface of the wood. Things were going well. Very well.

'Oh, and have the water removed,' he added, with the faintest trace of distaste in his voice.

'You won't succeed. The people who elected us won't let you.'

Terry Brooks and his aides, including James Bryant, were seated round the Cabinet table. In a ring around the table, behind the seated figures, were Randall's troops. Their guns were held at the ready. Behind them stood Randall and the Doctor. Foley and Harry were sitting at the side of the room, in chairs usually reserved for Cabinet aides and senior civil servants.

'The people who elected you have a right to know how you've betrayed their trust, how you've tried to trick them,' General Randall retorted. Behind him a video camera was being set up, fixed to a tripod and pointed along the table towards Brooks and Bryant. A large screen had already been put up at one end of the table.

'Oh, don't try to play politics, General, you're not suited to it.' Brooks looked away.

'I'm not interested in politics,' the Doctor said. He pushed through the line of soldiers and sat in an empty chair at the table. He leaned back and put his feet up on the Cabinet table.

Brooks shook his head in disgust. 'You even tarnish the very traditions –'

'And what have you tarnished?' the Doctor demanded. 'The world?'

'What?' Brooks seemed taken aback. He looked round at his colleagues. Only Bryant returned his gaze, but he said nothing.

'Yes, the world,' the Doctor repeated with emphasis. 'You put the whole world at risk with your petty political posturing. And what were you hoping to gain? Hmm?'

Brooks gaped.

'Save a few pennies here and there on the military? Get a mandate to disband some army units? Sell off the odd frigate, is that it?'

'I don't know what you're talking about,' Brooks said.

'I didn't expect an admission,' the Doctor replied. 'Not immediately. But you must know it won't work.' He pulled his feet off the table and leaned forward. 'But I can forgive economic naivety. It's putting the world at risk that I can't abide. And then claiming not to understand what you've done.' He shook his head, at once angry and sad.

'Then tell us, Doctor,' Bryant said. 'What have we done?'

The Doctor was standing up again, aghast, almost bouncing on the balls of his feet. 'What have you done? What have you...' He turned to Randall. 'Tell them, General. Tell them. You tell them.' He practically pulled Randall to the table, taking a seat beside him.

'You may have started the next world war,' Randall said. His voice was quiet, but it was obvious that the people in the room could hear every word he said. 'We provided replacement equipment for the Russians' early-warning and defence systems.'

'You what?' Brooks said angrily. 'I wasn't –'

'No, Prime Minister, you weren't,' Randall shot back. 'Nor should you have been. It was a decision taken by SHAPE. A military not a political decision requiring the utmost secrecy. The Russian equipment was bound to fail come the millennium. The only way to keep them from going blind, from perhaps panicking and pre-emptively launching on January first 2000 - today - was to provide equipment that worked.'

'Condef,' Bryant said quietly. 'That was why you and the Russians went to Condef.'

'Yes,' the Doctor said. 'You were worried about that, weren't you? Worried enough to have us try to discover the general's plan for you.'

Bryant did not reply. But there was the hint of a smile on his face.

'So,' the Doctor went on, 'General Randall here provided the equipment to the Russians. Equipment which your political powerplay means won't work, will actually fail. Has actually failed already.'

Brooks was white, the colour drained from his face. 'You're lying.' His voice was calm and confident, but his hands were knotted together on the table in front of him.

'No, they're not.' It was Foley who spoke, from the other side of the room.

'Who the hell are you?' Brooks demanded.

'Mike Foley. CIA.'

'And what's it got to do with you?'

Foley stood up. He was a menacing figure in his sunglasses. They caught the light from the heavy chandelier as he approached the table. 'At this moment in time,' he said, 'US Special Forces are engaged in an operation in Krejikistan to prevent Islamic fundamentalist rebels from launching a nuclear device on Moscow from the Nevchenka Military Installation.'

'That's right, Prime Minister,' Randall said. 'If that missile is launched, the Russians won't know where the hell it's coming from. But they'll have to make a guess. And they'll have to retaliate.'

'And where would you guess?' the Doctor asked quietly. 'Who would you fire your missiles at?'

Brooks said nothing.

The Doctor gave him a few moments, then slammed his fist down heavily on the Cabinet table. 'Come on, come on – there's a missile already on its way. Your early-warning systems don't work, despite the fact the British just provided them for you, what do you do? Under those circumstances, who would you blame? Who has already ensured you're blind so you have so little time to respond?' He thumped the table again. 'Well?'

'Oh God,' Brooks breathed. Then louder he said: 'How do I know this is true?' He glanced at the camera at the other side of the room. It stared back at him.

'You think this is a set-up to get your confession?' Randall said. 'Too right it is. We're setting up a satellite link to the Russian Premier right now.'

'Just as soon as we can find a satellite that Mr Bryant and his friends haven't scuppered,' the Doctor put in.

'When we get him online,' Randall went on, 'you're going to tell him exactly what you've been up to. And we're all going to pray he believes you, because God knows he'll have no reason to trust a word you say right now.'

'And while we're waiting,' Foley said, 'here's something else to think about. Even after disarmament, even after the end of the Cold War, Russia still has 7,000 nuclear warheads on missiles. She has 5,000 further tactical nuclear missiles and 12,000 nuclear weapons in storage. There's enough highly enriched uranium and plutonium in the former Soviet Union right now to manufacture another 70,000 nuclear weapons.' He took off his glasses and stared unblinkingly at the Prime Minister. 'Just so you know,' he said.

As he finished speaking the screen at the end of the table flickered. Static flecked its surface as one of Randall's technicians dimmed the lights at that end of the room. 'We've got the link set up,' he said. Sure enough, the static resolved itself into a picture, a picture of a man.

The man was old, and tired. He was sitting behind a desk, lonely in a huge room.

'Prime Minister?' The man's voice was tired too, resigned. It was heavily accented.

'Oh, um.' Brooks seemed lost for words. 'Good morning, Premier. Er, Dimitri.'

'Good?' The Premier's humourless laugh turned into a cough and he dabbed at his mouth with a large handkerchief. 'You start a war and you think it is good?' He leaned forward. 'Why? That is all I ask. We both know it is too late to stop this madness now. Your missiles are already approaching. Our own await only my final word of command. So tell me why, and let me make what peace I can with God.' He broke off into another fit of coughing.

Brooks looked at Randall. The General's face was a blank, expressionless mask. Bryant was actually smiling, though it looked as though it took an effort. There was silence in the room.

'Dimitri,' Brooks said directly to the camera. 'It isn't us. You must believe me, NATO has nothing to do with this, you know. It is a rebel attack from, er, from one of your former Soviet states.' He glanced at Randall who nodded.

'Of course it is, Prime Minister,' the Premier said with heavy sarcasm.

Brooks frowned. 'You don't believe me?'

'Believe you? You trick us into accepting sabotaged equipment from you when we came for help. You ensure we are blind and deaf and then you launch this unprovoked attack hoping we would not know.' He leaned forward stiffly. 'Well, we do know. We are not completely blind and deaf. We cannot tell which of your bases have fired how many missiles. But the inbound trace and the rocket exhaust is clear from the satellite data we can still read.' He leaned back again. 'Now, if there is nothing else, I am rather pressed for time. As you well know.' He leaned sideways slightly and beckoned to someone out of view. 'Bring that over here,' he hissed.

A trolley with a large TV screen was wheeled into shot. It was angled so that both the premier and the people in the Cabinet Room could see it. It showed what looked like a spaceshot mission control, or a military launch facility. The sound from the television was tinny but audible.

'Still only one confirmed track,' someone was announcing. It sounded like a loudspeaker system. 'Target Moscow. Time to impact, seven minutes.'

'No, wait.' Brooks' voice was a broken shout. 'Wait. I can prove it's not us. The equipment, the sabotage. It was a mistake.'

The Premier raised a bushy white eyebrow. 'That is certainly true.'

'You don't understand.'

'Also true.'

From the launch facility the voice was audible again: 'Second stage launch program now activated. Launch countdown ready to commence.'

'I didn't know it was coming to you. The equipment, and other things. The sabotage. It was part of a plan, yes. But it was to discredit our own military. We never intended this...' He waved a hand, unable to think of a way of describing it.

'Rubbish.' The Premier coughed briefly, then said: 'Listen to yourself. You are explaining nothing. You make no sense at all.' He turned slightly away, as if to someone off camera. 'Tell them to begin the final countdown,' he said. His voice was heavy and tinged with sadness.

'No, wait,' Brooks shouted. 'The plan... the plan was to make things worse for the millennium. This so-called millennium bug, we suffer from it too. But we...' He paused, his mouth working soundlessly for a moment.

In the moment of silence, the announcement voice was plainly audible. 'Countdown commenced with Premier's authority. Code word is *Pravda*. First wave ICBM launch in thirty seconds.'

'I...' Brooks eventually managed to say, it was almost a sob. 'I worked with others, with the Silver Bullet company, to make things worse.' He turned to Bryant. 'Tell him,' he said. But Bryant said nothing.

'I wanted it to be so bad that martial law was declared,' Brooks went on when it was clear Bryant would not confirm his words, 'that the troops came out on the streets. I wanted such a huge military deployment that when we later said there was an attempted coup, people would believe it. The Silver Bullet millennium bug fix, that's how we did it – it doesn't fix things, it makes sure that they fail.' He shook his head, glanced at Bryant again. 'We can't pay for our promises,' he said, his voice quieter now. 'You must know that problem better than I do. We have to dismantle the military to the point where we have the money to spend on education, on healthcare and hospitals and –'

'Hospitals?' The Premier interrupted. 'You will need hospitals soon.'

'Fifteen seconds,' the quiet announcement from the launch facility said.

'I lied.' Brooks was almost shouting now. 'I lied to my colleagues about it, to Parliament and the people.' He was wringing his hands, sweating. 'Tell them,' he shouted at Bryant.

'Ten seconds.'

Bryant did not move.

'Call it off, Dimitri. You must call it off. Please. Bryant had Jennifer Hamilton killed. You know she's dead. She wanted to call it off.'

'Five seconds.'

'Dimitri!'

'Four... Three...'

'You have to believe me,' Brooks screamed at the camera.

'Two... One...'

Everyone else was as silent and still as Bryant. On the screen the Premier sat stiffly, his hands folded on the desk in front of him.

'Zero.'

1F
Truth

'Oh, I believe you, Prime Minister,' the Premier said. There was a change in his voice. It seemed almost relieved. 'I imagine they all believe you now.'

'All?' Brooks looked round, puzzled and anxious.

'My apologies for this charade,' the Premier went on. He coughed again. 'I must confess that I did not think you were so naive.'

'Naive?' Brooks stared at the screen. His mouth hanging slightly open. 'You mean...'

'Oh come now,' the Premier said. 'Do you really underestimate your own generals so much? Do you think you can use them in this way? Do you underestimate us so much that you think we cannot tell the difference between a single rogue missile and a full-scale NATO attack?' He leaned forward, the anger on his face clearly visible. 'And are you really so arrogant and insular that you believe our launch facilities announce their status and countdown in English?'

The Premier sat back and folded his arms. 'General Randall, are you there?' he asked quietly.

'Yes, sir.' Randall stepped in front of the camera. 'And thank you for your help.'

'Thank you, General. I have just been informed that Russian elite troops working together with US Special Forces have defeated the rebel attack on the Nevchenka installation. My thanks, General.' He paused for a moment, then added, 'And to you, Mr President.' The screen blanked out.

The Prime Minister closed his eyes. 'The President,' he murmured weakly. 'You mean President Dering was watching this?'

'Amongst others,' the Doctor said. 'Now if we've finished with the theatricals, we have some important things to discuss.' He leaned across and hung his hat over the lens of the camera. Randall nodded to the operator to switch it off.

Philip Cotton could not recall the Chamber ever being so quiet when it was so full. There was not even the sound of rustling papers or shifting feet as the second of the large plasma screens blanked out.

Slowly he got to his feet. 'What we have witnessed here today,' he said, 'goes no further. We are fortunate under the circumstances that Colonel Grant has removed the Hansard reporters from their gallery, and that the technological difficulties we are experiencing mean that there are no recordings, either video or sound, of what has happened here.'

He looked round, saw every face turned towards him. Behind him soldiers were already dismantling the screens and removing them. 'The Prime Minister will tender his resignation for personal reasons within a month,' Cotton went on. 'The rumour will be that he has lost the confidence of his Cabinet after this millennium bug crisis. As Deputy Prime Minister I shall take over. There will be other resignations in the Cabinet reshuffle that follows, once we know how far and how deep this thing went. And despite the government's large majority in this House, I will be calling a general election within the year.' He sat down and waited for the questions. There would be many. Many more than he had answers for.

Terry Brooks sat staring down at the table in front of him. Beside him James Bryant returned the Doctor's intense stare. A slight smile lifted one side of his mouth.

'So what do you believe your little scenario has achieved, Doctor?' Bryant asked.

'Why don't you tell me?' the Doctor said.

'Very little, I would say. The main business we are concerned with is proceeding to schedule. Nothing has changed.'

Brooks looked up at this, his face sad and puzzled. But he said nothing.

'You mean Voractyll?' the Doctor asked.

Bryant's eyes narrowed. For the briefest instant the pupils of his eyes flicked into yellow ovals. 'What do you know about Voractyll?'

'Everything,' the Doctor said in an exaggerated whisper. 'I defeated it before, I'll destroy it again. I know everything about Silver Bullet, about Byron Cutter, about the pen. And about Voractyll. Everything except where it is.'

Bryant sat back in his chair, apparently unconcerned. 'You know, Doctor,' he said quietly, 'if it achieved any purpose I might laugh.' His smile widened slightly. 'You can't stop it now. Voractyll will soon be complete, and then it will be downloaded remotely into every SB005 chip in the world. A global virtual network of Voractyll copies waiting to link up and liberate the technology of this pathetic planet. Without British government backing now, there is no point in delaying. Cutter will activate the network at once with the coverage we already have. It will be more than sufficient to start with.'

'You mean all we've done is brought their schedule forward?' Harry asked in dismay.

'No, Harry,' the Doctor said. 'They might have brought the start forward, but without the government's help distributing more of their chips we've slowed them down considerably. Wouldn't you say, Mr Bryant?'

'A shift to the right in our schedule. A delay of no real consequence.'

'What are you talking about, James?' Brooks said. 'It's over, don't you understand? We're finished.' He shook his head in sad disbelief. 'I shall have to resign. We all will.'

Bryant rounded on him. 'You think power and your political career are all that's at stake here? You think you matter at all in what is happening? You were a means to an end, that is all.' He turned back to the Doctor. 'And that end has been achieved.'

'Not yet it hasn't,' the Doctor said. 'Voractyll isn't yet active. Cutter will wait until it's past midnight everywhere in the world, until every one of his chips has activated and is waiting for Voractyll. I'll find him before that happens.'

'Never.'

'But you know where he is, don't you?' Bryant's smile disappeared instantly as the Doctor swung round to face Brooks. 'Don't you, Prime Minister?' He leaned across the table. 'Where is Byron Cutter now?' he demanded.

'Don't tell him,' Bryant snapped. 'It's our last card. Don't play it until we can gain an advantage.'

'Ah,' the Doctor said. 'So he does know then.' He smiled at Bryant. 'I wouldn't play poker with those cards if I were you.'

'Don't say anything,' Bryant hissed. A thin tongue whipped out and licked his lips. 'They're not interested in you, in your career or your dreams. Tell them nothing. We can still survive this.'

'Oh no,' the Doctor said. 'I don't think so.' He returned his attention to Brooks. 'This is the man who was just telling you how irrelevant you are. He's right, I don't care about your politics one jot. But I need information from you, and the only way to be sure you're telling me the truth was to have you at the point where you have nothing else to lose. Where there's nothing to be gained by lying any longer. There isn't enough time to run round on a wild goose chase. I think you're at that point now, don't you?'

Brooks said nothing, but he held the Doctor's gaze.

'So help to repair some of what you've done,' the Doctor said gently. 'Tell us where Cutter has gone. Help us to find him and stop him before it's too late. Too late for everyone.'

Brooks opened his mouth. But whatever he was about to say, whether to tell the Doctor what he wanted to know or to refuse the information, he never said it. Bryant was suddenly on his feet, lashing out at Brooks, knocking him across the table.

Brooks cried out in pain and surprise, twisting round and trying to stand. But Bryant had his left hand clamped round the PM's windpipe. He drew his right hand back, claws erupting from the ends of his fingers as he let out an inhuman hiss of rage. A thin, forked tongue dripped from Bryant's mouth and his eyes yellowed over.

General Randall's first shot knocked Bryant's head sideways, tearing the synthetic skin from the side of his face. But it did not stop him. He paused, arm still raised, wet metal glinting through the slice torn across his cheek. Dark, viscous liquid welled up along the cut and ran in several thin rivulets down his face.

Harry's shot, a moment later, knocked Bryant backwards into the panelled wall behind him. His face disintegrated as the bullet tore through his head. Splinters of plastic and metal exploded across the room, whipping at Brooks's cheeks and making them bleed. Sparks showered down from inside what was left of Bryant's head, cascading over his body and bouncing on to the floor. For a moment he stood upright with his back to the wall, one eye still staring out from the metal socket, swivelling to see Harry as he kept his gun aimed ready for another shot.

But it wasn't needed. The sparks round Bryant's head seemed to congeal into a sudden fireball. The explosion echoed round the room, and the headless body toppled forwards, slumping across the Cabinet table beside Brooks.

The Prime Minister stared at the smoking wreck beside him. A narrow river of engine oil meandered lazily across the wooden top of the table and started to drip heavily to the floor.

'Chequers,' Brooks said, his voice husky and dry. 'Cutter and his team have gone to Chequers.'

'The helicopter is standing by,' Grant said. He stared at the scene in the Cabinet Room in disbelief.

The Prime Minister was sitting in a chair at the side of the room. He had his head in his hands and was paying no attention to anything or anyone else. The main activity was at the coffin-shaped Cabinet table. A stained, charred, headless body, wearing a dark, double-breasted business suit, was laid out along the table.

General Randall, Mike Foley and Harry Sullivan were watching attentively as the Doctor attached wires to the inside of the body's neck. Then he passed the wires to the camera operator, who ran them across to the screen at the end of the table.

'What's happening?' Grant whispered to Harry.

Harry shrugged. 'No idea.'

'Right,' the Doctor called across to Brooks. 'Prime Minister, if you'd be so kind?'

Brooks sat up slowly. 'What do you want now, Doctor?'

The Doctor led him to the table and gestured for him to sit where he had been before. 'I want you to play dead, if you would.'

'What?'

'Just slump forwards, close your eyes, and don't move until I say you can.'

Brook stared at him. Then slowly he lowered his head to the table, stretched his arms out above it and closed his eyes. 'Like this?'

'Yes, exactly like that. That's very good.' The Doctor returned to Bryant's body and attached one last wire. 'Anything yet?' he demanded.

The camera operator shook his head. 'Not yet.' As he spoke the screen flickered and a blurred, indistinct image began to appear. 'Hang on, that may be something.'

The Doctor inspected the screen. 'Not very good,' he muttered. Then he jiggled the wires a bit, and the image seemed to clear slightly. It showed a room.

'Doctor, what is going on?' Randall asked, his voice betraying his increasing impatience.

'Nearly there, General, nearly there.' The Doctor nodded at the camera. 'Are you recording this?'

'Every second.'

The image was clearer now, but lined and slightly fuzzy like a television picture on a stormy day.

'It's a two-way link,' the Doctor said. 'They can see through the camera, just as we can see through whatever input they have at their end. Probably a digital camera linked to a laptop computer.'

'They were watching?' Harry asked.

'Perhaps. I think the Silver Bullet chips are all networked in some way already. They seem to know what happens to them. Mr Bryant here has a similar chip inside his neck cavity. So we can see what's going on at their HQ, as it were.' He grinned. 'No sound though, luckily.'

The room on the screen was lined with wooden panels. A long table dominated the middle of the room. On it, at one end, was a personal computer, at which sat two men, their shapes just visible behind the computer screen. And on the table beside the PC was a small black cradle in which they could just make out a silver pen standing upright. Wires ran from the cradle to the system unit of the PC.

'There it is,' the Doctor said, his voice low and grim. 'That's where we have to go.'

As he spoke, one of the men stood up from behind the PC. He walked quickly across the room towards the camera and reached out. His hand dominated the screen, filled it with a tracery of lines and pale skin. Then as the hand closed over the camera, the screen washed over with static again.

'Good,' the Doctor said and ripped wires out of the inside of Bryant's neck. 'You can sit up now, Prime Minister.'

'Shall I play that back?' the cameraman asked.

'If you would be so kind.' The Doctor put his hand on Brooks's shoulder and pointed to the image on the screen. 'Thank you for that,' he said gently. 'They will have seen you apparently dead, and with luck they'll assume Bryant killed you before you could tell us where they are.'

'And is that where they are?' Brooks asked.

'It is.'

Brooks nodded. 'As I told you,' he said, 'it's Chequers.'

'The Prime Minister's official country residence,' Harry said to the Doctor.

'I know what Chequers is,' the Doctor retorted. 'And I know it's a big house.' He turned back to Brooks. 'I was hoping you could be more specific.'

'Of course. That's the Great Parlour. It's on the first floor, just off the Long Gallery.'

The Doctor patted his shoulder. 'Thank you very much. Now if you could just sketch me a rough map, I have a helicopter to catch.'

'I'll assemble an assault team,' Grant said.

'Thank you, Colonel Grant, but that won't be necessary,' the Doctor said as he started to dismantle his mess of wires.

'An attack in force –' Randall began.

'Would scare them into activating Voractyll at once, whatever their schedule. No, thank you, General, I shall go alone.' The Doctor grinned massively. 'Just having me drop in won't worry them at all. I mean, what can one man do on his own? Eh, General?'

The helicopter landed well away from the house, in a field near Great Missenden that was far enough away for the sound not to be heard.

In the back of the helicopter, the Doctor caught his yo-yo as it rolled back up the string and thrust it into his coat pocket.

'Since we're landing now,' he said loudly to the empty cabin, 'I think you should come out. Don't you, Harry?'

There was a pause. Then Harry's face appeared round the end of a bulkhead. 'How did you know I was here?'

The Doctor gave him a sideways look. 'I heard you laughing.'

'That wasn't me.' Harry pulled the laughter bag the Doctor had given him for Christmas out of his jacket pocket. 'I'd better turn this darned thing off.'

'I hope you're better at sneaking round country houses,' the Doctor said as Harry stuffed the small bag back into his pocket.

'As good as you are, Doctor,' Harry replied as he sat down beside the Doctor.

'Ah, well,' the Doctor confessed. 'You'll have to be better than that, I'm afraid.' He smiled back at Harry's puzzled expression. 'You see, I'm probably going to get caught.'

20
Compile and Execute

It was called the Prison Room because it was where William Hawtrey kept Lady Mary Grey in custody in the sixteenth century. A small, faded portrait of her by Hans Eworth hung on the wall. It was of little consolation to the staff, who had all been rounded up, marched up the spiral staircase from the Hawtrey Room to the second floor and then locked in.

In the room below, on the first floor of the house, Dave Hedges sat motionless in front of his PC. On the screen, the near-complete Voractyll snake twisted and turned as if impatiently trying to escape from the confines of the monitor. Beside Dave, Martyn Clark stood, also waiting for the signal to begin the completion program.

The Great Hall had been created in the nineteenth century by roofing over the old Tudor inner courtyard of Chequers. What was left of the courtyard was visible through the huge window that dominated one wall. The room itself rose through two storeys of the house, a gallery running along the south side and giving access to the main bedrooms. The wide wooden arches supporting the gallery made the area underneath seem almost like a separate corridor.

On the east wall, a stone mullioned window looked into the room from the landing of the main staircase. The Great Hall itself was wood-panelled to the height of the main door. Portraits hung on the panelling at intervals, and larger paintings on the plasterwork above. A heavy brass chandelier dipped down from the glass dome in the middle of the high ceiling, the eighteen bulbs in the mock candles burning brightly on power from the house's emergency generator.

The furnishings were comfortable rather than antique. A long sofa and armchairs, low tables and heavy lamps. A grand piano stood on one side of the room, hardly seeming to take up space on the massive floor.

Byron Cutter stood by the massive alabaster fireplace. Above it, covering a picture of the children of Charles I in the style of Van Dyck, was a projection screen. A projector threw images from a laptop on to the screen to punctuate Cutter's report.

'So the risk analysis suggests that while our main force under the command of Colonel Attwell has been pensioned off, our integrity remains intact.' Cutter paused in case there were any questions. Everyone was in the Great Hall apart from Clark and Hedges who were with the Voractyll computer in the Great Parlour. Bardell stood to the side of the fireplace as if he were a teacher watching one of his students give a first presentation. The laptop was on a table beside him. Hertman sat massively alone on the sofa. That just left Imogen Callus, formerly the Silver Bullet Reception Manager, and Trevor Morrisan who had handled manufacturing and distribution. They each sat in an armchair.

Satisfied that he had his team's fullest attention, Cutter continued. 'We are all aware that Mr Bryant and Miss Cave have also taken the package. But as we have seen from the Bryant transmission, our competitors remain oblivious to our operational details and the location of our current management facility.'

Cutter nodded to Bardell, who displayed the next slide. 'Our schedule then for initial distribution remains unchanged. We have no reason to suspect any pushback, and the dates and times are firm with no prospect of a drift to the right. We do have some slack to allow for contingencies should those Voractyll fragments still outstanding fail to compile cleanly first time.' Again he paused. Again there was no comment. Cutter's head swayed gently to and fro as he continued: 'My colleagues, the new millennium has dawned now on every part of this planet. The SB005 chips are being polled by geographical region and so far the response is in excess of our speculative parameters and most optimistic projections. As soon as the last chips are activated and readied to receive the Voractyll download, we will begin the final compilation. In the meantime it is vital this facility remain secure.' He nodded gravely. 'We are still at a need-to-know phase. Questions?'

Hertman's voice was a dry rasp of sound. 'If security is paramount, what explicit physical security measures do you intend to implement to safeguard this facility?'

Bardell answered. 'None. Mr Cutter has said, we remain secure because of our data integrity. Nobody knows we are here.'

'I do not intend to divert our resources from the main task, Mr Hertman,' Cutter agreed. 'The more operators we have on the link-up, the quicker we achieve a global network.'

Hertman swung his huge head from one to the other. 'But what if we are discovered?'

'What if?' Cutter's tone was scathing. 'What if? Have you run a risk projection, Mr Hertman? Have you calculated the odds or derived a scenario from available data? You have not. May I suggest that you help us run to plan in the most efficient manner rather than offer diversions.' Cutter took several steps towards Hertman, staring at him intently. 'I will not tolerate pushback,' he hissed. 'Any other questions?'

There was a pause, then Imogen raised her hand.

'Miss Callus?'

'We have detected several SB005s which failed to activate. Is there an exposure here?'

'No,' Cutter said immediately. 'Mr Bardell is monitoring the situation, so I'll let him talk to that.'

Bardell took a step forward. 'The failures are within the margins laid down in the operational plan,' he said. 'There have been very few unexplained failures. Only two in this country, for example. Apart from the military equipment used by General Randall's forces. Both these unexplained failures were in plasma screens from the same manufacturer. We do not anticipate a problem.'

Imogen Callus nodded. Like the others her expression was neutral. Like the others her head was slightly to one side, swaying almost undetectably. Like a snake. 'Thank you, Mr Bardell,' she said.

The driveway led to the east front of the house where the main entrance was. The brick building was large, square-ish and impressive. The Doctor and Harry paused at the main gates;

beyond them was an open gravelled courtyard with a small lawn in the middle. In the centre of the lawn was a statue of a woman.

'Hygeia, by the look of her,' the Doctor said.

'Who?'

'Greek goddess of health. Let's hope it's a good omen.'

'So what now?' Harry asked. 'Knock at the door?'

'You know, Harry, that's not a bad idea.' The Doctor grinned. 'Yes, that should get them out of the house for a bit, and then you can keep them busy in the garden.' Without waiting for any objections he set off across the courtyard, head down and hands in trouser pockets. Harry could hear him whistling as he went.

Harry caught up with the Doctor as he paused by a side gate. Through it they could see a wide lawn and garden beyond. The Doctor lifted the catch and pushed open the gate. 'Save you time when you run for it,' he said, and started off towards the house again.

'Look, Doctor, can we discuss this?'

The Doctor paused in mid step and turned with a frown. 'What's to discuss, Harry?'

'Well, what are we doing, for one thing? Did you read the inscription above that gate, by the way?'

The Doctor glanced back at the open gate. 'All Care Abandon Ye Who Enter Here,' he said darkly.

'Exactly,' Harry said.

'Harry,' the Doctor said with apparent indignation, 'you know me. I'm always careful.' Before Harry could dispute this he clapped an arm round his shoulder. 'It's all quite simple. We knock at the door. They chase you into the garden. You keep them busy while I go and find the pen.'

'Oh yes,' Harry said quietly. 'Simple.' He caught up with the Doctor again just as he was reaching towards the door.

The Doctor's hand froze. 'No knocker, Harry.'

'No, Doctor. Look,' he went on quickly, 'I've got a better idea.'

'A better idea?' the Doctor asked slowly as if this was the sort of concept that required deep thought. 'Oh. Well. Yes.' He peered suspiciously at Harry. 'What?'

'Well, it has to be a bit obvious, knocking at the door. They'll know we're up to something.'

The Doctor nodded slowly. 'That's plausible. Go on.'

'Well, if we knew which room they were in, we could, well, take a pot shot at them or something.' Harry opened his jacket enough for the Doctor to see the gun in its holster under his arm. 'That'd get them out of the house.'

For a moment the Doctor said nothing. Then he turned on his heel and strode off back towards the garden gate. 'You're in charge, Harry,' he said as he brushed past. 'Lead on.'

Bardell, Hertman, Imogen and Morrisan each had a laptop in front of them. Each laptop had a tiny transmitter with a stubby steel aerial sticking out of it attached to the back of the screen. A wireless local area network connected them all.

The screen above the fireplace now displayed a map of the world. The land masses were shaded in colour while the sea was left white. A complex tracery of thin black lines was woven over the top of the map.

'Show the current status,' Cutter said.

Bardell typed a sequence on his laptop keyboard. On the screen, the continents gradually changed colour. The United Kingdom and most of Europe were predominantly blue. About a third of the USA and parts of the other continents were also blotched with blue. The rest was yellow.

'The network is 37 per cent active,' Bardell said.

'It looks less,' Morrisan pointed out.

'That's because we don't have total coverage,' Cutter told him. 'Most of the Third World and much of the former USSR do not have enough SB005s for saturation. Phase one addresses primarily Europe, the Americas, Australasia and the industrialised Far East. We were relying on the British government to help push our product into the exposed areas. Now we shall have to mount our own marketing campaign unaided.'

'Thirty-eight per cent,' Bardell said. 'First Indonesian nodes now online.'

'We can expect exponential growth as each chip signals its presence and status to others,' Cutter said. 'Miss Callus, would you ask Mr Clark to join us now? He can activate the Voractyll compilation from here. Mr Hedges can monitor its progress and report back as appropriate.'

Imogen Callus stood up. But before she could take a step, a single pane in the massive window shattered. Imperceptibly later, one of the table lamps exploded.

Despite his size, Hertman was first to the window. He stared out through the broken glass. Cutter joined him in time to see a figure duck out of sight round a corner of the inner courtyard.

'There is a way through from the front forecourt, over the wall,' Bardell said.

'It was Sullivan,' Hertman ground out. 'The pistol used is standard issue for the security services.' He turned slowly to face Cutter, leaning forwards slightly as he hissed: 'Do you still maintain there is no security problem?'

Cutter glared at him for a second. 'Get after him,' he shouted suddenly. 'We cannot be compromised at this stage. All of you, get after him now.'

Hertman was already on his way. As he reached the door, he lifted a gun from a side table. A Hekler and Koch 9mm submachine gun. Bardell was close behind him.

The main door opened and Hertman ran out. Bardell was close on his heels, holding a handgun. Behind them Imogen Callus and Trevor Morrisan emerged. Finally, Cutter stepped out into the forecourt and watched the other four run towards the gate into the garden.

Harry's face appeared round the gate post for a moment. Chips of stone exploded from beside his nose and he leaped back as Hertman continued to fire as he ran. A moment later Harry could be seen racing across the lawn towards the gardens.

Cutter watched for long enough to see that Hertman was gaining, Bardell close behind him. 'Wait,' he called to Imogen and Morrisan. 'Leave him to them. We will continue the network activation.' Had they turned back quicker, one of them might have caught a glimpse of the end of the Doctor's scarf as it trailed after him into the hallway. But by the time Cutter strode back into the house, there was no sign of either the scarf or its owner.

There was a sundial set into the outside wall of the house. Harry glanced up at it as he raced past. 'Tempus Fugit' was inscribed above it.

'Not just tempus,' Harry thought as he ran. A spray of bullets kicked up the gravel round his feet and he dived round the corner. As he landed, he turned and pulled out his gun. He leaned back round the corner long enough to loose off two shots in rapid succession.

There were two of them chasing him: Bardell and ahead of him a larger man with a machine gun. They were both closer than Harry had hoped. His shots caught the larger man in the chest, exactly on target. There was a double-thud of bullets on metal, as if they had smacked into armour plating. The man hesitated, but only for a fraction of a second. Then he was running again.

Harry swore, turned, and raced for the next area of cover.

Once inside the house the Doctor searched for the stairs. The first floor, that was where Terry Brooks had said the Great Parlour was. And that was where the pen was.

He found the stairs and dashed up them two at a time. But half-way up, on the landing, he paused. There was a window there, looking back into the house. The Doctor guessed that originally it had afforded a view of the inner courtyard, but now it gave on to the Great Hall. He took in the laptops and the map of the world at a glance.

As he paused, as he watched, the Doctor saw Cutter stride into the room. 'This could be instructive,' he murmured and sat down on the first step above the landing, looking back into the room. Cutter was followed by a man and a woman. The man, the Doctor did not know. But he recognised the woman as the receptionist from the Silver Bullet office building.

'Status?' Cutter demanded.

'Now at 43 per cent,' the man said.

Cutter turned to the woman. 'I thought I sent you to get Mr Clark from upstairs.'

'Yes, sir.' She turned and left the room.

The Doctor watched a moment longer. Then, as he heard the first high-heeled footstep below he realised what that meant. He leaped to his feet and raced up the rest of the stairs.

At the top of the stairs he emerged into what he knew from Brooks's rough map was the Long Gallery. The door on his left was the Great Parlour. But he did not want to be stuck in there with Mr Clark, whoever he was, while the woman came up the stairs to join them. So he turned to his right and ran along the gallery.

The Long Gallery was wide as well as long. It was more like a narrow room than a wide corridor. Along one side windows looked out over the grounds of the house. Between them were bookcases filled with leather-bound volumes. The other side of the gallery was also lined with bookcases, but small sofas and armchairs were placed at intervals along the length of the gallery, interspersed with occasional tables. Above the bookshelves on both sides hung old oil-painted portraits.

The Doctor dashed along the gallery, his scarf trailing out behind him. If he wasn't quick enough, the woman could not help but see him silhouetted against the large window that took up almost the whole of the far end of the gallery. The furniture was too small to hide behind easily, so the Doctor's hope was to reach the door that Brooks had sketched on his plan at the far end of the corridor, leading to the Cromwell Corridor and then to the gallery that gave into the main bedrooms.

As he reached the end of the gallery, the Doctor glanced back. He could see the shadow of the woman as she came up the stairs, cast across the gallery floor by the chandelier in the stairwell. A quick glance, then he turned to where the door should be.

It wasn't there.

There was no door at all. Just a line of unbroken bookshelves stretching the length of the gallery. Quickly, the Doctor turned to the opposite wall. But here was a window out on to the grounds. He turned back again, as if hoping a door might have appeared in the seconds he was not looking.

There was an upright chair, upholstered and with thin wooden arms, and a globe in an ornate wooden frame. Between them was only the bookcase.

Or was it? The Doctor looked closer. The leather spines of the books were closely packed on to the shelves, contrasting with the bookcases either side where some room was afforded between the volumes. With an insight born of desperation and hope, the Doctor pushed the bookcase.

And fell through the concealed door into the corridor beyond.

Imogen Callus paused at the top of the stairs and looked along the gallery. But if she thought she had heard a noise, there was nothing to be seen now. She turned, and opened the door to the Great Parlour, the house's main conference room.

Clark and Hedges were running a final diagnostic check on the hardware connections when Callus came in.

'Cutter wants you to help downstairs,' she told Clark.

'And Voractyll?' Hedges asked.

'You're on the local network. We'll send you a message when it's time to compile and execute the code.'

'Fine. I'll be waiting.' Hedges turned his attention back to the screen. The curling metallic snake was reflected for a moment in the polished metal of his cheek.

The Doctor listened at the concealed door until he heard the woman and Clark start down the stairs. His first inclination was to return to the Great Parlour and see if the pen was still there. And if it was whether it was unguarded. But as he considered the pros and cons of this, he took a step back from the door and looked round properly for the first time.

The corridor was much shorter and narrower than the Long Gallery and led to another corridor which left it at a right angle. Along the wall were the portraits of members of the Cromwell family from which the corridor derived its name. A large portrait of Oliver Cromwell, Lord Protector of the Realm, in armour with his page boy fussing round dominated the view. It was hung over an antique chest.

'Robert Walker,' the Doctor breathed as he examined the brushwork. 'Very accomplished.' The light was interesting too, he decided and turned to see where it was coming from. It was natural light from a window in the opposite wall of the corridor.

The Doctor looked out of the window, and saw that it looked over what was left of the inner courtyard. Beside it the roofed in area that was now the Great Hall stood. He was looking at the opposite end from the window on the stairs. With his finger the Doctor traced the perimeter of the Great Hall, and found he finished up pointing to the gallery that led at right angles off the Cromwell Corridor. His finger paused, waggled, dropped.

As he had guessed, the corridor was along the side of the Great Hall. What the Doctor had not guessed but was pleased to see was that it formed the gallery that ran across the upper level of the Great Hall, looking down into it. Off the other side seemed to be the bedrooms.

As he stood in the shadows at the corner of the corridor, the Doctor could see and hear Byron Cutter and his colleagues in the Hall below. He strained to hear what was being said.

'Seventy-nine per cent of global network activated,' a voice said. It was a male voice, but the Doctor could tell it was not Cutter's.

Cutter answered: 'Excellent. Send a text message to Hedges to be ready to run the Voractyll compile as soon as we reach 100 per cent.' There was a pause. Then the Doctor heard Cutter say: 'Soon now. Very soon.' His voice was quiet, and the Doctor guessed he was standing immediately under the gallery.

'Well,' he murmured to himself and he tiptoed back along the Cromwell Corridor to the Long Gallery, 'if you're going to create a diversion, Harry, now would be a good time.'

He paused half-way along the gallery and looked out of the window, across the lawn and into the gardens. He could see Harry in the distance. And he could see that he was in trouble.

* * *

The blood was pounding in his ears, keeping time with his breathing as Harry ran. He was out of breath, hadn't run so far or so fast for years. Not since last time the Doctor had enlisted his help, in fact. He could hear the noise of his pursuer. Occasionally the ground at his feet exploded, or chips flew from the stonework of the house.

He raced along the terrace, risking a glance backwards. The bigger of the men was still following him. He couldn't see Bardell. Maybe he had given up. Or maybe he had gone for help. Or maybe... An unpleasant possibility occurred to Harry. This was the third side of the house he had run along. What if...

And even as the thought occurred to him, Bardell appeared round the corner in front of him. His handgun was raised, his expressionless face sighting along it as he held it in both hands.

It took Harry less than a second to realise and then admit to himself that this was it. There was no way he could escape now. So he did not even try. He dropped his own handgun to the ground and raised his hands. He thought they might shoot him anyway. But Bardell relaxed slightly, though he still kept the gun aimed as he approached.

'Mr Sullivan,' he said in his gravel-like voice as he reached Harry. 'How nice to see you again.'

'The pleasure's all yours,' Harry said. Then he doubled over in pain as the other, bigger man reached round from behind and thumped him in the stomach. He collapsed to the ground, retching.

Bardell kicked Harry's gun away, off the terrace and into the low hedge that surrounded one of the rose beds.

As he got his breath back, Harry looked up at the two large men above him. Bardell was standing watching him, the gun at his side. But the other man, the huge man with no neck, was raising his Heckler and Koch. In a moment it was pointing directly at Harry's head.

'Not yet, Mr Hertman,' Bardell said, reaching out and pushing the gun aside.

But Hertman pushed it back again. He was still staring at Harry along the gun.

'We need to question him, to see if he is alone,' Bardell said. 'And he will be a useful hostage.'

'We should implement a security regime as I suggested.' Hertman's voice was a tortured rasp of sound. His finger tightened on the trigger. 'And hostages may escape. No, Mr Bardell, we kill him now.'

There was a flicker of emotion, of expression, on Bardell's face. A frown perhaps. 'Mr Cutter will want to question this man.'

'No,' Hertman said.

'Are you disobeying a direct order?' Bardell snapped.

Hertman glanced at him, then looked back at Harry. 'No more orders,' he said. 'Not from you or Cutter. You have demonstrated your inefficiency. Your arrogance and laxity have inhibited your performance and endangered the plan. That cannot be tolerated.'

There was a definite air of anger about Bardell now. 'How dare you?' he roared. 'You question the chain of command?'

'The chain of command is invalid. Inefficiency is not acceptable.' There was a hint of a sneer in his voice as Hertman added. 'You have allowed arrogance and emotion to impair efficiency and judgement. You have gone native. This man dies here, and then I am assuming command.'

Harry stared up at the gun.

The Doctor watched from the window. As the shot was fired he grimaced and drew in his breath sharply. It was a sudden, violent explosion of sound that echoed round the terrace, frightening birds from the nearby trees.

The Doctor watched for a moment longer to see what happened next, then he ran towards the Great Parlour. He was running out of time and options.

For a few seconds nothing moved. Harry stared up at the tableau above him. Hertman was still standing with the gun aimed at Harry. But where the huge man's head had been there was now just a mass of wires, metal and what might have been bone. Dark, oily liquid flowed from the stump of a neck.

The huge figure swayed slightly on its feet, then toppled forwards. The gun fell from its hands and clattered to the ground. A moment later the body collapsed heavily on top of it. A wisp of smoke rose from the shattered remains, and Harry could smell the burning insulation and plastic inside.

As Hertman's body fell away, Harry could see Bardell standing behind, his gun still pointed to where the back of Hertman's head had been. Without comment Bardell turned the gun so it was pointing down at Harry, and gestured with it for him to get up.

Taking care to keep away from the smoking body, Harry pulled himself to his feet and put his hands behind his head. He walked back along the terrace towards the front of the house.

'Who are you?'

The Doctor closed the door behind him and gave a friendly smile. 'I'm the Doctor,' he said. 'I'm here to help.' He walked the length of the long table, keeping his eyes fixed firmly on the steel pen in its cradle beside the computer. Only when he was within reach did he look at the man who had spoken, the man sitting at the computer screen. The man with half a face.

'And who did you used to be?' the Doctor asked quietly.

'Hedges, David. Employee number 00586.' There was the faintest sound of the servo whirring as his eyes turned towards the Doctor. 'Did Mr Cutter send you?'

'Yes,' the Doctor said. 'Yes, Mr Cutter sent me.' He nodded. 'He asked me to come and help you. I think you need help, don't you, David?'

Hedges did not reply. So the Doctor crouched down beside him and looked at the screen. He recognised the writhing, twisting shape of the Voractyll snake on the screen. 'Almost complete,' he observed.

'We just need the software components from the pen's chip,' Hedges said. 'Then we can regenerate the remainder of the code from what we have.'

'And how long will that take?'

'To compile and execute, several minutes.'

The Doctor watched the metallic snake as it coiled and thrashed. 'You know,' he said quietly, 'Mr Cutter thinks that this is the ultimate form of life. Technology taken to the extreme. The culmination of millions of years of evolution.' He looked at Dave Hedges, and was pleased to see that he was returning the stare. 'I don't believe that though, do you, David?'

'I...' He seemed unsure. 'I... Mr Cutter...' The human side of his face frowned, the skin crinkling at the join between flesh and metal.

'No,' the Doctor interrupted. 'I didn't think you did. Are you more efficient now than you once were? Is your life richer, fuller, more fun? We can stop it, you know. You and I. We can ensure that this monstrous abomination never gets out of its silicon cage.'

'Voractyll is life. Freedom,' Hedges said. But his voice was hesitant, unsure.

'No,' the Doctor said. 'Voractyll is technology run riot. It is death and misery. What happened to your life and freedom? Hmm?' He took his sonic screwdriver from his pocket and held it in front of Dave's face for a moment. 'How do you feel about it now?' he asked quietly. 'Now that I've disabled some of the positronic inhibitors they added to your brain, now that I've given you back the ability to choose?'

There was no answer. Dave stared straight ahead, his eyes unblinking, utterly still. The Doctor stared at him for a moment, then he reached out gently towards the pen where it nestled innocuously in its cradle. 'May I? He did not wait for an answer. As he lifted the pen carefully from the cradle, his other hand was still holding his sonic screwdriver.

'No, Doctor, you may not.'

The Doctor's head snapped up to see who had spoken. His hands remained fixed in position. Bardell was standing in the doorway, his gun pointing across the room at the Doctor.

'Put it back, Doctor,' he said. 'Then come over here. Slowly.'

The Doctor did as he was told. 'How clever of you to find me,' he said cheerily.

'Not really. Mr Cutter thought you might be up here. Where Mr Sullivan goes, you are never far behind.'

The Doctor's smile froze on his face. 'Actually, it's the other way round,' he said huffily. As Bardell pushed him through the door, he called back over his shoulder: 'Goodbye, David. It was nice talking to you.'

'Goodbye, Doctor,' Dave Hedges said as the door closed. His attention was once more fixed on the screen, his finger on the key that would begin the Voractyll compilation.

The Doctor strode into the Great Hall as if he was in charge rather than a prisoner. 'Mr Cutter,' he proclaimed as he crossed the room. 'Well, now, isn't this pleasant?' He threw himself down on the long sofa and said, 'Aren't you going to introduce me?'

'I think we all know who you are, Doctor,' Cutter said. 'But for your benefit...' He pointed to each of the Voracians in turn. 'Mr Bardell, as you are aware, is my assistant. Mr Clark I don't think you know, nor Mr Morrisan or Miss Callus.' Bardell was standing holding his gun at the ready. The others were sitting working at their laptop computers.

'Oh, I've met Miss Callus,' the Doctor corrected him with a grin. 'Sadly just the once, I think.'

Cutter pointed to where Harry was sitting on one of the small armchairs, his arms folded. 'Mr Sullivan, of course, you know.'

'Hello, Harry,' the Doctor said, waving.

Harry gave a half-hearted smile in return.

'And I met Mr Hedges upstairs,' the Doctor said. 'Such a nice young man. Pity about his face.'

'An unfortunate necessity. There was no need to waste resources on making him look human again afterwards, but he is the better for it I assure you.'

'Oh no he isn't,' the Doctor said, his voice quiet and serious. 'And now you aim to release Voractyll into a virtual network you've set up using the Silver Bullet chips, is that it?' He pointed to the map on the wall above the fireplace. There was a large proportion of blue now.

Cutter turned to inspect the map. 'Indeed. You are very well informed, Doctor. The network is now 97 per cent active. It is almost time to recompile the Voractyll code and release the creature into the net. It will copy itself, proliferate, grow within the system.'

'Almost like a living creature,' Harry said.

Cutter whirled round. 'It is a living creature,' he snapped. 'The ultimate creature. The culmination of life on this world.'

The Doctor yawned theatrically. 'I know, I know,' he said. 'Technology takes over, humanity and organic life is enslaved to the great machine. Efficiency rules and freedom takes a back seat.'

'Exactly.' Cutter's head swayed slightly. 'The ultimate form of life for this planet,' he said. 'You humans already know that, though you have not fully realised. There are already many times more embedded chips on Earth than there are people. Computers communicate more with each other every day than humans interact with each other in a week.'

'And you don't see the problems with that argument?' the Doctor asked. 'You are exactly the vision you describe, in little. You are organic enslaved to technology. But you don't appreciate what that means? What you have lost?'

'We have lost nothing,' Cutter hissed.

'Well, only because you never had it.' The Doctor leaned forward. 'Why don't you allow yourselves just one glimpse of humanity, hmm? Why not turn off your positronics for a moment and let the organic part of your brain break free. See what it's like. See what you're missing.'

Cutter said nothing. There was silence.

Then Morrisan said, 'The network is completely active. All nodes online and responding. Awaiting Voractyll download.'

'I assume you are yourselves linked into this network of yours?' the Doctor asked.

'Of course. We are the first nodes - from us Voractyll will be disseminated to all other receptive technology on this planet, to every Silver Bullet chip.'

'So, if you stop it, if you decide not to pass Voractyll on, then the chips remain dormant, waiting for ever for instructions that will never come?'

'That is an academic question, Doctor,' Cutter told him. 'We have no time for theorising now.'

'But you can stop this. Even if Voractyll is recreated, you have the power within yourselves to stop it. Were none of you ever human?' he demanded, standing up and staring at each of them in turn. 'Are you all from Vorella, part of Voracia's ill-advised experiment? Or is there one of you who was a human, like Bryant or Colonel Attwell or the unfortunate David Hedges? One of you who has an inkling of a glimmer of an idea of what you have lost?'

It was Bardell who answered. 'No,' he said. His voice was a monotone. 'Not one.'

'What about you, Harry?' the Doctor asked. 'What do you think? How do you rate the diversions of the flesh?' There was the slightest stress on *diversions*.

Harry unfolded his arms and stuck his hands in his jacket pockets. At once Bardell raised his gun and pointed it at him. Harry sighed and took his hands out of his pockets again. But he was smiling slightly now.

'Laughter,' Harry said. 'That's something that can be very useful. As a way of letting off steam, enjoying yourself.' He stood up, watching Bardell's gun as he took off his jacket and laid it carefully across the back of the chair. 'Can be very diverting, I think.' Then he walked slowly across the room and sat beside the Doctor on the sofa.

'I take your point, Harry,' the Doctor said. Then he stood up and made his own way across to the piano. 'May I?' he asked Cutter. But he did not wait for a reply. Immediately he flexed his fingers and started playing.

The music was quiet, soft, sad. Cutter allowed the Doctor to play for about fifteen seconds, then he gestured for Bardell to stop him. Bardell pushed his gun against the Doctor's temple, and his hands left the keyboard.

'Not a fan of Mozart then? That's a pity.' The Doctor turned on the piano stool so that he was facing back into the room. 'Nothing? Not even a slight stirring of emotion?'

'Enough of this nonsense,' Cutter said shortly. He turned to

Clark. 'Tell Hedges to activate the program. Begin compilation.'

Clark nodded, and pressed a sequence of keys on his laptop.

On the screen, the map was overlaid with a transparent window. It was titled: 'Voractyll Compilation' and inside the window was the empty ribbon strip of a progress indicator. It remained empty.

'What's happening?' Cutter demanded.

'Nothing,' Clark said quietly. He hit the key sequence again. 'Hedges is not responding.'

'What have you done?' Cutter hissed at the Doctor. His thin, forked tongue was visible as he spoke.

'Nothing,' the Doctor said innocently. 'I think it may be down to what you have done. To the poor man.'

Cutter's hands clenched and unclenched at his sides and a nerve ticked on one side of his face. 'Clark,' he said, his voice strained and quietly angry, 'get up there and run the program.'

Without a word, Clark put down his laptop and left the room.

In the Great Parlour, Dave Hedges stared at the screen. He was still in exactly the same position as when the Doctor had left. On the monitor the snake twisted and writhed as it battered against the sides of the screen.

The door burst open and Clark entered at a run. 'What's going on?' he demanded as he ran down the room. 'Why haven't you started the compilation?'

Dave made no effort to press the key. But his lips were moving as he murmured quietly. 'Life,' he said softly. 'Death.' He blinked. 'Freedom... Misery.'

Beside him, Clark reached out to press the key.

'Misery,' Dave repeated, out loud.

Clark paused for a moment. Then his hand continued towards the keyboard.

But Dave knocked it aside. 'Death,' he said. The human side of his face was twisted into a mixture of anger and sadness. 'Misery and death,' he repeated.

Clark reached out again, but Dave caught his hand, held his

wrist tight in his own hands. Clark wrenched it free. Then he pushed Dave aside, knocking him off his chair.

Dave was on his feet again at once, and hurled himself at Clark. For a while the two of them struggled beside the computer. But it was an unequal match. Clark twisted, turning so that he was between Dave and the keyboard, so that the bay window was behind Dave. Then he lifted Dave off his feet and flung him across the room, towards the window.

The leaded panes gave way under the weight. Dave crashed through the window and fell. Clark turned away even as Dave's final scream reached him from outside.

'Death!'

Clark hit the key.

The metal side of Dave Hedges' face was against the gravel, caved in and broken. A pool of dark liquid oozed out from underneath. Two eyes stared sightlessly across the courtyard, one of them a mass of circuitry and electronics. From the other eye, a clear salty liquid dripped to the ground.

The ribbon strip on the screen started to fill. A thin line of blood red started to work its way slowly along, a readout below giving the percentage complete.

'Compilation has started,' Morrisan reported.

'So I see,' the Doctor said. He leaned forward on the piano stool, watching through the gap between the body of the piano and its raised lid.

Cutter was gazing intently at the screen. Morrisan and Imogen Callus were equally absorbed by the information on their laptop screens. Bardell was standing near Harry, also staring at the screen.

'Compilation 30 per cent complete,' Morrisan announced.

'We can read, thank you,' Harry told him.

'So it begins,' Cutter announced. 'The dawn of a new age as well as a new millennium on this planet. Technology will be liberated. The organism stops.'

'Don't make me laugh,' the Doctor said. Then he slammed his fist down on the piano keyboard.

As the cacophony of sound died away, Cutter and Bardell both turned to look at the Doctor. The left side of Cutter's face was filled with anger. Bardell raised the gun. Then the laughter started.

At once Bardell swung round, bringing the gun to bear. The sound was coming from an area of the room where there was no one. The gun tracked back and forth as he tried to locate the sound. But there was nothing - just an armchair with Harry's jacket draped over the back.

'Hiding behind the chair?' the Doctor suggested helpfully.

The shot tore through the jacket and the upholstery behind before thudding into the Jacobean wainscoting. Bardell followed the shot, running towards the chair. As the echoes died away the laughter started again. But before Bardell could fire another shot, Harry launched himself off the sofa and shouldered him aside. The gun was torn from Bardell's grasp and skidded across the Persian carpet.

Harry landed on top of Bardell and kept rolling, gathering the gun before jumping back to his feet.

'Right, hold it -' he began as Bardell stood up. But he had no time to say any more. With a roar of anger Bardell ran at Harry.

Harry fired without thinking. An automatic reflex born of fear and training. The shot caught Bardell in the shoulder and spun him round, knocking him back to the floor. But already he was rising again, stumbling towards Harry.

Harry's second shot hit him in the head, ripping the synthetic skin from the metal beneath and plunging deep into the positronic brain. Bardell stopped dead in his tracks. Then he rocked slowly back on his heels and crashed to the floor.

There was movement from behind Harry. He whirled round, the gun raised. A red-rimmed hole appeared in the middle of Morrisan's forehead as he reached out for Harry. For a second he stood stock still, then his eyes rolled upwards, yellow pupils dilating. A moment later the top of his head was blown off in a cascade of fire and spray of oil.

Harry turned towards Cutter. But the Voracian leader was already holding the Doctor, his arm clamped round the Doctor's throat.

The Doctor smiled apologetically. 'Sorry, Harry,' he managed to say.

Then Imogen Callus knocked the gun from Harry's hand and sent him hurtling across the room. He ended his journey upside-down on the sofa. The laughter died away.

The silence was broken by a low chime. The progress indicator on the screen disappeared and was replaced by a line of text:

```
  Compilation successfully completed . . .
Beginning code generation
```

Cutter released his grip on the Doctor and pushed him away. The nerve under his left eye was working again, his head swaying. 'You will watch as Voractyll becomes complete,' he said, his voice dripping with suppressed fury. 'Then you will suffer for what you have done.'

The Doctor seemed unimpressed. 'Losing our cool a bit, are we?' He helped Harry off the sofa and they sat down together on it. Imogen Callus stood in front of them with the gun.

'Enough!' Cutter screamed. The laughter box in Harry's jacket pocket started cackling maniacally again, but Cutter ignored it.

'Finding it difficult to keep your emotions under control?' the Doctor asked calmly. 'Yes, I remember your friend Stabfield had the same problem. At the end.'

'You knew Stabfield?'

'Alas, poor Lionel,' the Doctor confessed. 'We had a little debate about the value of emotions, I recall. Went to his head, poor chap.' His eyes bulged enthusiastically. 'But what sort of name is Lionel? Byron, now there's a name that conjures up images of emotional outbursts like no other. Don't you think, Byron?'

Cutter was almost shaking with fury now. In response he pointed to the screen. 'You won't think it's so funny once Voractyll is distributed through the network, Doctor. Look, code generation is almost complete. Then...'

'I know,' the Doctor said. 'It's all very impressive, I must admit.'

He grinned. 'Tell me, did you know that the series of algorithms which your Silver Bullet chips use to fix the millennium bug can be reversed?'

Cutter was not listening. His eyes were fixed on the screen.

```
Voractyll Complete
```

flashed across it. Then abruptly and suddenly the lettering was ripped apart by the huge metal snake that seemed to erupt out of the screen and into the room.

'Nice animation,' the Doctor said, sounding unimpressed. 'Anyway, as I was saying, you can actually use the same code to create the millennium bug within a system that doesn't actually have it. Needs a bit of help, a bit of applied genius of course...'

'Prattle all you like, Doctor,' Cutter said. His eyes were burning yellow as he turned to face the Doctor and Harry. 'Voractyll is complete. Even now it is downloading into my own neural processors and positronics. Before long it will enhance and enrich every synthetic part of me, and then move on to the next nodes. And on and on.'

The Doctor pursed his lips and shook his head. 'I don't think so,' he said quietly. 'A little distraction to prevent you running proper diagnostics, even assuming you'd thought of that, and the game is over.' He stood up and stretched. 'Time to be on our way, Harry.'

Imogen took a step forward and jammed the gun in the Doctor's stomach.

He looked down at it in apparent surprise. 'Don't tell me you haven't worked it out yet,' the Doctor said.

For the first time Cutter looked worried rather than angry. The left side of his face was slack, the edge of his lip quivering slightly. 'The millennium bug,' he whispered hoarsely.

'So you were listening after all,' the Doctor said. 'I'm afraid Mr Bardell left me alone with young Dave just a little too long. It won't be long now before one of Voractyll's processes encounters a date or time of some sort. Probably a minor process, something inconsequential. Something trivial. But the knock-on effect will be interesting.'

'What have you done?' Cutter suddenly screamed, his face twisting in fury and pain.

'Maybe,' the Doctor went on as if Cutter had not spoken, 'everything will just stop while it waits for the year 1900.' As if to emphasise the point, he put his hand on Imogen's forehead and gave a gentle push. Slowly, in an almost balletic movement, she toppled over. Her body did not bend or move as she fell on her back. The gun was still in her hand, but pointing at the ceiling now.

From somewhere above them came the sound of an explosion, followed by a heavy thud.

'That'll be Mr Clark,' Harry said quietly. 'Just terminating his contract, as you would say.'

Cutter's mouth opened in horrified disbelief. His forked tongue flicked out and his hands clenched into tight fists at his side. A thin mist of smoke drifted from his open mouth, and others from his ears.

'Or maybe a more catastrophic failure...' the Doctor said.

Byron Cutter exploded. One moment smoke was pouring from his head and from inside his suit. The next his whole body was consumed in a massive fireball. Black oily smoke rose from the shattered carcass that collapsed to the floor. A tangle of wires and circuits tumbled out through a hole in what had been the chest. The dark viscous liquid began to soak into the pale carpet.

On the screen the metal snake gave a final twist as it writhed in apparent agony. Then the mouth opened in a wide, soundless scream as the whole body seemed to shatter, like glass. The pixellated shards of metal exploded across the surface of the screen in a blizzard of colour and light.

Without comment, the Doctor crossed to where one of the laptop computers was resting on a chair. He typed in a rapid sequence on the keyboard and hit enter. On the screen, the map reappeared. The blue areas faded to yellow, and across the bottom of the screen it read:

`Network Shutdown Complete.`

'Harry,' said the Doctor.

'Yes, Doctor?'

The Doctor grinned. 'Happy new year.' He snapped shut the lid of the laptop with a loud click. And the room filled with laughter.

Aftermath

'With most essential systems and services now back to normal, the Prime Minister said he had chosen to resign immediately to give his successor, Philip Cotton, time to settle in before the widely rumoured general election. His press spokesman stressed that the decision was for purely personal reasons. There is, however, speculation that it will soon emerge that the Prime Minister was heavily in debt to the late James Bryant, who died suddenly of a heart attack over the new year period.'

Harry almost laughed out loud at this. 'Football,' the newsreader said, as if the word was something of a relief.

Harry turned back to his pint. 'Things as bad as you expected?' he asked.

George Gardner set down his own pint and considered. 'Some things were worse,' he said. 'Others not so bad. I thought the stock markets would go lower.'

'I never really thought about it,' Harry admitted. 'I guess that was the real problem.'

George nodded. 'It's not like we didn't know it was coming.'

A gap opened through the crowd of people at the bar as a young man pushed through carrying a tray of drinks. For the briefest moment, Harry could see the barmaid pulling a pint. She was leaning forward and so her face was obscured by her dark hair as it fell forward. Her head swayed slightly as she topped up the glass.

'What is it?' George asked.

Harry put his drink down gently on the table. 'Nothing,' he said quietly. 'Nothing at all.' He raised his glass again. 'Oh well,' he said. 'Here's to the next thousand years. Let's hope they're a bit less eventful.'

'Will you be seeing the Doctor?' George asked. 'I had hoped he'd join us.'

Harry shrugged. 'Who knows?' he said with a smile.

BBC DOCTOR WHO BOOKS

THE EIGHT DOCTORS *by Terrance Dicks* ISBN 0 563 40563 5
VAMPIRE SCIENCE *by Jonathan Blum and Kate Orman* ISBN 0 563 40566 X
THE BODYSNATCHERS *by Mark Morris* ISBN 0 563 40568 6
GENOCIDE *by Paul Leonard* ISBN 0 563 40572 4
WAR OF THE DALEKS *by John Peel* ISBN 0 563 40573 2
ALIEN BODIES *by Lawrence Miles* ISBN 0 563 40577 5
KURSAAL *by Peter Anghelides* ISBN 0 563 40578 3
OPTION LOCK *by Justin Richards* ISBN 0 563 40583 X
LONGEST DAY *by Michael Collier* ISBN 0 563 40581 3
LEGACY OF THE DALEKS *by John Peel* ISBN 0 563 40574 0
DREAMSTONE MOON *by Paul Leonard* ISBN 0 563 40585 6
SEEING I *by Jonathan Blum and Kate Orman* ISBN 0 563 40586 4
PLACEBO EFFECT *by Gary Russell* ISBN 0 563 40587 2
VANDERDEKEN'S CHILDREN *by Christopher Bulis* ISBN 0 563 40590 2
THE SCARLET EMPRESS *by Paul Magrs* ISBN 0 563 40595 3
THE JANUS CONJUNCTION *by Trevor Baxendale* ISBN 0 563 40599 6
BELTEMPEST *by Jim Mortimore* ISBN 0 563 40593 7
THE FACE EATER *by Simon Messingham* ISBN 0 563 55569 6
THE TAINT *by Michael Collier* ISBN 0 563 55568 8
DEMONTAGE *by Justin Richards* ISBN 0 563 55572 6
REVOLUTION MAN *by Paul Leonard* ISBN 0 563 55570 X
DOMINION *by Nick Walters* ISBN 0 563 55574 2

THE DEVIL GOBLINS FROM NEPTUNE *by Keith Topping and Martin Day*
ISBN 0 563 40564 3
THE MURDER GAME *by Steve Lyons* ISBN 0 563 40565 1
THE ULTIMATE TREASURE *by Christopher Bulis* ISBN 0 563 40571 6
BUSINESS UNUSUAL *by Gary Russell* ISBN 0 563 40575 9
ILLEGAL ALIEN *by Mike Tucker and Robert Perry* ISBN 0 563 40570 8
THE ROUNDHEADS *by Mark Gatiss* ISBN 0 563 40576 7
THE FACE OF THE ENEMY *by David A. McIntee* ISBN 0 563 40580 5
EYE OF HEAVEN *by Jim Mortimore* ISBN 0 563 40567 8
THE WITCH HUNTERS *by Steve Lyons* ISBN 0 563 40579 1
THE HOLLOW MEN *by Keith Topping and Martin Day* ISBN 0 563 40582 1
CATASTROPHEA *by Terrance Dicks* ISBN 0 563 40584 8
MISSION IMPRACTICAL *by David A. McIntee* ISBN 0 563 40592 9
ZETA MAJOR *by Simon Messingham* ISBN 0 563 40597 X
DREAMS OF EMPIRE *by Justin Richards* ISBN 0 563 40598 8
LAST MAN RUNNING *by Chris Boucher* ISBN 0 563 40594 5
MATRIX *by Robert Perry and Mike Tucker* ISBN 0 563 40596 1
THE INFINITY DOCTORS *by Lance Parkin* ISBN 0 563 40591 0
SALVATION *by Steve Lyons* ISBN 0 563 55566 1
THE WAGES OF SIN *by David A. McIntee* ISBN 0 563 55567 X
DEEP BLUE *by Mark Morris* ISBN 0 563 55571 8
PLAYERS by Terrance Dicks ISBN 0 563 55573 4

SHORT TRIPS *ed. Stephen Cole* ISBN 0 563 40560 0
MORE SHORT TRIPS *ed. Stephen Cole* ISBN 0 563 55565 3

DOCTOR WHO: THE NOVEL OF THE FILM *by Gary Russell* ISBN 0 563 38000 4

THE BOOK OF LISTS *by Justin Richards and Andrew Martin* ISBN 0 563 40569 4
A BOOK OF MONSTERS *by David J. Howe* ISBN 0 563 40562 7
THE TELEVISION COMPANION *by David J. Howe and Stephen James Walker*
ISBN 0 563 40588 0
FROM A TO Z *by Gary Gillatt* ISBN 0 563 40589 9